praise for
WARRIOR

"I really enjoyed this no spice Christian romantic suspense novel. It was a great installment in this series set in Colorado. I loved the protective, veteran MMC and the doctor FMC who is struggling to trust. There was plenty of faith woven in with danger - WITSEC, medical procedures, the cartel, and more. This book added a lot to the web of the overarching series mystery while also satisfyingly getting these two through trials and danger and on to their HEA. I'm excited for more of this series!"

—MICHAELA, GOODREADS

"A gripping romantic suspense that will have you keep you up until the last page! You don't want to miss Luca and Kira!"

—LARAMEE, GOODREADS

"Get ready for pulse-pounding suspense, a fresh examination of courage, and the reminder that we are all capable of brave acts. Luca Saxon exemplifies the warrior mindset. I love how he confronts his fears and doubts, takes action with intention and commitment, and balances this with compassion and vulnerability. In my mind, he's a perfect hero and warrior."

—THE LITERATE LEPRECHAUN, GOODREADS

"Besides the captivating storyline, the page-turning mystery, and the romance with sweet banter and chemistry, this is a beautiful story about courage, and trusting God in all situations, especially the ones we have no control over. I highly recommend *Warrior*, and the whole Heroes of Renegade series!"

—JEANNE, GOODREADS

WARRIOR

HEROES OF RENEGADE

RENEGADE
WARRIOR

WARRIOR

LISA PHILLIPS

Warrior
Heroes of Renegade: Book 2 | The Brave

But God demonstrates his own love for us in this:
While we were still sinners, Christ died for us.

ROMANS 5:8 NIV

ONE

Northern Syria

LUCA SAXON HAD BEEN BORN IN THIS DIRT. IT stood to reason he was going to die here as well.

His back hit the ground, and he rolled. Sand and dust coated everything. He coughed against the wave of grit but was unable to hear it over the sound of his ears ringing. Someone pulled him up roughly, lifting him by his vest to his feet.

The bearded face of his sergeant swam in front of him. Luca watched Hammer's lips form the words *not today*.

Luca could barely breathe, but he coughed out the words, repeating them back to his team leader. "Not today."

Hammer slapped the back of his shoulder, and they were on the move, weaving through rows of white tents while the oppressive July sun beat down on them. Away from the tent that was in flames and what remained of the camp stove, nothing but charred debris now. All thanks to a member of an ISIS sleeper cell working in this forsaken part of the world.

A woman hurried past them in a black niqab, completely covered except for the slit of her eyes. Clinging to her hand was a little boy who couldn't be more than six years old. Both of them needed a full meal and a peaceful night of sleep—neither of which were commodities that could be easily obtained in the back alleys of this refugee camp.

The comms earbud in one ear hummed to life. "Trigger One, this is Trigger Three. I have visual."

Sweet. Kane, a member of their team and one of Saxon's best friends, had the suspect in sight. But this was far from over. They needed to get their hands on Namir Hassan Al-Hijazi, fleeing through the camp up ahead, before the ISIS terror cell members that remained after last night's raid caught him first. Namir needed to be in prison for what he'd done, betraying those Marines for such a deadly cause. And while he was at least partially responsible for the death of six US soldiers, he had also stolen sensitive information that was now on a flash drive in his pocket.

Not only could they not lose Namir, but they also couldn't afford to lose the information he carried.

Running full speed ahead of Saxon, Hammer called on the radio. "Trigger Three, give me his twenty. Over."

Kane responded, "Three rows west of the medical tent."

Saxon could see the Red Cross flag flying high in the center of the refugee camp and made a beeline toward it, catching up to Hammer so they were almost side by side. His buddy glanced over and grinned, as if this was just your average footrace through a war-torn country.

Up ahead, in the direction they were going, gunshots rang out. Someone screamed. Answering gunfire sounded across the open air.

"We've got company," Elias said over the radio. The fourth man of their team, Redding, wasn't someone Saxon would have called a friend. The guy was too edgy for his taste. But the US Army had seen fit to put them together on a team. Considering how well he liked Hammer and Kane, Saxon wasn't going to complain about one team member.

Hammer raced around the corner of the next tent, almost colliding with an armed insurgent. The two faced off against each other for a second before the other man slammed into the Delta Force team leader. They hit the ground in a cloud of dust.

Another man stepped between two tents about twenty feet up the row.

Saxon lifted his rifle and squeezed the trigger for a split second. But it was too late. The man's gun fired, and the bullet slammed into the left side of Saxon's arm. Tearing through flesh with heat and pain.

He cried out, almost going down, but managed to keep his wits about him. He aimed again with the rifle and squeezed off another grouping of shots. His left arm hung loose by his side, trickling blood down to his elbow.

The man collapsed to the ground in a pool of regret and bad choices.

Saxon turned to Hammer. The sergeant was on his feet now, blood running from a cut on his temple, his gun aimed at the man on the ground. The insurgent looked at Saxon, fully aware of what was about to happen.

He said the word *brother* in Arabic. More of a question than anything else.

"I'm not your brother," Saxon replied in the same language, turning away so he could go and help Kane and Elias.

The shot exploded behind him, and a second later, Hammer caught up. "You need to get that arm looked at."

Saxon wouldn't have said he did, except that now Hammer pointed it out, the whole thing started to throb. "Let's secure Namir and I'll put some cream on it or something."

Hammer snorted. "I will make it an order."

"Did you get a picture of that guy?" They were supposed to photograph everyone they killed. With most of them being high-value targets, the higher-ups always wanted proof when a target was taken out.

"I recognized him from the briefing. Last year the guy blew up a home for orphans about a hundred miles east of here."

Up ahead, the gunfire had eased off. Which could mean good or bad things for Kane.

"This is a lot of fuss just for a flash drive." Saxon checked around the next corner. The opening of the tent flapped in the nonexistent breeze. The scent of curry spices hung in the air with a current of charred wood and the smell of too many bodies packed together with poor hygiene conditions.

His head swam, the heat beading drops of sweat across his forehead. He lifted a hand and swiped at his skin.

The world seemed to shift around him. Blood coated his fingers where it had dripped all the way down from the outside of his arm. He moved his fingers on that hand against one another, rubbing his thumb across his fingertips. Smearing the blood.

Hammer grabbed his elbow. "Easy."

Kane's voice came over the radio. "Package secure."

"Meet us at the medical tent. Saxon needs a bandage." Hammer's arm snaked around his waist, and his buddy walked him under the flap of the tent. A long room flanked with medical beds on either side. Equipment seemed too sparse in here, except where crates had been stacked in one corner.

He didn't need a hospital.

"Just put . . ." The name of the bandage eluded him. Saxon couldn't string two thoughts together. "The thing on it. Let's go."

They had something with them that would go over his wound and stop the bleeding. At least long enough so they could get back to the rendezvous point and get picked up. There was a packet of it in the right thigh pocket of his cargos. He reached down and patted it.

Hammer grunted. "And I went to the trouble of bringing you all the way to the finest hospital in Syria."

A woman in a white lab coat over blue scrubs came over, her hair covered with a blue scarf. She had dark eyes that were like huge midnight pools trying to suck him under the surface. He tried to blink or look away, but she drew him in. She said something, but he couldn't make out the words that seemed to swim around him.

Hammer walked to the bed she indicated and dumped Saxon down on his back.

He hissed out a breath between clenched teeth and tried to focus on the woman, because she was the best-looking thing in this place. Like a single flower in a garden that was nothing but neglected shrubs and trampled bushes. One of those plants that only bloomed at night.

Hammer leaned over him. "You're going to wanna stop talking, buddy."

Great. Whatever he'd been thinking just now, he'd apparently been saying it out loud as well. The doctor lady tapped a syringe, then stuck the needle into the outside of his arm.

Saxon hissed out another breath.

She patted his chest. "Just a few minutes and you'll be good to go."

He couldn't look away. "Does it cost extra for the express service?"

She smiled at him, and so many things in his life seemed to fall into place. "Only because you showed up in the middle of a malaria outbreak and I need to get back to treating patients. Not because you're the only Americans in the place." She spoke with a crisp British accent that made him want to ask her what her favorite kind of tea was.

A commotion over by the entrance to the tent drew his attention.

He could feel her begin to irrigate the wound on the outside of his arm. *Ouch.*

He attempted to pay more attention to Kane and Elias striding down the center aisle of the hospital tent with dark looks on their faces, coming over to where Hammer stood at the end of the bed.

Elias had dirt smeared across his forehead and the side of his head, and Kane had grazes on the knuckles of his left hand.

"Tell me, Doc…" Kane clasped Saxon's hand and pushed something small and made of hard plastic between their palms. When Kane pulled his hand away, Saxon closed his fingers around the flash drive. "Are you going to be able to reattach his brain?"

Saxon snorted. "Even if she doesn't, I'll still be smarter than you."

Behind Kane, Elias and Hammer spoke in low tones too quiet for him to hear. Saxon slipped the flash drive into his pants pocket.

The doctor said, "If you're going to demand the express service, it requires minimal questions."

Kane stared at the woman like he'd fallen in love. Saxon cleared his throat, and Kane looked down at him.

"Understood." Kane replied to the woman's comment, but Saxon knew it was meant for him. As usual, they were on the same page.

Saxon wasn't here to find the love of his life. But if she was going to show up suddenly, he wouldn't argue.

Saxon said, "Get lost."

Kane grinned. "Don't worry, you'll live. After all, only the good die young." He turned and wandered back to the huddle of Hammer and Elias. Whatever had happened with Namir, it seemed they had the flash drive but not the man himself. Had he escaped?

Saxon didn't like the sound of that, with members of the terror cells still scouring the refugee camp, looking for all of them. The bad guys were trying to take out Namir before the Delta Force team could grab the guy and drag both him and his information out of here.

"I won't bother asking if you're US military." The doctor's dark eyebrows drew together, all her attention on the stitches she was putting in the outside of his arm. "Or what you're doing here."

"Good call. I'm Luca." Saxon studied her Middle Eastern features and the casual adherence to cultural strictures. "British?"

She nodded. "Born in Iran, raised in England. Harvard Medical School, then straight to the Red Cross. I'm Kira Yassan."

Nice to meet you sounded so lame. "That's an impressive résumé."

"You haven't even seen what I can do with phyllo pastry." She looked up for a second and winked at him.

Saxon pretty much fell in love right at that moment.

Hammer wandered over and said, "We're going to do a quick sweep. Try to find him." He squeezed Saxon's shoulder. "We'll be back in less than twenty minutes."

When Hammer got that look in his eye, there was no point arguing with him.

"Understood."

They were leaving the flash drive in his safekeeping and giving it one more shot to locate Namir. Saxon didn't have any choice but to comply—at least, not until Dr. Kira Yassan finished stitching him up.

He glanced at her, about to say something corny like *Do you come here often?* Figure out how to maybe email her or something later. Get to know each other and see what happened after.

Except, when did that ever develop into something solid for a guy like him?

She snipped the edge of the thread with a pair of scissors. "Stitches are all done. I'm going to cover it with a bandage."

He glanced at the front entrance to the tent, but his teammates had already left without him.

"The drug that I put in that syringe is going to knock you out for a couple of minutes." She taped down the bandage. "I'm surprised you're still awake. But you'll be all set to go just as soon as you wake up."

Saxon started to argue, but everything around him sucked down into darkness, and he passed out.

Dr. Kira Yassan watched Luca's eyes roll back in his head. It really was easier this way. Apart from the fact that he seemed like a nice guy and he might actually be attracted to her, it was best that he passed out. Attraction wasn't something that happened often in her world.

Actually, maybe that made this whole situation worse.

She glanced around to make sure no one else on the medical staff team was watching, then reached over and pulled out the flash drive that she'd seen him tuck into his pocket. The one his friend passed to him. The reason they were here, most likely, given how he'd safeguarded it.

She'd known what she had to do the moment she saw it. There would be just enough time before he woke up and his teammates returned. She needed to make a copy of the flash drive on her computer and then return the storage device to his pocket.

Kira ducked into the back, where a tall curtain that hung from a frame covered the area in the rear of the tent from view of the main room. Back here, it was occasionally necessary to perform surgery on a patient or deliver a baby. That or a hundred other things that occurred when people lived in such close proximity in horrible conditions.

Maybe she was growing jaded.

Kira sat on the stool and scooted up to her laptop, inserting the flash drive into the port on the side. Passing along whatever was on this storage device had to earn her some credit with the government. After the high-value target the Brits had been after had passed away on her operating table, they hadn't been entirely pleased with losing their shot at intelligence. Whatever the Americans were after with this thing, it had to be valuable enough for them to risk their lives to obtain it and the person who'd been carrying it.

She tapped her foot on the groundsheet tarp under her sneaker while the files transferred. Didn't look at the framed photo of her at age nine with her parents on holiday in Egypt. She'd been so excited to see the pyramids, and in the months before they went, she'd read everything she could get her hands on about pharaohs.

In the end, it was the last time they'd ever had fun together as a family.

She leaned back on the stool and looked out at the soldier. He really was a good-looking guy. Middle Eastern like her, but she'd guess from his features that he was Syrian. How a man like him ended up in the US Army—or whatever branch of the American military he was in—she couldn't even fathom. So many who lived here would consider that a betrayal of all they stood for.

Luca Saxon.

He'd been self-assured enough that she knew he didn't consider the life he lived as a betrayal of anything. More likely, Luca was one of those hero types who thought every mission was to right all the wrongs in the world and restore the balance of justice.

As if that was how the world worked.

Still, she had to admit that, without people like him, the world would be a pretty sorry place.

"Dr. Yassan?" Simon, one of their nurses who was originally from Australia, stuck his head around the curtain.

Kira tried to pretend he hadn't startled her out of her skin. "What is it?"

"Dr. Chen is bringing in a family. All of them have fevers and nausea."

"I'll be right there." She checked the file transfer and saw it was complete, copied the files to a password-protected drive that only belonged to her, and attached everything to an email she left in her draft folder.

Kira pulled out the flash drive, then tucked it into her pocket, leaving the surgical area and stepping back into the main room. Luca was still unconscious, this soldier with his ropey arms and thick chest. Dark hair that was short and fell over his forehead in a way that begged her to brush it back and made her wonder what it would look like long and in need of cutting.

As if her life would ever be conducive to a relationship. But then, that was the entire point of being here. Because it was as far from the person she had been in the Western world as she could get. Out here in the forgotten places of the world, giving all her sweat and tears to people that no one else seemed to care about.

She pretended to adjust his bandage, then wandered around the bed so she would be close to his pocket in order to return the flash drive. She glanced around again, ensuring no one was watching her, and slipped the flash drive back into the folds of his dark cargos.

His hand whipped up and grasped her wrist. Those strong fingers squeezed the fine bones in her hand. "Who do you work for?"

She loosened her grip on the flash drive, moving her hand away from his pocket. He didn't let go of her wrist. Those dark eyes of his bored into her. She wanted to tell him everything. Just open her mouth and unburden her soul on someone—anyone. But he wouldn't understand.

"Answer the question."

"I'm not your enemy." She forced the words from her mouth, trying to figure out how to explain this without incriminating herself.

His dark gaze assessed her, just a hint of betrayal in his eyes. And why would that be? They didn't even know each other. They wouldn't ever see each other again.

"Saxon!" Someone called out from by the entrance.

The other three men on his team rushed into the tent, moving fast. The one in front with the light-brown beard covering the bottom half of his face came first. The leader of this team. "Gotta go, we have incoming."

The man's gaze swept across Saxon holding her wrist.

A second later, she had been released. Saxon sat up on the bed and swung his boots onto the floor. She wanted to step forward, help him steady himself as he stood. He'd lost a lot of blood and hadn't eaten anything. But instead of supporting him, she folded her arms across her chest. She had what she wanted, and now it was time for him to leave.

Outside the front entrance of the tent, gunfire sounded in quick succession.

All four of the men shifted, a deadly intention overwhelming their body language.

"We can't get out that way," one of the men said. "They'll kill us before we even step into the light."

Kira cleared her throat. "You can leave out the back, if you want."

Her patient turned to her. "And walk right into unfriendly fire?"

"I told you I wasn't your enemy." She lifted her hands, palms up, and then let them fall back to her sides. "I'm just a doctor."

Saxon's gaze narrowed, the skin around his eyes contracting. "You can't expect me to believe that."

"I don't think you have time for anything else." Kira lifted her chin.

The team leader tugged on Saxon's good arm. "Let's go."

He clearly didn't want to, but he complied with the instruction from his boss. The group of four men moved to the rear of the tent, where they would find the back exit. He didn't even look back. None of them did.

A second after they disappeared behind the curtain, two men

strode into the medical tent. Rifles across their bodies and sweat-soaked hair on their foreheads. She knew the type. Had seen them in the shadows every day since she got here. The kind of men who showed up when danger happened and capitalized on the suffering of others.

She crossed to the center aisle and stood in their path, her palms raised as she had done with Saxon. But this time Kira was certain her life was in danger. She used the language her father had taught her, speaking in their native Arabic. "This is a place of healing. You are not welcome here."

The man on the right, the older of the two, though not by much, replied in the same language, "We go where we please. The will of God Almighty will be done in this place, as it will be done everywhere in the coming days."

Now there was a terrifying thought. Was this all about some impending attack? She would have to ask her contact at MI6 if they'd heard anything.

"What do you want?" She needed to delay them as long as possible, giving that American team as much of a head start as possible. "You cannot steal our supplies. There are people here in need."

"We do not want the kind of hope you offer, that only weak people are willing to accept. Our cause is just. We will kill the infidels who invade our country."

And they'd do it caring nothing for the people in their way. Innocents they viewed as nothing but collateral damage.

"There haven't been any of those people in here." She shook her head, playing the dumb female they considered her to be—or someone with too much to lose if she spoke the truth.

But what did she have to lose? Everything she valued was on her person. There was nothing for her anywhere else in the world other than here.

The thought struck her with something a lot like grief. But it was the loss of something she'd never had.

A dream she had long since given up on.

"I have patients coming in who need to be treated. You both need to leave." She squared her shoulders and lifted her chin.

The older of the two muttered something that would have made her gasp if she wasn't already on high alert. She couldn't give away that she was anything more than a doctor in a war-torn country.

He crossed the space between them in a second and brought his gun down on her temple. She swung her arm up to block the blow, but it was far too late to do anything about it. Pain exploded in her skull, and she started to collapse.

A gunshot went off inside the tent, so loud it sounded like fireworks. The pain felt like it was fracturing her head, but she couldn't get up.

The man who struck her fell to the ground, his lifeless eyes staring at her from where he had slumped. His friend turned and didn't even take one step before more bullets slammed into his back. He tripped and landed on the ground.

Someone in the tent started screaming, the sound far too close to her splitting head.

Kira was rolled to her back. She tried to focus on the person over her and managed to discern Simon's features. Saxon knelt on the other side of her. Both of them stared at her with similar expressions on their faces.

"That looks bad." Saxon glanced at Simon.

The nurse palpated the edges of the wound on her forehead. Kira screamed at the pain that whipped around inside her head. "It's bad," Simon said. "And our X-ray machine is on the fritz. I'll have to call for a medevac chopper to take her to the hospital."

She felt moisture run from the corners of her eyes.

"Sax, we have to go. There's a change of plans." The other man came over, his face swimming into view. "That was a brave thing you did."

"More like stupid."

"Sometimes those two things look the same." The team leader grasped the collar of Saxon's bulletproof vest and tugged. "Come on. Time to go."

"Not until I know she's going to be okay." He was tugged all the way to his feet, whether he liked it or not.

The team leader said, "Right now, we have to go save someone else's life. Someone who doesn't have a medevac chopper coming for her."

Saxon knelt again quickly. "I'm sorry you got hurt."

Kira tried to think past the pain.

Strong fingers squeezed her hand, and then he was gone.

TWO

THE BUZZER SOUNDED, AND THE DOOR FOR cellblock four swung open. Luca Saxon watched the prisoner shuffle into the room, jingling chains from the shackles that held him here. Six weeks until his trial, and already Alden Jenkins didn't look anything like the man who had tried to destroy Rowan "Hammer" Wallace's family just four short months ago.

"I'll be right outside," the corrections officer said.

Luca nodded. "Thanks."

Jenkins settled into the chair like it was the seat behind the mayor's desk—the one from which he'd run the city of Renegade, Colorado, for years. At least, that's who he'd been on the surface. Underneath, he was responsible for multiple murders and a massive land grab, all for the mineral rights to build his personal criminal enterprise.

Jenkins lifted his chin and stared down Luca. "You don't look like my lawyer."

"He's busy trying to figure out how to defend you when the evidence is clear." Luca adjusted the sleeve of his thick black shirt, the one with pearl buttons, over his smartwatch. "That and the fact there's more I believe you've done that no one knows about."

"So you came to gloat?"

"You think I care about you enough for that?" Luca asked. "Hammer has moved on. He and Sierra got married just before Christmas. Maybe you haven't heard that they're expecting now. Their second baby together. Huck is so excited to have a little brother or sister to teach how to rope and ride."

But of course, Alden didn't care about that. His connection to the family had only been about getting his hands on their land.

A tendon flexed in Alden's jaw. "Just tell me what you want."

"You're facing some big charges." Luca whistled. "Then there's the whole mayoral race going on, and your deputy mayor telling everyone who will listen that he always knew you were corrupt. The whole campaign—on both sides—is about undoing what you did to this city."

"Why do you care? You aren't even from here."

Luca had wondered that himself. For about the first ten minutes after he and Hammer arrived in Renegade last fall. After that, he'd decided to put down roots here and make a life for himself.

He'd helped Hammer fight against the thugs stealing land from people. Sabotaging equipment, poisoning cattle, even arranging "accidents" to take care of anyone who got too close to the truth. Crimes Jenkins would go down for.

Meanwhile, Ralph Rousseau, who'd been named in all the evidence Sierra's grandfather had collected, was claiming he'd been framed and talking deals with the cops.

Luca needed the truth. Would this man give it to him?

Alden Jenkins stared at him from across the table. Probably trying to figure out which way to play this.

Alden had not only targeted landowners whose property he wanted for himself but also taken his frustration out on teenage Hammer with his fists. Helping his best friend save Sierra and Huck from Jenkins hadn't just been the right thing to do; it had been the best use of Luca's skills. All that military training in action, saving good people who should have someone around to stand up for them but didn't.

"Maybe I don't care about Renegade." Luca shrugged. "But it's somewhere to be. Good as anywhere, I figure."

Alden didn't need to know that Luca had decided to stay, or that he'd spent the last few months since Sierra and Hammer reunited working this case. Finally getting his private investigator license and digging in with the people in Renegade, working to uncover the corruption of this "shadow syndicate," whoever they were.

But the whole thing was proving more than frustrating. He and Detective Michael Martinelli, who he'd been working closely with on the investigation, just couldn't seem to get traction beyond what they already knew about this shadowy syndicate operating in Renegade.

Far as they could tell, Jenkins and Rousseau had both been working for the syndicate. Problem was, none of the evidence they had linked back to anyone else but them. Just Rocky Mountain Land Development—Rousseau's company—and the conglomerate Meridian Holdings, which put Jenkins in the mix, thanks to his legitimate business interests in both companies.

Whoever was in charge had taken pains to hide their identity.

Alden's eyes flared. "If you don't care about Renegade, then get lost. This city doesn't need people like you in it."

"People who don't care?" Luca fired back. "Because clearly you cared so much that you wanted it all for yourself." Before Alden could argue with him, Luca said, "We know what's really going on in this city."

After his kidnapping a few months ago, Ralph Rousseau had told them that there was more to the crime world in Renegade than anyone realized. It had been enough to convince Luca to look for power players in Renegade. Ralph had been kidnapped and shot, but why? Detective Martinelli wasn't convinced the syndicate had ordered it, so Luca had a hunch he was here to play.

"We know about the Shadow Syndicate." Luca watched for Alden's reaction.

Another clench of his jaw.

"The DA could find you somewhere cushy to spend your sentence. Somewhere out of the syndicate's reach."

Alden scoffed. "With all those charges you mentioned?" He shook his head. "No one's gonna give me nothin'. They haven't even offered me a deal."

"I could talk to the DA on your behalf. Find out what kind of concessions they're willing to make in exchange for the names of whoever's in charge of this shadow syndicate."

Alden's expression hardened. "What makes you think I'm not the head of the Shadow Syndicate?"

"If you were, I doubt you'd have allowed yourself to be arrested." Jenkins had let his emotions get the better of him and used violence to solve his problem rather than being cold and calculating.

Luca had met all kinds of evil people in his life. The ones who let feelings control their actions were the ones who slipped up and got caught. Those who acted with zero emotion were so much more disturbing.

Luca shifted in his seat. "I think you know who they are, or at least you have an idea. You made a deal to sell your lithium to them, didn't you? But I also think Rousseau wasn't happy doing your dirty work and wanted in on the profits. When Elway brought you the evidence he'd found, you discovered Ralph trying to undercut your agreement with the syndicate, so you decided to remove him from the equation. Did I get that right?"

"You think I'm the chump who got double-crossed?"

Luca leaned forward. "I think you're the chump who'll go down for all of it."

"Can't prove it, or I'd be facing more charges."

"Speaking of that," Luca began, "all the evidence we've got points to Rousseau, but I don't see him behind bars. Why's that?"

A tendon in Alden's jaw flexed.

"I'm surprised they didn't already come up with proof that you're the head of the syndicate. That way you go down and no one's the wiser." Luca shrugged. "I figured they'd have pinned it all on you by now."

Given the shift in his expression, Alden didn't like that. "They aren't pinning anything on me. Rousseau can rot for all I care."

Ralph Rousseau had been the first person to mention the Shadow Syndicate. If he hadn't opened his mouth, they might not have paid much attention to the words Elway had scribbled on a sticky note. Even Rousseau's statement was hardly conclusive.

But it was a start.

In the months since then, for all their looking, they hadn't come up with more than what already implicated Rousseau. Documents that Rousseau's lawyers argued were forged versions of his legitimate business accounts and which Rousseau contended were evidence that he'd been framed. That he was merely the victim of a crime.

"Now's your chance to do yourself a favor before you go down, Rousseau makes a deal of his own, and the syndicate gets away with everything." Luca leaned back in his seat. "Fight this battle on your terms with the only leverage you have left, before you go down for all of it."

He figured appealing to the man's inherent selfishness was the best play here.

What he wanted to do was persuade Alden to do the right thing, but that wasn't going to be effective. Luca wanted to practice the speech he would give if his brother Amir was the one sitting across this table. But Amir was currently serving eight years in federal prison in Texas, hundreds of miles from here, and Luca couldn't do anything about that.

But he could do something about this.

"Maybe I'll take you up on that offer of a cushy cell. Get them to wheel me in a TV so I can watch whatever I want." Alden's tone dripped with disdain. "That would've been an easier sell than getting me to betray people who would retaliate and kill me."

"You think we can't protect you?"

Alden leaned forward, the shackles jingling. "I think once you have what you want, you don't need me. I'm only alive now because I've kept my mouth shut this far."

"No one has to know that you said anything," Luca said. "We can ensure your safety. But do you really not want to play the one card you have left—the knowledge of the syndicate and their names? Why not make sure they all go down?"

The other man shook his head. "Just talking to you puts my life at risk in a place like this."

"Then why did you agree to meet?" Luca got the feeling there was something Alden wanted. Something he hadn't asked for yet.

And given the look in his eyes, it might be the first real thing Jenkins said in this whole conversation.

Luca waited, the clock on the wall marking each second while he watched the expression on Alden's face. It almost made him seem vulnerable, or at least a tiny bit human. A man who had been the mayor, who got whatever he wanted, and now he wore a jumpsuit and chains. He knew he didn't have much left to lose.

Finally, Alden said, "I'll tell you what you want to know if you get Mack to come and see me."

Luca didn't allow his thoughts to reach the expression on his face. Alden couldn't know how Luca felt about the idea of bringing his friend here to see his father. Hammer's half brother, a kid who was barely twenty-one, didn't need to come into the prison to see the man who had shattered his perception of what a father should be.

They hadn't talked about it much, but since Alden had shown his true colors to Mack, the kid hadn't been the same. He'd withdrawn the past few months, and even when Hammer reached out over and over, the kid rarely showed up. He'd been getting an EMT cert and starting work, but he couldn't carve out time for family?

Alden pushed back his chair and stood. "Guard!"

Luca watched the corrections officer lead him out, and the door shut. After Alden and his escort were out of sight, the door on the other side of the room opened, and Detective Mike Martinelli stepped in.

"You actually got somewhere." Mike didn't look happy about it. He paced the floor on the other side of the table, running a hand through his hair. "But we need action."

"This is taking way too long." Luca pushed his own chair back and stood, stretching his arms above his head, almost able to touch the ceiling. "It's like he's feeding us crumbs that we're begging for, and every time he gives us something, we have to jump on it. We've got a group of people who have been under the radar for so long we can't even grasp whether they're real or not. It's not going to get solved in a matter of days."

"And you're fine with them operating for years to come?" Mike asked.

Luca didn't want to live in a city like that. "I'd rather kick down every door in Renegade and figure out who they are."

Mike shot him a look. "But of course, you aren't going to do that. Because it would be illegal and your private investigator license would be revoked."

"You're no fun."

They both knew Luca had no intention of breaking the law. Mike just didn't know the real reason why he always did the right thing. He knew what his life would be like if he'd made different choices and not gone into the Army, because that life was being lived in a federal prison in Texas.

"Are you going to talk to Mack? See if he's willing to meet with his father so we can get a break on this case?"

Luca sighed. "I'll track the kid down and see what he says. But don't get your hopes up."

Mike held the door, and they made their way out of cellblock four at the Renegade Correctional Facility. Thankfully, Luca had driven himself here, so he'd have the hour-long drive back to his place through morning traffic to figure out a plan of action.

"In the meantime, I got a call from the US Marshals in town. They need someone in the private sector for a job. You have an appointment tomorrow morning, first thing, at the federal courthouse."

Luca glanced over at him. "You vouched for me?"

"Don't get all misty-eyed about it."

Luca laughed. "I'm surprised you didn't ask Hammer to do it. He's got the same training I do."

"Are you kidding me? Sierra would kill me if I let the guy put himself in danger."

"Good point," Luca said. "I think she's had enough of that for a lifetime." He pushed the door open, and they both stepped into the late-morning sun. Luca planned to spend the rest of the day working a couple of cases he had on his desk.

Background checks on three new hires for a local finance company, and a young woman trying to locate her grandfather. Somewhere in there he planned to track down Mack and see what the kid thought about visiting his stepdad in prison in exchange for information about the Shadow Syndicate.

"I'll send you the info for that appointment." Mike held out his hand and they shook.

"Happy hunting."

The detective walked away to his unmarked police car, and Luca headed for his old truck, the one he had bought from Dolly at the diner.

He needed answers.

One way or another, he would figure out how to break this case.

***

Dr. Kira Yassan said a quick thank-you and climbed out of the rideshare in front of Renegade's hottest new restaurant, the Gilded Lily. At least there was something newer in this city than her. With less potential staying power as well. Made her feel downright settled, but then, it had been several years since she moved here.

This place should probably feel like home by now.

She adjusted her purse and brushed her long dark-brown hair back off her other shoulder. One glance to her left gave her a view of the mountains in this part of Colorado. Capped with a dusting of snow from the storm that had rolled in over the past weekend, the peaks west of the city reminded her every day that majesty existed.

She lived only six blocks from here but had never ventured to this restaurant until now, and certainly wouldn't have done so in these heels. Considering she worked long shifts in rubber-soled shoes, Kira took every opportunity she could to wear a pair from her extensive collection of heels.

One day she might feel as if she wasn't an impostor anywhere outside of the hospital, where she wore a lab coat over scrubs and those comfy shoes on her feet. But was it so bad that, inside the walls of the emergency department of Renegade Mercy General Hospital, she knew exactly where she belonged?

"Dr. Yassan!"

She glanced toward the voice and spotted the woman she was meeting for lunch. Destiny climbed out of a town car that had pulled over to the curb behind where Kira's rideshare had stopped. A driver in black held the door for the woman and then closed it behind her.

Kira waited for the woman to saunter over in her own heels, a light-pink dress highlighting her thin frame. "Mrs. Rousseau."

The other woman kissed her cheek. "Please, it's far past time you call me Destiny."

She probably didn't intend to intimidate Kira. Destiny was who she was, and one could argue that was a good thing for the world, given the work she did. But Kira would always be the scrawny girl from Iran, growing up in South London in a small house with far too many people taking up space. Always looking for ways to make herself as small as possible. Walking an hour to the library and back by herself, usually with a backpack of books.

That isn't who you are now.

Kira had a prestigious position as the head of the emergency department at Renegade Mercy General Hospital, and her work all over the world had saved lives.

Kind of like this woman she was meeting.

"Let's go inside." Destiny led the way to the doors, which opened thanks to a maître d' holding the door for them.

The older man wore all black, slacks and a shirt, and had a mustache threaded with gray across his upper lip. "Good afternoon, ladies."

Destiny spoke over her shoulder. "We have a reservation. At my usual table." She grinned in Kira's direction. "I've been here twice a week since they opened!"

Kira smiled, following her acquaintance—she wouldn't go so far as to call Destiny a friend—into the restaurant, all the way to a table at the far end. A place of prominence, where at least six people could sit. But no one else was joining them. Despite the fact there were only two of them, this was where they were going to have lunch.

Hopefully without Destiny using it as a photo opportunity to build buzz for her foundation.

Kira would certainly look the part, with these wide-leg slacks and the gold blouse she had tucked in. Assimilating and blending in anywhere in the world, no matter the situation, was one of her skills. She had been using the art of camouflage this way for years. And thankfully, lately it wasn't to keep herself safe.

Her life wasn't in danger here.

She settled her purse on the seat beside her and surreptitiously reached up to run a finger across the scar just above her left eyebrow. No amount of plastic surgery had been able to completely remove the daily reminder of that refugee camp in Northern Syria. No matter where she went or who she became, it would always be with her.

Reminding her of what was real, just in case she ever forgot.

She didn't have to be a vapid doctor with no care for people and an inflated pride in having power over life and death. She could be more than what a lot of doctors became. So she'd traded that kind of career for refugee camps and outbreaks and finding heroes who made her want to help the world be a better place.

Now she was in yet another fresh start, and it was high time to figure out where she fit here.

Kira cleared her throat. "What's good here?"

"Oh, just about everything. But they have the most divine oysters." Destiny settled a pair of reading glasses onto her nose and peered at the menu. "I try to order something different every time though. It's not good to get into a rut."

Kira swallowed back honesty. "That sounds like an adventurous way to live."

And didn't that just make her sound incredibly pathetic? All she did was work at the hospital and read books at home, mostly watching church services online when she could, or listening to podcasts.

What was an everyday occurrence for this woman and her high-society lifestyle was probably going to be the highlight of Kira's week—and her social life for the month.

Destiny laughed lightly. "If you want an adventurous life, Renegade, Colorado, is probably not the place to find it."

"I've lived in enough spots in the world with far too much adventure. Finding somewhere with just enough life to be interesting suits me just fine."

Hopefully that didn't sound too much like she was hiding from real life.

When the server had taken their orders, Destiny said, "This city used to be so backward. Now that more people have moved here, we actually have some semblance of a downtown and society life. Otherwise, I would have moved away a long time ago." Destiny took a sip of her ice water. "But I still take every chance I can to go on trips with my husband."

"How is Ralph doing?" They'd never discussed the fact he had been kidnapped and shot months ago, and Destiny probably wasn't going to mention it now. Or the fact he hadn't been brought to the hospital where Kira worked—he'd been flown to Denver and treated at a private facility. He'd been back in Renegade nearly two months, surprisingly well recovered for a man who'd been gut-shot.

Kira knew from previous conversations they'd had that Ralph was currently out on bail and had been extensively interviewed, first by the police and then by the FBI, during his recovery. Despite paperwork implicating him in shady business, his team of high-priced lawyers were arguing he was the victim of a crime. That he'd been framed for all the land grabbing, harassment, and sabotage that had been going on in Renegade, and was only an overeager real-estate developer.

"Oh, fine, fine. Resting plenty, so don't worry." Destiny waved a hand. "Fussing far too much about this gala we're having this weekend. Which is what I wanted to talk to you about."

"It's for your foundation?" Maybe Destiny believed that as the head of an emergency department, she had the income to make huge donations to Destiny's nonprofit.

Destiny nodded. "That's right. I wanted to talk about the foundation with you."

The server came over and took their lunch orders. When he had taken their menus away, she said, "We strive tirelessly to provide treatments for people in developing nations who don't have the access to medical care that the Western world does. I know you've worked at refugee camps, so you're certainly aware of what it's like to face an outbreak of disease with little access to pharmaceutical supplies."

Kira nodded. "Local hospitals in the US have their own share of issues, but access to medical supplies isn't one of them."

"What made you decide to take a job in the emergency department?"

After trying to start her own practice and meeting only roadblocks, she had been offered a position with a cardiac team on the other side of the city, at a medical center with a private client list. But that sort of thing had never been what Kira wanted. The people with the money to solve their problems and get the care they needed weren't the ones she was here to help.

Kira took a sip from her own water glass, the condensation leaving a wet stain on the white tablecloth. "I've always preferred an environment that is fast-paced, and day-to-day, you never know what you're going to face in the ER."

"And you work evenings?"

"My shifts are always six at night to six in the morning, which I've found suits me best." Not only because it was usually busier at night and on the weekends, but also because people were less inclined to hang around and make small talk in the middle of the night.

Busy shifts went quickly, and interesting cases were like puzzles to solve. In the end, the result was saving a person's life.

Destiny cleared her throat. "I hope you don't think this too forward or like I'm bragging, but you know I'm friends with the hospital's administrator and I'm one of their biggest donors. If you wanted to move out of the emergency department, I could put in a good word for you."

"Thank you. I know I had the job offer in the first place because of your influence and our connection after that fortuitous day at the country club." Kira smiled. They'd been tennis partners since. "But I'm very happy where I am."

She expected the words to taste not quite right in her mouth. But they didn't, because she *was* happy. She liked her job, even if she didn't quite feel like she fit in Renegade.

Not yet, anyway.

After all, surely it wouldn't seem this way forever. One day she would realize she'd been here long enough to put down roots, and this city might even start to feel like home.

"What made you choose Renegade out of all the places in the world you could've picked to practice medicine?" Destiny smiled, but it didn't seem to be completely natural. "Not that I'm complaining, since it seems like kismet that you fell right into my lap."

Whatever that was about, Kira wasn't going to explain that she had thoroughly researched the four-man team of Delta Force soldiers who had stormed into the medical tent at the refugee camp that day. Or that she had discovered where they were from and who they were. Months after she had met them, they'd been declared dead—killed in action. That was a whole other story she didn't want to think about right now, but looking into those men had put Renegade, Colorado, on her radar.

"I researched all the open positions that I might like at hospitals all across the country, and as soon as I saw pictures of Renegade, I knew I wanted to move here. The combination of a metropolitan area with a small-town feel and a short drive to reach mountains and the wilderness sold me on moving here."

"I'm so glad you did." Destiny reached over and patted her hand. "I won't beat around the bush, dear. The Healing Hearts Foundation is desperately in need of a fresh face to be our spokesperson. I hope you will come to the gala and get to know the staff, as well as see what we are about. And then I hope you'll give serious consideration to joining me on staff and helping to get sufficient medical supplies to people who really are in desperate need of them."

The server deposited their plates in front of them with a flourish. Kira stared down at the small portion of white fish surrounded by leafy greens she couldn't have named. All of it was covered in a sauce that was an odd orange color.

Before she went to work tonight, she was going to stop off at her favorite hole-in-the-wall drive-through burger place and get a large fries with her bacon double cheeseburger. With all the walking she did on shift, she would burn off those calories by morning.

Tomorrow, right around dawn, she would run four miles on her favorite trail to bleed off the stress and strain of her job. She would get seven hours of sleep, and then she would do it all over again. Rinse, repeat.

She liked her life and the predictability of it. She would've said everything was fine and that she didn't need anything else.

But why did thinking about her routine make her so sad?

"What do you say?"

Kira smiled at her lunch companion. "I would love to attend the gala."

THREE

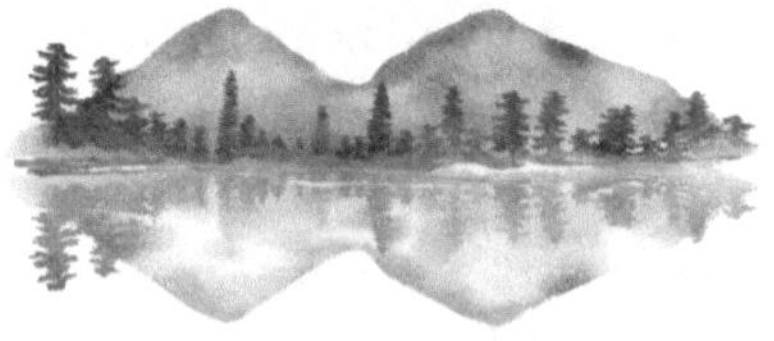

THE BASKETBALL BOUNCED OFF RED BRICK AND sent a dusting of concrete into the air. Luca snatched the ball and turned, tossing it toward the basket so that it sailed over Hammer's head. It bounced off the rim and sank into the net. Overhead, the night sky was threaded with clouds obscuring whatever stars might be visible.

Probably he should start thinking of the guy as "Rowan," since that's how everyone here referred to Hammer.

"Looks like I'm going to win." He raced over to face off with Hammer, who bounced the ball, doing that steady stare thing. Trying to psych out Luca because he knew he wouldn't win unless he threw Luca off his game.

"You always say that in every game, and then you end up losing." Hammer bounced the ball a couple more times, then faked out Luca and made a run for the net.

There was something about basketball that enabled him to push out everything that was happening and focus on the physical exertion. Challenging both of them. He and Hammer had been doing this for years, whenever they could. Though less now that Hammer was married with a kid and a baby on the way.

Luca wasn't going to begrudge the guy not spending as much time with a ball in his hands in favor of being with his family. But Luca needed the moment of clarity that came when he saw Hammer's move coming, intercepted it, and got the ball. When there was nothing in his mind but the game and anticipating his friend's move. Besting him. Luca turned and gave the jump shot everything he had.

Hammer whistled. "That was sweet."

Luca wandered over and got the ball. He wanted to gloat, but what came out of his mouth was "I went to see Jenkins today."

Hammer's brows rose.

"Detective Martinelli is still trying to get information out of him." Luca wandered over and set the ball next to the dumpster by the back door of the Chinese restaurant. The one below the office space he rented.

Way too much room for one guy, but commercial rentals in this city were hard to come by if you didn't have two hundred employees. The two-thousand-square-foot apartment had been converted into a travel agency years ago, but it had gone bust and they'd left everything behind—including a prehistoric printer that didn't work but liked to rattle at random moments.

The back door banged open, and Andrew, the restaurant owner's oldest son, came out. His jet-black hair had been cut super short on the sides but left to hang long over his eyebrows. The kid sniffed and lifted his head. "Hey." He swung the bulging trash bag and tossed it into the dumpster.

Luca said, "How's it going?"

"Can't complain." Andrew grabbed the door handle and swung it open, heading back inside.

Luca called out, "Have a good one."

Andrew waved a hand over his shoulder before the door shut.

Hammer slapped a hand down on Luca's shoulder. "You have such a way with people."

"It's a gift."

The fact was, he spoke more with Andrew's elderly uncle than anyone else who worked in the restaurant. They played checkers every Wednesday afternoon before the older man went downstairs to the restaurant to prep for the weekend. He had caught Andrew tossing the basketball through the hoop a few times, which was why Luca left the ball out on purpose now.

"I have all the friends that I need in this city. Everyone else is considered a suspect until they get ruled out." He opened the door for Hammer, and they both headed inside, taking the stairs up to the second-floor apartment.

Hammer went to the refrigerator in the kitchen and grabbed two bottled waters, one of which he tossed across the breakfast bar.

Luca didn't twist off the lid just yet. "I noticed you didn't argue with me that everyone in this city is a suspect."

Hammer finished the water bottle, his throat working as he drained the last drops. When he lowered the water bottle and crunched it between his hands, he said, "Not sure I disagree with you. Even if there are some people I'd love to trust and believe in."

"You have roots in this city and people you've known since you were a kid. There are plenty of good folks here."

"I'm glad. Because I trust them with Huck when I'm not around. And I'm going to be trusting them with Sierra and the care of my baby. Hospital staff. The nursery people at church. Teachers and staff at the school. I can't be around the kids twenty-four seven to make sure they're protected."

Luca got a read on his friend's body language. "We know more than most people that the world is a dangerous place. But that's why you do what you can to make it safe, so you don't have to worry about the worst things happening. You can just rest in the peace that you did what you could."

"And God will cover the rest." Hammer folded his arms, leaning his hip against the counter.

Luca nodded. He hadn't accounted for that part, but he should have. His faith was a new thing and not so natural yet. Right now, it was another item on his to-do list, like studying the Bible and going to church. Once he had all those boxes checked, he would find that peace he'd been looking for.

"Alden is in prison now, and he isn't getting out anytime soon. So that's one part of it you don't have to worry about." Once Luca took down the rest of the Shadow Syndicate, Hammer would be able to breathe even easier.

His family would be a little bit safer.

"What did he have to say to you?"

Luca shrugged. "He's still pretty tight-lipped about this whole shadow syndicate thing. Enough for me to wonder if Rousseau was only throwing us off, sending us on a wild-goose chase when there's actually nothing to it."

Just because it wasn't a good theory didn't mean he should outright dismiss it, but Luca wasn't going to base anything on the idea. It was far more likely both men knew who was behind the Shadow Syndicate and were refusing to talk out of fear.

Luca grabbed his phone off the breakfast bar and checked it, but Mack hadn't called him back. "Any idea where your brother is?"

Hammer pulled out his own phone. "Looks like he's at work. His GPS has him at the ambulance station."

"Thanks. That explains why he hasn't called me back." The kid didn't usually answer his phone, or even look at it much, if he was on shift as a rookie EMT. "Alden told me he'll give us information about the Shadow Syndicate if Mack agrees to come and see him."

Hammer winced. "I have no idea what the kid is gonna say to that. He's been avoiding the whole subject of his dad for the past few months, telling me he was just focusing on getting his certification and becoming an EMT. But we all know it was a smokescreen.

Sooner or later, he's going to have to deal with the fact that the father he thought he had doesn't even exist."

"Getting him to go talk to Alden might be the only way to get this case moving again." Luca wandered across the waiting area, past the conference table he'd put in the center of the room, to his office in the corner. Not the one he used to have private conversations with clients, but the spot where he actually did most of his work.

Two of the walls were now covered in newspaper articles, copies of police files, and every other piece of evidence he'd managed to assemble related to this case. A ratty armchair in the corner was the only piece of furniture.

"It feels like we're spinning our wheels. And I'm wondering why I ever thought I could actually be an investigator."

Hammer clapped him on the shoulder, then went to look at the information, even though Luca knew he'd read it all several times before. A lot of it was his lived experience, like the newspaper article that detailed the fire where Sierra and Huck had almost died. "You love puzzles and figuring stuff out."

"This is definitely a puzzle, but I don't have enough pieces to see what the picture is. And I haven't even started figuring out how to put them together."

"If getting Mack to talk to Alden is what does it, then the kid is just going to have to suck it up and face his dad."

Saxon turned to his buddy. "Practicing your drawing-the-line dad speeches?"

"It's easier with Mack, that's for sure. Huck looks at me with those big eyes, and all I can think is how much of his life I've missed. Sierra keeps calling me on it, saying I'm being too easy-going with him." Hammer lifted his hand and squeezed the back of his neck.

"It hasn't been long, and she's been raising him for ten years."

Hammer might be the kid's father, but he was new to the dad

game. Meanwhile, Sierra had done an amazing job teaching Huck everything he needed to know to be Luca's favorite kid. Not that he was biased or anything.

Actually, he was hoping they would ask him to be godfather to their baby.

"We'll figure it out." Hammer sighed. "Want me to talk to Mack?"

Luca shook his head. "I've got it. I'll track him down and have a face-to-face. You go home and enjoy your time with your family."

"Sure?"

Luca nodded. "Tomorrow I'll probably try to track down Ralph and ask him more questions about what he told us. See what else he might have to say about this shadow syndicate."

Hammer headed out, leaving Luca with his wall of puzzle pieces that didn't fit. And the burning need to do what he could to ensure Hammer's family was safe. It was what life had instilled in him. Spending his childhood looking out for his brother, whether Amir cared to remember or not. Taking care of things after his father . . . Joining the military so he could be someone else and build a different life than the one he'd been working on. Then it all went wrong.

Betrayed by one of their teammates.

Reported killed in action.

Hammer, Luca, and their friend Kane had taken Mack and gone to Montana, where they'd fought wildfires because it enabled them to keep below the radar and make sure Maria Sanchez was safe. They'd done a season in Alaska after that, found Maria's father, and wrapped up that summer with Kane and Maria engaged.

No one had expected Hammer to be the first to get married after that, but Kane and Maria had already decided to wait until summer this year.

Now his life had changed again. Things were shifting and his friends were moving on. All Luca needed to worry about was making sure they were safe.

Which meant solving this case.

He headed for his desk and fired up the computer, logging onto his email. The message from the US Marshals had been written by Deputy Marshal Ethan Butler, confirming the meeting was set for oh seven thirty at the federal courthouse. In Judge Mullinax's chambers.

He looked at the address line, seeing who else he could expect at the meeting. One of the names made his breath catch in his throat. *No way.*

Dr. Kira Yassan.

Luca muttered, "What are you doing here?"

"How's the kid in four?" Kira stopped at the counter behind which Nurse Rebecca and Nurse Martin sat. The two of them had rolled their stools toward each other and were no doubt discussing last night's episode of some reality TV show Kira had never seen.

Rebecca shook the mouse and woke up the computer. "His blood work came back clear. And he managed to keep some juice down."

"That's good. If he can get some sleep and his numbers are good tomorrow, I'll be comfortable letting him go home in the morning."

"Yes, Doctor."

"I'm about to hit the cafeteria." Martin stood. "Did either of you need anything?"

"I'll go when you get back," Rebecca said.

Kira shook her head. "I had a big dinner."

When she needed to stretch her legs later, she would hit the vending machine in the break room and grab herself a diet soda. At three in the morning, the need for caffeine with no sugar was always very real.

The side entrance door down the hall opened, and two EMTs entered, one pushing a wheelchair they used to transport patients. Kira smiled at seeing Mack Jenkins in front, carrying the clipboard, his partner Eric Valletta behind him.

The two men couldn't be more different. According to Mack, he had some of his mother's dark features, but it was those serious eyes that made you wonder what he'd seen. He had the kind of demeanor that gave you the impression he was a quiet guy who considered his words carefully. Meanwhile, Eric had three kids and an ex-wife and chattered almost incessantly.

She let them check in with Rebecca and do what they needed to do before she met them in the second bay, currently the only one that was open. So far tonight, they'd treated the victim of a car accident, who'd headed straight up to surgery for the removal of his spleen—something she had done in the back of a pickup truck before—an older man with a broken leg, and the kid in four, who had thrown up all over the table at the restaurant where his family was eating dinner.

Kira pulled back the curtain and waited for them to wheel the patient into the room before she slid it closed. The woman's shirt had been removed, and the EMTs had a blanket around her shoulders. Her face and hands were a mess of small bruises and lacerations.

Mack looked at the clipboard. "Frankie Hesburgh. Twenty-seven, female. Domestic-violence situation. She's fifty-seven kilograms. Heart rate, one twenty-seven. Blood pressure, one thirty over eighty-five, and respirations are rapid and shallow. Suspected broken ribs, but her chest is clear in all fields. She didn't lose consciousness, and no suspected head injury. We gave her ketamine, fifteen milligrams, slowly over a minute. The pain returned before we arrived, but we were close enough we held off giving her any more."

"Very good." She nodded, watching Rebecca hook a pulse

oximeter to the woman's index finger. "And the person who did this to her?"

"We left him talking to the police." She didn't miss the tone in Eric's voice, the sound of distaste.

She had to agree, considering that whoever he was, he had done this. Frankie might have fought back, but she was a slight woman who hadn't been able to match the strength of her attacker.

Kira assisted the patient as she climbed onto the hospital bed, Mack and Eric standing close by. Mack ended up steadying her arm, and Kira caught the distraught look on his face. She wasn't sure that boded well for the kid. He was new at this EMT thing and had to be able to separate his empathy from the plight of a patient, or every victim would weigh on his heart until it crumbled.

Not that Kira was immune. A child with malaria would always swell up in her a need to not quit until the patient was out of the woods. It was probably a trauma response, but she hadn't stuck around therapy long enough to unpack the whole issue.

She'd just gone back to work.

Kira slid the stethoscope from around her neck. "Frankie, I'm Dr. Yassan. We're going to take good care of you, okay?"

The patient nodded, gasping a little and wincing on the inhale.

Kira checked her chest, listening to her breathe, and confirmed that Mack's read on the situation was likely correct. Possible broken ribs, but no risk of a pneumothorax, where the broken rib would have collapsed the lung.

Kira hooked the stethoscope back around her neck, tugging out her braids. "Rebecca, take all of her vitals again and order a chest X-ray. Let's give her another fifteen milligrams of ketamine."

"Yes, Doctor." Rebecca continued hooking Frankie up to the machines that would enable the nurse to monitor her vitals from behind her desk.

Kira waited a beat, just to see. The patient glanced at her.

Kira said, "You're safe here. You can get some rest, and we'll take care of everything else."

The woman's eyes fluttered closed.

Kira headed back out to the hallway, where Eric and Mack were filling out paperwork. She didn't wish on any unsuspecting member of the public the kind of night where she would be able to lose herself in back-to-back trauma cases. That would be wishing for someone else to get hurt and suffer immense pain just so that she could be distracted.

But this was a decent shift nonetheless—one where she hadn't thought much about Destiny's offer. Not that it was far from her mind. There might not even be anything to decide now. She really needed to attend the gala so she could see the whole thing for herself. Find out what this foundation was really about.

She'd been on the website and everything, and it all looked good on the surface. Something Kira should be invested in. But she still wasn't entirely convinced.

Kira headed for the soda now so that she could have it close by later when she needed the hit of caffeine. She tugged a couple of dollar bills from her pocket and fed them into the machine.

"You should go down to the cafeteria and at least get a smoothie."

She glanced over her shoulder and saw Mack swagger over. The kid was far too young for her, but she could tell he was the kind of guy who had been a heartbreaker most of his life. Probably since middle school. He just had that loose-hipped Western style going on, even in his EMT uniform and boots.

Who would have thought she'd ever develop a thing for cowboys?

No, that wasn't who had captured her attention.

Her soda tumbled to the bottom, and she crouched to retrieve it. "How is your family?"

Since they'd met, every time he stopped by, he'd told her a little bit more about his half brother Hammer. Sorry, *Rowan*. As well as

Rowan's wife and their kids. The whole story about how he'd never known he had a son and now they were expecting a second child. Everything was all about happily ever after for the Wallace family.

Trying to marry that with the man she had met in a refugee camp in Syria had proven difficult until she'd seen his picture in the paper, holding on to his now wife with their son tucked between them. Now she knew this was the real guy. The real Rowan. The man Kira had met overseas was Hammer, the soldier.

"They're all fine." Mack shrugged, making his drink selection.

What the kid didn't know was that Kira knew exactly who he was the first day he rolled in here wearing that same uniform. Because when she'd looked up the team who'd invaded her life for an hour and forever changed who she was, she'd discovered that Hammer had a half brother. The same way she'd found out that Luca Saxon's older brother, Amir, was currently serving time in Texas for unlawful weapon sales.

"Just fine?"

He shrugged, bending for his orange soda. He'd told her all about the past two years, where he'd been fighting wildfires. About the "Trouble Boys" and how they'd saved Maria's father from terrorists led by the teammate who had betrayed them.

She'd guessed which of the four that'd been, and the newspaper articles she'd read had confirmed it.

"Lexi still hasn't texted me back."

"Oh no." Kira touched his forearm. "I'm sorry."

He'd told her a few weeks back about the girl he'd met a couple of summers ago in Montana. The daughter of one of the other wildland firefighters. They'd hit it off and stayed in touch. For a while, at least.

"I guess it's over." Mack shrugged. "Not that I was all that excited about the long-distance thing, but I thought we were making it work. Building something. We were talking about meeting up for a weekend somewhere in Wyoming. Hanging out."

"I'd love to give you advice about moving on and keeping yourself open to finding love, but I have no idea how to do that." She made a face.

After all, she'd been pining for some guy for years now. Even though she knew he wasn't dead anymore, that didn't mean she was going to do anything crazy like look him up. He thought she'd betrayed him, probably. Had likely been glad to see the back of her—until she got herself hurt moments later. What followed was weeks of pain and physical therapy. Headaches. She'd clawed her way back to health and eventually back to work.

She said, "Seriously, no clue. My love life is pathetic."

Mack's lips curled up into a smile. "Are you serious? I'm probably not supposed to say this, because it's like, against regulations or whatever. But you're gorgeous, and you should probably know that if you don't already."

Kira chuckled. "Thank you." She nodded her head slightly, but that only drew attention to the sick, ugly scar above her left eyebrow. "It's nice of you to say."

"It's the truth. Even with the scar. Because to be honest, it actually kind of makes you look mysterious and maybe a little vulnerable. It makes me wonder how somebody can go through that and be as strong as you are."

She didn't like the traitorous tears that gathered in her eyes, burning and blurring her vision. Given everything she had been and what she had gone through, there should be no reason for her to react like this. Or maybe it was simply this man in front of her and the connection she had to that team of heroes. The kind of people she wanted to be like. She just hadn't figured out how to do that.

She knew how to be a doctor, but the rest of it was more like who they were as people, rather than the things they did.

If God had any advice for her on the subject, He'd been surprisingly quiet about it. No matter how many times she'd asked.

Kira touched Mack's shoulder and spoke a word in her native language because she needed to remember who she was.

"What does that mean?" His head tipped to the side.

"It means 'thank you.'"

Eric knocked on the open door. "Time to go."

That sounded like they had another callout to attend. Kira said, "Be safe."

Meanwhile, she would be here doing the things she knew how to do. Making a difference across the world had been distilled down to doing the same thing but on a local level. One patient at a time. She'd made peace with knowing that she would never be a true hero. Not after everything she'd done for the British government and then, after, for the Americans, until she'd packed it all in and told them no more.

She was done using her skills like that. Done daydreaming about a dark-eyed man she had no business wanting and definitely didn't plan to run into in a city this size.

After all, if she did run into him . . .

What on earth would she say?

FOUR

THE HALLS OF THE FEDERAL COURTHOUSE WERE all wood wainscoting and gray tile floors. Luca's shoes clipped as he made his way to Judge Mullinax's chambers. He carried a hot cup of coffee and had his backpack over the shoulder of his suit jacket. He still didn't know what this meeting was about, but he figured he would look the part no matter what.

After transitioning out of the military and coming back from the dead all at the same time, he had been approached by a couple of international private security firms. But Luca had found himself turning down offers. Choosing to operate more on a local level—which had turned out to be a good thing when Hammer's family was in danger.

Working by himself as a private investigator wasn't as satisfying as being part of a team, but he still got to coordinate with local cops like Detective Martinelli and his friends.

He wondered if he was early when he knocked on the chamber door, but it opened quickly, and a young woman with long blonde hair, wearing a skirt suit, waved him in. "Thank you for coming, Mr. Saxon. Everyone else is here."

Luca frowned. "I'm not late, am I?"

"Depends on your definition." She closed the door behind him. "The judge always says to be early is to be on time. But he's also older than my father."

He stuck his hand out. "Luca Saxon."

She shook his hand. "Nice to meet you. I'm Claire Carnforth." She led him to an inner door, past her desk. "I'm the judge's assistant." She knocked gently on the door, then opened it. "Mr. Saxon is here."

Luca gave her a small smile and stepped into the judge's chambers. More wood wainscoting, a couple of floor lamps, and more bookshelves than he'd ever seen in his life. All of it filled with leather-bound volumes that were probably older than the judge— and Claire's father.

A woman with dark hair sat in one of the chairs in front of the desk, and a tall guy in a suit was to the right, leaning against a sideboard. The guy had a silver star badge on his belt, his cowboy hat on the surface beside his hand, where he gripped the edge of the piece of furniture.

Judge Mullinax sat behind the desk, looking like a guy he'd seen in an old Western, but Luca couldn't remember which one. He had dark hair threaded with the same gray that wove through the mustache and full beard on his chin. His big form filled the chair in a way that told Luca this guy had some heft behind him, like a man who'd spent years building muscle and made sure he didn't lose it, even into his sixties.

"Glad you could join us." The judge lifted his chin and indicated the man. "This is Deputy Marshal Ethan Butler. He'll be coordinating things. And Dr. Kira Yassan from Renegade Mercy General Hospital."

She turned and stood, facing him.

Kira.

To her credit, she managed to cover the flinch. Yeah. She hadn't been expecting him. *Turns out I'm not dead.*

He had no idea what she thought.

"Do the two of you know each other?" Deputy Marshal Butler asked. "Because that would explain a lot about the fact you have exactly the same security clearance. It's why you're both here. The two of you are the only people in town with the skills to do what I need and the necessary background."

Luca looked at Butler. "Dr. Yassan and I have met once, very briefly." He looked at her, determined to keep all his feelings to himself. He could've held out his hand and shaken hers, but touching her was a slippery slope to betraying a little of what was going on in his head. "Good to see you." He managed to nod.

"You as well." She nodded back to him, her expression flat. Utilizing all the skills she'd amassed doing . . . whatever it was she'd been doing years ago in that refugee camp.

Was she even a real doctor?

She could have been faking it and using the situation for some kind of covert operation. Now she was here? Yeah, that wasn't suspicious at all.

"You can have a seat." Deputy Marshal Butler motioned to the other chair, and Luca and Kira both sat. He wandered around to the other side of the desk, standing beside the judge.

The older man with his silver-streaked hair leaned back in his chair and interlaced his fingers over his shirt buttons. He looked over at the marshal.

Ethan cleared his throat. "As I said before, the two of you are the only people qualified to assist me in a sensitive operation. All you need to know is that a patient will be arriving at the hospital two days from now to receive treatment for his specific type of blood disorder. The treatment will be administered by a specialist. Dr. Yassan will be on hand to assist the specialist in whatever way they need and ensure the patient comes through the procedure to the best of her ability. Luca, you'll be in charge of security."

A patient.

One under the protection of the US Marshals, authorized by a federal judge.

Luca would guess that the patient was in witness protection. Or some kind of high-value target. A criminal testifying against others in exchange for a deal—like cutting-edge treatment for a rare disorder.

Either way, this could be a potentially risky situation.

Ethan looked at Luca. "We would like you to do a full assessment of hospital security prior to the patient's arrival in order to identify any potential points of threat. During the patient's stay, we would like you to oversee security and protection along with a rotating team of those you authorize to work with you or off-duty marshals who volunteer their time."

"You don't have the personnel for full detail?" That explained why they were outsourcing the job.

The judge said, "The agreement with the patient isn't yet signed. I can't authorize the personnel without the deal, and he won't sign the paperwork until he receives the treatment."

Ethan shook his head and sighed. "A couple of our agents are either ill or on vacation. We're also one marshal short and looking for someone to transfer in, but that won't happen soon enough to have this covered."

This whole thing actually sounded like a pretty good use of Luca's skills. "As long as the hospital understands what I'm there to do, I can give you a quote for the job."

Ethan's lips twitched. "Your envelope is on the desk. All the details are inside."

He figured that meant there was a flat payment for the job and the terms weren't negotiable.

Beside him, Kira shifted in her seat. Not nervous, but he got the sense she was intrigued by the idea of this opportunity. "Am I going to receive the patient's medical history, even with the name being redacted?"

Luca wondered if she would recognize the person as soon as she saw them. Did she keep up with the Most Wanted lists?

He didn't want this woman beside him to be intriguing, but the fact was, he had thought about her off and on since they met. Mostly in order to try and figure out who she worked for or why she'd taken his flash drive, even if it was only for a few minutes. But he'd never discovered any answers. On the surface, this woman had been, by all accounts, a legitimate doctor.

Except he knew different.

Ethan said, "We have a secure drive, on which is everything you'll need to know about the patient and the treatment he will be receiving. If any of this information is leaked, all culpability will fall on your shoulders."

Luca figured that was a reasonable warning, given what he knew about Kira. Even if it wasn't much.

She lifted her chin. "I assure you I can keep my mouth shut."

"If you couldn't," the Judge said, "you wouldn't be here."

So they had done a thorough check on her and found out who she really was. Luca wondered if it was worth asking Ethan for a copy of that report. They evidently had access to things restricted from Luca. Because he wouldn't have said he trusted her.

Not until she'd stood up in front of those two insurgents and risked her life to give his team enough time to get away.

But Luca hadn't been doing that.

Something had held him fast behind the curtain, watching to see what would happen to her. Observing her in action as she talked the men down and tried to get them to leave, waylaying them in order that men she didn't even know could survive the encounter and complete their mission.

And then one of the insurgents hammered the butt of his rifle into her face. Seeing her crumple to the ground was one of the most harrowing things he'd ever experienced. Though by far not the worst. Still, it was bad enough he'd nearly launched himself through the curtain and out into the main hospital room.

Hammer and Kane had acted quickly, neutralizing the threat. Enabling him to go to her.

The guy had practically caved in her skull.

And again, when he'd tried to find out where she was and what happened to her—if she'd even survived—there had been nothing to discover. No records. No files.

She'd completely disappeared.

Kira turned to him now, and he saw the line of the scar over her left eye, where that guy had hit her. She turned away from him, retrieved her envelope from the desk, and stood. "Thank you for the offer, gentlemen. I'm happy to assist."

Deputy Marshal Butler nodded.

Kira headed for the door.

Luca grabbed his envelope. "Me too." He nodded. "Marshal. Judge." As quickly as he could, he gathered his things and made his way through the receptionist's area to the hall outside.

Just in time to see Kira turn the corner and disappear out of sight.

Too late.

Luca caught up to her by the rear exit door, where he watched her hammer the button for the door with her index finger. "Dr. Yassan?"

She glanced over at him but said nothing.

"What are you doing here?"

The door swung open, and she frowned at him. "I've lived here for a few years. What are *you* doing here?"

As if she knew he had only moved here recently. "I have a lot of questions. Maybe we could go out for coffee and talk about—"

"I don't think that's a good idea." She stepped outside into the parking lot, red shade trees around the perimeter.

Well, at least she wasn't here in order to stalk him.

He didn't want to stare at her, but all that long, dark hair reflected different shades of red and brown in the overhead light. She wore a slim white blouse with no sleeves, tucked into high-waisted black pants. Tall red heels on her feet. Makeup understated. Fancy purse.

He was suddenly very glad he had worn a suit today and not his usual jeans and shirt. Even if he shopped from the higher-end section of the Western wear store, he still drove an older-model truck. Not the kind of thing a woman like her rode in.

"When I decided to live here, I had no idea where you were." He softened his tone. "I didn't even know that you'd survived what happened." His gaze drifted to the scar.

"Thank you for drawing attention to it. Again." She turned to the street and stepped off the curb. Luca followed her, unwilling to let her get away another time. "I'm sure whatever overlap there is between us on this job, we can be professionals about it." She lifted her chin and headed for the center of the lot.

"I'm sorry, I wasn't trying to point out that you have a scar." He touched the outside of her arm with the hand holding the hot cup of coffee, keeping it careful and gentle. "I have one as well from the same day."

"Then you know what it's like to be constantly reminded of something you would rather forget."

"Was it so bad?" He'd thought there were some sparks between them, but once she'd taken the flash drive from his pocket, all that had gone out the window in the face of mission security.

"Like I said, I'd rather not be reminded of it." She beeped the locks on a gray compact and walked away.

Kira didn't look back at him or that long hair he had pulled back in a ponytail. No longer the military soldier, now he was a handsome man in a suit. But she wasn't sure if that change was a good or a bad thing.

She pulled her three-year-old Mazda out of the court parking lot and onto the street, between an SUV and a mom van. Whatever she might've thought about Luca Saxon and the hero he had seemed to be on the day she met him, he wasn't that man anymore.

If he'd ever been.

The first thing he'd mentioned was money. As if getting paid was his only reason for being there, and not helping the Marshals with a high-profile operation. She was more intrigued by the patient's condition and the treatment he was going to receive than how big the offer in her envelope might be.

At the first stoplight, she used the dash screen to call an old contact. Jordan Witherspoon had worked for the CIA for more than twenty years, and in the short time Kira had been one of their assets, Jordan had become a friend. Someone she was determined not to lose contact with.

"Hello?" Jordan answered.

Kira gripped the steering wheel, trying to squeeze her frustration out on the hard plastic. "It's me. Can you talk?"

There was a faint click, and she said, "The line is secure."

Kira let out a big sigh.

"What happened?" Jordan asked. "I haven't heard any chatter in your neck of the Colorado woods."

"Good, because that's exactly how I want things to stay." Kira turned onto Broadway toward the high-rise where she lived. "Maybe this is all based on the fact I worked all night and then went to a meeting instead of going home and going to bed, but my brain is spinning right now."

"We can talk after you get some sleep."

Kira slowed for a parcel truck to pull out in front of her. "I just need to know what exactly the Marshals know about the work I've done in the past. They mentioned my security clearance, so I know they ran a check on me."

"Let me see." Jordan went quiet for a second.

It wasn't as if Kira was going to bring up her previous work for any government agency to that judge and a marshal. It was enough that they knew she had been a doctor in all kinds of conditions, under a whole lot of hair-raising situations. That was probably enough to make her qualified for this particular assignment. But she still needed to talk to her bosses at the hospital, just to make sure they knew she had taken on additional duties for a short period of time.

Jordan came back on the line. "It looks like they just did an in-depth background check. Which wouldn't have given them more than what's on your résumé, at least officially. Unofficially, the CIA didn't divulge anything, and neither did any other agency."

"Thanks."

"Were you really worried about some of your secrets being leaked?"

Kira pulled into the underground parking lot in the basement of her building and pushed her sunglasses to the top of her head when the area around her plunged into dim light. Her numbered space was down one level, in the corner. Far enough from the elevator that she always walked with her keys between her fingers, just in case someone came up behind her with ill intentions.

"I just ran into someone I met a long time ago, and it kind of threw me. All of it colliding in the same conversation where they are mentioning my clearance."

"Right." Jordan paused. "Do I need to run a background check on someone?"

"Not as far as I'm concerned. My plan is to steer clear of him as much as possible during this job. Besides, he'll be on security, and

I'll be taking care of the patient." That meant they didn't necessarily have to see each other, right?

Kira didn't need the constant reminder that she might have been completely wrong about Luca Saxon. That the person she had built up in her mind as a hero could be far from it. It seemed more likely, from the stories Mack had told her, that Hammer—the team leader—was the heroic one. He was the guy who'd saved his family from a burning house. Luca had settled into civilian life, and now he was trying to build his nest egg. That wasn't necessarily a bad thing, considering everyone needed money to live. But it definitely rubbed her the wrong way.

Which meant it was high time that she set aside those fantastical daydreams about being swept off her feet by a hero, and let go of the idea that a man could be everything she dreamed he was.

"That may be so," Jordan said. "But I still want his information so I can do some checks of my own. Just in case something happens to you, I'd like to be prepared."

"You're so sweet." Kira gave her friend Luca's name. "He spent the last couple of years fighting wildfires, I guess—"

"Oh." Jordan paused. "I know who he is."

"You do?" Kira frowned. She only knew about the wildfire thing because Mack had been telling her stories of his brother and the rest of the team. Everything that'd happened during their summer in Montana, then in Alaska, and all about people in some place called Last Chance County.

If she didn't think Mack was more honest than a lot of people she'd met, she might not believe him. She might think he'd been making it up. Or at least embellishing stories.

Jordan said, "Those guys were all over the papers for a while. They made national news after they took down some conspiracy to poison the food supply last year, or something like that. But I know about it because there was a CIA agent involved. One of my assets, though she dropped off the radar a few years ago and no one knew what had happened to her."

"Really?"

"I figured she'd been killed, and honestly, it bothered me for a long time. Thinking that maybe I could've done something to save her life."

Kira swallowed against the lump in her throat. "But she's okay now?"

"We connected recently, and she's doing great," Jordan said. "I keep my people safe. That's the deal, isn't it?"

As far as friendship with Jordan went, that was pretty much a declaration of undying devotion. Kira smiled to herself. "Love you too, girlie."

It was also a measure of Jordan's dedication to her job at the CIA that she worked so hard to keep people safe. Jordan was going to work for the agency for her entire career because she believed that much in the work they did. In keeping assets safe and ensuring missions were completed with as little loss of life as possible.

Kira said, "Now I have an appointment with half a chapter of a sweet romance novel and a pile of blankets. Otherwise, when my shift rolls around tonight, I'll be exhausted."

Jordan said, "Falling asleep thinking about some guy might not be a bad thing."

"I've done way too much thinking about this guy. It's time to find a new hobby." She hung up the phone and headed from her car to the elevator and up to her apartment.

The lobby between the elevator doors and her front door echoed, the temperature lower than necessary so that it raised goosebumps on her forearms. She ducked into her apartment and toed off her heels by the front door.

Her feet, in her nylons, pressed against the warm tile where she had underfloor heating. Kira turned on the kettle to heat water for decaf tea and changed into her comfiest pajamas. Yesterday's mail sat on the counter in a stack she hadn't gone through yet, but she would do that while she ate breakfast this afternoon, before her shift.

When most people were waking up and getting ready for the day, Kira was lowering her blinds and darkening the apartment so she could get a few hours of sleep.

This was what she'd needed for so many years, working overseas. Quiet space that she controlled. Minimal decoration, because too many things cluttering a room didn't allow her mind to relax. In the hospital, she was constantly overwhelmed by sights and sounds and movement. Here, in her personal space, she found a sense of peace, enough that she could rest.

First, she would check her email for the patient's file and do some research on the condition they had. Then maybe after that, she would turn on the audio Bible instead of reading the sweet romance she'd mentioned to Jordan.

Her friend was the one who had suggested that Kira exit the covert ops world and the contract work she had been doing. Go back to just practicing medicine and nothing else. Jordan had seen how that life was starting to affect Kira and cautioned her that things wouldn't get better unless she made a change. Took a break.

It was like being given a new lease on life.

Probably a lot like Luca and his journey, being declared dead and then coming back to life. Getting a second chance to make a life for himself. That would take money, wouldn't it? Especially if a person hadn't built up a nest egg.

Maybe she shouldn't judge him too harshly, considering the things she had done. The Bible was pretty clear about not condemning another person when she had plenty in her life that would condemn her, but for the blood of Jesus.

She used her iPad to do some research on the doctor who would be administering the procedure. She'd never heard of Dr. Torres, but recognized some of the research he had conducted from medical journals she had read. Turned out he was local to Renegade and well known for his cutting-edge ideas.

This was certainly going to be an interesting job.

Once it was done, her life would go back to its normal, steady state. Peace and quiet—something she had desperately needed after spending years in a war zone—was now a given. She'd eventually realized that her heart and soul had been battered by the constant conflict and ever-present fear, and that Jordan was right. She'd needed a change.

She'd clung to her faith as best she could, but that had felt thin as well when she finally walked away from the work she'd been doing.

The last few years working in Renegade, seeing the mountains every day and helping people who lived in this city, some of them for their whole lives, had been a kind of therapy for her. She had spent so much time just trying to rebuild who she was and sort of put herself back together.

Seeing Luca wasn't going to set back the progress she'd made. It wasn't going to interfere with her peace or her carefully ordered world.

At least, not if she could help it.

Her iPad pinged with a new message. Sent to her hospital email account from Saxon Investigations. She frowned and tapped the notification.

> I'm sorry for how our conversation ended this morning. The answer to your question is yes, we can be professionals about this. Working together doesn't have to mean being at odds with each other. I'm sure we can find a way to get along.

She'd been so thrown by his mentioning money that early in the conversation that when he'd asked her out for coffee, she'd immediately shut him down. How on earth was she supposed to understand his intentions?

But apparently, she didn't need to worry about that. He was there to do his job, just like her. Which meant she'd have to stick to her word about being a professional. As long as Jordan didn't come up with something that Kira needed to worry about, everything would be fine. They would do the job, and as soon as it was over, he would be out of her life again. A good way to test the efficacy of everything she had been building the last few years.

Otherwise, how else would she know that she was who she needed to be now?

And not the woman who had failed to save so many people's lives.

FIVE

LUCA TORE OPEN THE PACKET OF SUGAR AND dumped it into his black coffee, stirring his spoon around in the small diner mug. Determining not to think about Kira or their conversation, especially since he was here to have lunch with Mack.

Luca had done a little research into her background, even connecting with someone he knew who was a tech whiz and CEO—Jamie Winters. They'd met in Alaska last year, and Jamie had helped them figure out that whole deal with the bioweapon and the terrorist group. In fact, she'd been an integral part in getting to the truth that their old teammate, Elias Redding, and his family were working to destabilize the USA.

Jamie had sent him a packet of information she'd found about Kira. Added to what he'd uncovered locally, it didn't amount to much. She had extensive investments, and three years ago she'd signed a lease on a downtown apartment in a brand-new high-rise. She was paid well by the hospital, and every annual review seemed positive.

Jamie had told him it all came across as clean—almost too clean—but he'd told her not to dig anymore. If there were secrets in Kira's life, he wanted to discover them himself. Preferably by getting to know her and her choosing to trust him enough to share those things herself, rather than him uncovering anything she didn't want the world to know.

Dolly wandered past him, her sneakers squeaking on the linoleum floor. She winked as she went by, already aware he was waiting for Hammer's half brother.

The lunchtime crowd included a couple of moms in a booth, strollers next to their table. Toddlers climbed on them and the bench seat while they chatted and caught up with each other. Two older men talked over open Bibles at their table in the corner. Dolly took the empty plates from the gentlemen and said something Luca was too far away to hear.

The door swung open, ringing the bell above it.

Dolly glanced over. "Hey, sweetie."

Mack waved to her, then found Luca in the room and headed over. When he slid into the seat across the table, Luca got a look at the dark circles under his eyes.

"Long shift?"

"I got off late last night. It's been a long few days, so I slept until about an hour ago."

Luca nodded. "Smart, resting while you can."

"I have today off. I might go see a movie later or something. And get some food, because there's nothing in my apartment." He glanced aside at Dolly, who held out her carafe of coffee. Mack upended his mug, and she poured. "Thanks, Dolly. I'll have the ham and Swiss sandwich."

"You got it." She glanced at Luca. "And for you?"

"Cheeseburger and fries."

"I'll be back." She turned and wandered away.

"How is it going, being an EMT? You like it?"

Mack shrugged one shoulder. "It isn't exactly what I expected, and I'm still a rookie, but being closer to downtown means some nights are back-to-back calls. I'm pretty sure Hammer expected me to go back to school, not just get an EMT cert and go to work."

"I think he just wants you to find something you enjoy doing. Preferably something legal." Luca smiled.

"I knew for a fact it wasn't going to be something boring." Mack shook his head. "Not after fighting wildfires for two years and everything that happened."

Luca took a sip of his coffee. "Boring can be good sometimes. A little bit of peace is good for the soul. But I get what you mean about needing something high-energy. Transitioning to being an investigator has been interesting."

"I'm just glad things have settled down a bit." Mack sniffed. "Hammer is here, and he's with his family. Dad is . . . whatever."

"Have you talked to him at all?"

Mack shot him a look. "I know you're still investigating that whole thing and you went to talk to him. One of the old ladies at church, her son is a corrections officer. He said he saw you come in and talk to my dad."

"Sorry. I could've given you a heads-up," Luca said. "But I need him to tell me what he knows about this shadow syndicate. Rousseau isn't giving us anything."

"You really think there's some criminal empire in Renegade?"

"If there is, I want to know. I don't want to bury my head in the sand."

"Seems like you're just asking for trouble, digging up things people don't want anyone to know."

Luca studied the guy. Barely into his twenties, but in some ways, he seemed like he was much older. And yet in others, as if he was more vulnerable than he should be. "You've had to face a lot the last few months. Realizing the kind of man your dad is and him going to jail. All those charges."

"That doesn't mean I'm anything like him."

"No one would ever believe you were." Luca wondered something. "Did you become an EMT to help people, to try and convince everyone that you're a good guy?" If someone in his life was hassling him about being the son of Alden Jenkins, Luca wanted to have a word with that person.

"I already have a big brother, Sax. I don't need another one breathing down my neck."

"Fine." Luca spread his fingers, showing his palms. "I'll back down. But seriously, if anyone is giving you a hard time, you should tell me or Hammer."

Dolly delivered their plates, and Luca reached for the ketchup, squirting some beside his fries.

Mack lifted one half of his sandwich. "Because I need my big brothers wading in to fight my battles for me?"

"I know what it's like to take a job so you can be someone other than who everyone thinks you are. That's why I joined the Army, so I could figure out who I wanted to be and everyone would know I was on the right side because of what uniform I was wearing."

Mack eyed him, taking a big bite.

"My older brother was already in jail by then. I finished out high school in foster care because it was better than being on the streets. Soon as I was done, I signed up."

"I never knew that."

Luca shrugged. "Your dad said that he'll consider telling me what I need to know about the Shadow Syndicate . . . if you come and see him at the prison."

Mack's expression hardened. He wiped his mouth with the back of his hand.

Luca watched him absorb the information, but the kid didn't say anything. He probably didn't know what to say. Mack was the kind of guy who thought a whole lot and then measured his words carefully. It was nice on a rough day, when everyone was tired and overwhelmed by what'd happened. Out in the backcountry somewhere, exhausted from fighting fires and dealing with the loss of someone they weren't able to save. The kid's natural quietness had been a kind of peace they'd all needed.

But right now, Luca needed someone to give him something. "I don't even know if he has information or if he's stringing me along. I just wanted you to know what he said."

"You aren't going to tell me to go see him?" Mack seemed surprised.

Luca shrugged. "That's up to you. I'm not going to force you to do something you don't want to do just because it might get me an answer on my case."

"I'll think about it." He took a big bite of his sandwich.

"Thanks." Luca finished his burger and wiped his hands on his napkin. "Want some company for that movie later? I need to go to the hospital and get started on a security job I was contracted for, assessing all the measures they already have in place and making some suggestions. But I could move some things around and come with you."

Mack shrugged. "If you want. When you go by the hospital, see if my friend Kira is there. She's a doctor in the ER. She seems kind of lonely, so I always talk to her when I go in. She's super nice."

Luca forced himself to not react. "Dr. Kira Yassan?"

Mack frowned. "You know her?"

"A little bit." How else was he supposed to explain their encounter years ago? Or the one this morning. "You think she's lonely?"

Mack shrugged one shoulder. "Whenever we take a patient into her ER, she and I grab a soda from the vending machine and chat for a minute. I've told her all about Hammer and Sierra, and you and Kane. Not all the sensitive stuff about Maria and her father. That stuff seems pretty top secret, and it wasn't in the news articles."

"Did she ask you about all that stuff?"

"I don't remember. We just started talking about it, and like I said, she seems kind of lonely. Like she needs someone to talk to."

This didn't sound good at all. If Kira was going around questioning people connected to Luca about all the things that'd happened the last few years, it could be because she was here as a covert operative to gather information. Even the paper trail of her having been here for a few years could be fake. She may have shown up recently, purely to get close to the Trouble Boys in Renegade—Hammer and Luca.

"Could you do me a favor?" When Mack nodded, Luca continued. "Maybe pull back a little on telling her stuff. Just for a while. Until I figure something out."

Mack's expression shifted to something that looked like worry. "There's something about her that I need to know?"

"I don't have an answer for that yet. But I'll keep you posted."

Mack rolled his eyes. "Maybe *you* just don't know her. She's not some kind of bad guy like the people we've met before, terrorists and whatnot. She's just a doctor. And a nice lady."

Of course the kid would call someone ten years older than him a "lady." But Luca still needed him to be careful. At least until Luca knew who Kira really was and what she was doing here in Renegade.

"I hope you're right."

Mack shook his head. "You know, she's pretty good-looking as well. If you're going to be so cynical, thinking everyone you meet is a bad guy, you'll never end up with a date. You're way too suspicious."

The kid probably thought he knew Kira a whole lot better than Luca did. But there were too many things Mack didn't know about her. Mack didn't seem worried at all that Kira would turn out to be someone with ulterior motives.

That's what had burned him with his father. Believing Alden Jenkins was a nice guy, when in the background, he was terrorizing people and arranging their deaths. Eventually, Mack had been forced to face the fact that his father was abusive to his family as well.

In time, he would realize that he was in denial about Kira in the same way. Luca would break it to him gently, but Mack needed to realize that people were usually someone other than who you thought they were. And most folks couldn't be trusted. That was just the way this fallen world worked.

He'd seen way too much evil to believe otherwise.

Luca knew who the people were in this world that he could trust, and he would happily lay his life down for them. He didn't need to widen his circle of who he put faith in. That would only burn him when someone inevitably stabbed him in the back—like a doctor who wasn't just a doctor.

Making the world a safer place for people to raise their families was the reason he did everything he did. And that included keeping Mack safe from himself.

"Maybe I am too suspicious," Luca said. "But it's kept me alive this far."

And for everyone's safety, he needed to find out what Kira was up to.

Kira stood at the end of the hospital bed. "As far as I'm concerned, you're good to go home." She looked down at the iPad in her hands and the last set of test results. "Your vitals are good, and your blood work came back clear. But if you have any more lightheadedness, go see your primary care physician. Okay?"

The patient nodded, relief on his face. His wife stood beside his bed, holding on to his arm, a whole lot more worry in her features than in his. She sniffed, brushing hair back from her face with one hand. "You're sure he's going to be okay?"

"As long as he's keeping down food and doesn't take a fall, you should be good." Kira looked at the patient. "Just take it easy for a few days and get some rest."

"Thanks, Doc."

The wife nodded. "Yes, thank you, Doctor."

Kira headed out to the nurses' station and handed the iPad over to Martin. "No partner in crime today?"

He grinned, revealing a cracked tooth in front. "Rebecca went away for the weekend with her sister."

"Oh boy. I don't want to know what the two of them are going to get up to."

Martin tipped his head back and laughed.

"Could you draw up discharge papers for Mr. Salazar, please?"

He nodded. "Yeah, no problem."

"Thanks," she said. "Anything new come in?"

The last thing she needed after yesterday was a quiet night. But that seemed like what was going to happen, whether she liked it or not. It made her want to take a break, sit and have a discussion with the Lord about what she needed versus what He was giving her.

But maybe that was a bad idea. Not the part where she was being honest with Him about how she felt about her life. The problem was more that she knew God would do what was best for her, which wasn't always what she wanted, and she'd rather complain about it.

I do want to grow. To build a stronger faith. Even if I don't like how that happens.

Martin clicked the mouse on his computer. "Dr. Barnett took the new patient that came in. Fifty-seven-year-old male in cardiac distress."

"Let me know if anyone else comes in." She had a few patients she could check on, awaiting X-rays or tests. Or simply people they were observing for a little while before they were either admitted or discharged. But it felt a whole lot like doing laps of the same area and expecting to find something different every time she swung by a patient's bay.

She walked over to check on Dr. Barnett and his patient, but before she even reached the curtain, Destiny Rousseau stepped out. The woman flushed when she saw Kira.

"I'm so glad it's you." Destiny rushed over and flung her twiggy arms around Kira. Kira hugged the other woman back, and Destiny said, "It's Ralph. He just collapsed, saying his arm hurt. I had no idea what to do. Thankfully, an associate of Ralph's showed up and called an ambulance. I was just so—" She waved her hands in front of her face, the movement almost frantic.

"I understand." Kira touched Destiny's shoulders and looked into the bay to see Dr. Barnett talking to the nurse. Kira's gaze drifted to the monitors, but she couldn't read the heart rate from this distance. They didn't need her help. She didn't need to go in there and take over. She would be of more use talking to Destiny right now.

She said, "Does he have a history of heart problems?"

"The EMTs asked me the same thing. I have no idea! Ralph has always been as healthy as a horse. That's why he bounced back so fast after those bullies tried to kill him."

Kira nodded, thinking it might also have been the exorbitant sum they'd paid for top-tier private care in Denver. "It does seem like he got his strength back quickly. That's good. It could help him recover from this in the same way."

"Assuming whoever did this to him doesn't try again." Destiny pushed back her hair with both hands and touched her cheeks, looking a little shellshocked.

Kira frowned. "Do you think someone did this to him?" She pointed toward Ralph, passed out on the bed.

"Ralph isn't just going to grab his arm and fall over for no reason. Obviously someone tried to poison him." Destiny gasped. "It's because he's a threat to their business. But he hasn't told anyone anything!"

"If you suspect this was a personal attack, you should tell the police what you know." They would be able to reassure Destiny that there was no reason for her to worry. Unless she was right and Ralph had been receiving continued death threats in the months since his capture. Still, from everything Kira could see, this looked more like a run-of-the-mill heart attack. One that had nothing to do with him being shot months ago. "If you believe his life is in danger, perhaps you could seek protection."

Destiny nodded. "I'm going to tell the police he's in danger. It's because they haven't caught the culprit yet."

"I can call the police department for you and have a couple of detectives come by to interview you. Once Ralph is stable, of course."

"If they figure out what was done to him, the doctors will be able to reverse it. Right?"

"It's usually not that straightforward. But everyone will do everything they can to make sure Ralph is stabilized and that he pulls through." She touched Destiny's shoulder. "Don't worry."

Most of the time, it was pointless to tell someone not to worry. But people still needed to hear it. They needed to rest in the fact that the professionals were taking care of the situation and that their loved one was in good hands.

"Do you want me to make a call to the police?"

Destiny wavered. "Let's wait until Ralph wakes up. Then he can decide what to do."

Kira had never heard Destiny defer to her husband in this way before, but it made sense in this situation. Acting rashly and declaring this to have been attempted murder might not be the best way for Ralph to recover without stress in his life.

"You just let me know." At the end of the hall, a familiar figure stepped into view. Luca Saxon, wearing dark blue khakis and a polo shirt with a white embroidered logo she couldn't make out. He carried a clipboard and pen and had his phone clipped to his belt. A security badge hung from his left pocket.

She squeezed Destiny's shoulder and strode over to Luca. "May I ask what you're doing in my department?"

She shouldn't like the way his hair looked, pulled back like that and secured behind his head in a bun. When she'd first met him, his hair had been short and more of a military style. Since then, he had grown it out long enough he could tie it back, and now she could honestly say she preferred it long—and wanted to see what it looked like down.

She shouldn't like anything about him.

"Yes, you may." Humor lit his gaze. As if she had been trying to be funny. "But if you think about it, you already know."

And here she'd assumed that he'd come to spy on her or something. "Right, the Marshals job."

"I'm doing an inventory of the hospital security system and all measures in place, and then we need to find the best spot where the patient can be protected."

She nodded. "I took a look at the procedure. It's cutting-edge but has a lot of promise. The doctor who's going to treat him is one of the best in his field, and he's a local. Although, he's very aloof and not many people know much about him."

"That sounds about right for a clandestine operation like this." He looked around at the nurses' station, then the bays that lined the hallway.

She didn't glance back to see if Destiny was watching them. She had probably gone back into the room with her husband.

"You like it here?"

Kira wasn't sure he needed a rundown of every issue she had or all the ways she thought this was a great place to work. "In a sense, one emergency department is like any other. There are differences, but medicine is medicine. People get hurt or sick, and we treat them to the best of our ability."

Okay, so the end of that sounded a little defensive. But why wouldn't she feel the need to do that? He stood four inches taller than her and was currently looking down his nose with a slight frown between his brows.

"So Renegade is what brought you here?"

"It seemed like as good a place as any to start over."

The skin around his eyes contracted. Yeah, because she'd just told him there was a reason she felt the need to start over.

"And it just happened to be where I live?"

She folded her arms. "You didn't live here when I moved here." This was Hammer's hometown, not Luca's. "So the real question is, why did *you* move to a city that just happened to be where *I* live?"

"We may be at an impasse on that one."

"I don't have any ulterior motives. I live here, and I'm good at my job. I'm not sure why you'd have a problem with any of that." Or why it seemed like he thought she might've moved here because of him.

It just happened to be a place she had come across when looking into his team's backgrounds. She could just as easily have wound up in Baltimore, where Luca actually grew up. Or in Last Chance County, where Kane was from. So she had chosen this spot. So what?

"Did I say I had a problem with that?"

She rolled her eyes. "I should go check on some of my patients."

Because that was better than standing here, going around and around in this conversation with him.

"I'll get back to work as well."

"So great to talk to you." She laced the words with sarcasm, not quite sure why he was bringing this out in her.

Okay, fine. The mix of him not being who she thought he was, or who she wanted him to be, and her trying to live a life where she was something completely different than who she had been before . . . It was all jumbling together and making her defensive. As if she had to prove to him that she was a good person now.

She turned away.

"Kira."

She didn't want to turn back, but she did, because otherwise it would be rude, and she was trying to convince him she was a nice person. "Yes?"

Those dark eyes stared at her. Did the man have to be completely handsome and one hundred percent someone a mother might have approved of? That's how she knew the world wasn't built to be fair—because she had no idea what kind of person her mother would've been if she'd lived.

And she probably wasn't ever going to catch a break.

"If you're here for some nefarious reason, I'm going to figure out what it is." He took a step toward her and spoke in a low tone. "I don't know what you did with that flash drive you took from me, and I doubt I ever will unless you tell me. But I sincerely hope you're not on some kind of mission here in Renegade. Because if you are, you have to know that I'm going to stop you doing whatever it is before someone I care about gets hurt."

She stared at him, her eyes suddenly burning with unshed tears. She'd worked so hard not to be that person anymore. To do her job trying to save lives and push everything else out so that she could wake up in the morning and go to bed at night feeling good about herself.

The skin around his eyes flexed, and she saw the beginning of a frown. "Kira—"

"Like I said, I have to get back to work."

She turned and strode away, ignoring the nurses behind the desk looking at her. Destiny and her husband. Dr. Barnett and anyone else. She ignored them all and rushed to a quiet corner where she could shed a couple of tears.

And then she got back to work.

SIX

LUCA WALKED OUT OF THE OFFICE OF THE HEAD of security after a meeting that had gone pretty well, considering he was seriously encroaching on the guy's territory. And also considering it was after midnight. He was still thinking about Kira's reaction to what he'd said and found himself automatically heading toward the elevator so he could go back down to the emergency department.

Ralph Rousseau should be stable by now—he hoped. Luca had gone by the Rousseau house to talk to him late last night, and Destiny had answered the door flustered because Ralph had collapsed. As the person who had called 911 for them, he would trade on some goodwill to ask the guy a couple of questions if he was awake. Or he'd arrange to swing by tomorrow so they could talk.

He hit the button for the elevator and stepped inside when the doors opened.

It was almost as though Kira thought she was being falsely accused. Which was crazy. She'd reacted like someone brought to tears by the idea that they were being treated like a guilty person.

With her too-clean background check, which was suspicious all on its own, he had no idea who she'd been working for back when they first met. Or what her role had been in that refugee camp.

There was no way she was completely innocent.

She was someone. An operative. The kind of person who used her femininity and fake tears to throw a guy like him off.

But even that didn't seem quite right. He would rather believe she really was innocent, but that didn't match up with the fact she'd taken the flash drive from his pocket. If he took her word for it, he ran the risk of being deceived.

Luca had far too much at stake to let this go. He just needed to find a way to get her to tell him what she was hiding.

He stepped out into the hallway and immediately heard yelling. A nurse ran from one of the rooms at the end of the hall, close to where the doors to the waiting area were. The entry was controlled by a buzzer so that only people who were authorized to enter were allowed in the emergency department.

The nurse ran back to the room, pushing a heavy cart.

"We're losing him," he heard Kira yell.

Luca figured it wasn't a good idea to disturb her right now if someone's life hung in the balance, so he kept himself from walking all the way over to see what was going on. She already thought he was entirely too nosy and suspicious of her motives.

But was it such a bad thing to be cautious?

Destiny pushed the curtain back and looked out into the hall. She spotted him. "Oh, hello."

Luca wasn't sure if she was aware he was one of the men who had rescued her husband after he was kidnapped a few months ago.

Ralph called out from behind her. "Who's there?"

"Mr. Rousseau." Luca stepped into view. "How are you feeling?"

Destiny looked at the embroidered Saxon Investigations logo on his polo shirt. She moved aside, and Luca headed into the bay. Ralph was sitting up in the bed, his phone in his hand.

"I feel a whole lot better than I did earlier." Ralph looked at the monitors beside him. "Now I'm hooked up to all this, stuck here for who knows how long."

Behind Luca, Destiny said, "You nearly died!" She came around the side of the bed to stare disapprovingly at her husband.

"It takes more than poison or a gunshot to kill me." Ralph slapped a hand on his chest. "You're just getting to see how tough I am."

Luca wasn't sure she appreciated that sentiment. The woman looked worried out of her mind. The fancy clothes she wore were rumpled, and her hair was out of place. She'd been through something, and Ralph already considered himself to be a survivor.

If he'd been poisoned, did that mean the syndicate was no longer happy with him?

Luca turned to her. "I can keep your husband company for a few minutes if you'd like to stretch your legs. Get yourself a cup of tea from the cafeteria."

She moved to Ralph's side and took his hand. "I can't possibly leave my husband at a time like this."

Ralph said, "Anything you want to talk to me about, Destiny can hear it." He patted his wife's hand. "I wouldn't be the man I am if it wasn't for her. I'd be lost without her."

"I don't want to put too much strain on you if you aren't feeling well." He had to say it so they knew he didn't want to push Ralph beyond what he was capable of right now. Especially if his health hung in the balance. "But I have been meaning to ask you some questions. Just to follow up on what happened to you a few months ago and the police questioning."

"People always assume I don't want to talk about it anymore. It was a terrible time, being tied to a chair, held against my will. Beaten and shot. Having you guys come in and rescue me, only to discover that someone was blaming the whole operation on my company."

Luca didn't react to that. It was the way Rousseau and his lawyers had decided to play it.

Destiny gasped. "You're one of the men who rescued my husband." She touched her free hand to the buttons on her shirt. "I'm so grateful you got him back for me before the worst happened."

Luca nodded to her. "I was glad to be able to do it."

"Ask me anything," Ralph said. "You've earned it."

"I've been looking into what you said about the Shadow Syndicate. About how they're the ones behind everything in Renegade—like a criminal empire."

Destiny twisted around to her husband. "Do you think these shadow people are the ones who just tried to kill you?"

Luca frowned, silently asking Ralph the same question.

"Someone must have slipped something in my drink at the restaurant, and by the time I got home, I was about done for," Ralph said. "The hospital is running tests to see what I was poisoned with, but it mimicked a heart attack. They nearly killed me tonight."

"Has anyone been sending you death threats recently?"

Destiny said, "Our investment company is very lucrative. Enough that I am able to spend most of my time working on the foundation, helping people in developing countries who need medical supplies. Of course there will be people who are jealous of our success and want to take Ralph down a peg or two."

Ralph glanced at his wife, then back at Luca. "I think they also found out that I was considering running for mayor when the election rolled around. Of course, that's all in a shambles now that snake Jenkins is in prison."

Luca kept his mouth shut. Had Ralph really thought that would actually work? Even if Luca hadn't known then about the evidence out there implicating Ralph and Rocky Mountain Land Development in exactly what Jenkins had gone down for, Luca still couldn't see a guy with Rousseau's reputation winning an election.

"Whoever these shadow people are," Destiny said, "they don't want you to become mayor. They want to destroy your business and kill you before you can be elected. They know what a good mayor you would be."

He patted his wife's hand.

Luca said, "Do you have any idea who the Shadow Syndicate are?"

Ralph shook his head. "I've heard scuttlebutt about them, and when I was taken, I assumed they were the ones behind it. Now it's clear they were trying to frame me."

Luca nodded, but not because he agreed that's what was happening. He needed to press Ralph until he admitted something or contradicted what the police could prove. That would be more difficult if Ralph became defensive. "How did you hear about them in the first place?"

Destiny stroked a hand down his arm. Ralph said, "Here and there, at the country club or at wine club. Anywhere that the Renegade elite congregates, you will hear rumors of powerful people in charge. Guys like me can't seem to get ahead easily. There's always some kind of block. It has to be them stopping us from taking what they consider to be their territory." He sighed. "I must have got too close, which was why they trumped up all that evidence indicating I was the one behind everything. Now innocents are dead, and I think I'm going to be next."

Luca didn't want this going back to him being a victim, so he said, "Do you have any specific names of people you think might be part of it? Anyone at all that you suspect?"

Destiny's hand on his arm stilled. "If we went around pointing fingers, that would put Ralph in even more danger. All this is happening because he told you about the Shadow Syndicate in the first place. If he'd kept his mouth shut, we wouldn't be here."

"Now, dear. We can't just do nothing in the face of all this corruption."

"I see." Luca nodded. "So you don't care that they tried to kill you before, or now. All you care about is standing up for justice." He paused. "That night when we rescued you, we heard you saying that you hurt people. That you did everything they asked."

"I was a victim. I just told them whatever I thought they wanted to hear. I played along." Ralph swallowed, sucking in a choppy breath. "They're bullies. They shouldn't get away with what they've done anymore. Hurting innocent people."

Luca shifted his weight, trying to figure out how to salvage something from this conversation. "I've been trying to gather details and figure out who they are, but so far, my investigation has come up empty. Unless you have any proof that Jenkins was connected to them that I can look into? Or have they ever threatened you directly since, or sent some kind of warning?"

"Not unless you count almost being run off the road a few weeks ago."

Luca worked his mouth back and forth. "If you haven't filed a police report, I think you should do that now. Every time something happens. If you even suspect that someone is deliberately trying to hurt you or kill you, then you need to take measures for your own protection."

Destiny nodded. "That's an excellent idea." She looked at her husband, turning to face him. "We should hire somebody to keep you safe. Like a bodyguard. Someone who will make sure nobody does anything like this again."

Ralph said nothing. He glanced at Luca.

"It doesn't mean you can't protect yourself," Luca said. "It just means you want to ensure your safety and also get on with your life."

Destiny turned to Luca. "What do you say?"

"Excuse me?" He glanced between her and her husband. Given the look on Ralph's face, he had no intention of hiring protection.

"We can hire you as Ralph's bodyguard. He knows you, and

we both trust you because you've saved his life before. So what do you say? Because I think you're the perfect person to keep my husband safe."

"I have a number of cases and clients currently on my desk." He needed a better reason to turn her down. He waited for Ralph to tell her no or argue with her, but the guy said nothing.

"I'll pay you double to get rid of them."

"I'm afraid one of the jobs is with federal law enforcement, and it's time sensitive. But I can find someone with the same level of training as me who is available, if you'd like me to do that." He looked at Ralph, wondering if the guy would speak up at all.

Luca had no intention of protecting a guy mixed up with the Shadow Syndicate. And he would put money down that Ralph didn't want Luca in his business either.

No matter what his wife said.

Destiny frowned. "But I wouldn't trust them. I trust you." She lifted her chin, as if that was enough for him to rearrange his entire schedule.

"I'll inform hospital security that there's a possibility the two of you are in danger. Make sure they come by regularly and ensure you're safe."

He hoped that would placate her for now and prevent her from convincing herself he was her only option. Luca needed to come up with a good plan B for these two.

"Until tomorrow." Destiny nodded, certain of what she said. Convinced that he was going to figure out a way to personally protect Ralph.

He stepped out of the bay and almost collided with Kira. She had sweat across her hairline and was breathing hard. He reached for her, but she shifted away from him. "Is everything okay?"

Her mouth opened, but she said nothing. Still trying to catch her breath.

Luca held out a hand. "Come on, we can find somewhere quiet to talk about whatever it is."

She shook her head. "Why would I want to do that?"

Kira turned and walked away.

———

Dawn lit the sky with swatches of orange and white, marbled across the horizon. Kira pumped her arms and legs back and forth. Each foot strike on the asphalt of the greenbelt path was more purposeful than usual. Focusing on form and the cool of early morning helped her keep out errant thoughts.

What she could've done differently.

What more she might've tried.

Patients die sometimes, and there's nothing we can do about it.

She banished Dr. Barnett's face from her mind. As if she didn't know that. Kira had been a doctor long enough to have accepted facts she couldn't change. What mattered was that she never lost the sense of grief that came with losing a patient. The moment she grew cold to loss, she might as well give up being a doctor, because she'd lost her compassion.

The truth was that a nine-year-old boy had died, and now his family would be faced with having to live all the days to come without him in their life. With memories fading and the constant, nagging absence of their loved one.

Because she couldn't save him.

A dog across the park barked a couple of times. The owner threw a tennis ball, and the dog shot across the stretch of grass between the path and the kids' playground. Life moved on. Another day, another chance to save someone's life—except she wasn't working tonight.

Lord, comfort the brokenhearted today.

She blinked and the child's face filled her mind. She saw Rebecca on the gurney, administering CPR, trying to do everything she could to keep the kid alive. The bacterial infection had simply been too bad, too far gone.

A tear escaped the corner of her eye. Kira swiped it away and ran faster. Until sweat beaded at the small of her back and her leggings seemed overly warm.

Her thoughts drifted to Luca, and she let them.

Did the guy really have to be so good-looking? It was almost unfair, considering she had objections to so many other things about him. Her fault though, considering she'd built him up in her mind as the epitome of the American military warrior hero. What was even sadder was the fact she'd agreed to work with the US government because of his team. The way they'd clearly looked out for each other like brothers, and how they'd come back to check on her after she was struck.

Care and concern.

The same kind of concern he'd shown her in the hospital last night. It had thrown her when he'd suggested they go somewhere quiet so she could tell him what had happened and why she was upset. She hadn't had anyone in her life who cared about her like that in years. She hadn't known what to do with it, and in the emotion-laden heat of the moment, she'd chosen solitude rather than facing her feelings in front of someone else.

She had no idea what he'd do with an emotional woman dealing with something heavy. Kira didn't need any more disappointment when it came to Luca.

She spotted a woman running the opposite direction and recognized her from other mornings, though the woman didn't run on the same days each week. Not that Kira was obsessively keeping track, but it seemed like the woman's schedule shifted days from week to week. She looked to be about the same age, her hair a dark blonde that looked almost brown, tied back behind her head. She wore shorts and a Renegade Fire Department T-shirt.

The woman nodded. "Morning."

Kira sniffed. "Morning."

They passed each other, and she focused on her form again, slowing at the four-mile mark, where there was a fountain by the fishing pond. She got a drink, then wandered around a little in an off-center circle, just to keep moving. Cooling down from the hard run.

Not too far away, on one of the benches that lined the path, a young woman sat hugging herself. She wore black jeans and flat canvas shoes, a gray zippered hoodie over her shirt. Hair hanging forward, covering the sides of her face. She looked a little familiar, but that wasn't surprising considering Kira saw so many different people every time she worked a shift at the hospital.

But it was the way the woman held herself that drew her attention.

Kira wandered over, keeping her distance and giving the woman a chance to notice her. The woman drew in a sharp breath and looked up. Eyes wide, one of them rimmed with a blue bruise. Her lip was split, and she had a gash on her cheek. Those looked to have been tended to at one point, which made sense. This was the woman from the other night, the domestic-violence victim Kira had treated—the one Mack brought in.

Her ribs hadn't been cracked, just bruised. Still extremely painful. Now she held her elbow to her body with her other arm, which was new.

"Hi." Kira kept her distance and didn't get closer, not wanting to spook the woman and cause her to leave quickly. "I'm Dr. Yassan. From the hospital?"

The woman nodded slightly. "Hi."

"What was your name?"

"Frankie."

Kira took a half step toward her. "Did you hurt your arm, Frankie?"

Her nose wrinkled and she said nothing.

"Can I take a look?" She motioned to the arm.

"I heard it pop."

Kira crouched in front of her, barely close enough to touch. "You might need an X-ray if you think there's damage to it." She needed to phrase things carefully, or it would sound like an accusation. "You might need a cast to keep it secure until it heals."

And Frankie might need to file another police report, if she'd even done that the other day. The police had shown up to talk to her after the nurse had called them, but Kira didn't hear what happened after that. What happened next was this woman's choice, whether she felt like she had one or not. She had to grasp the fact that she had the power to change her own life.

When a person felt stuck or trapped, they often believed they had no choices available to them. Whether there weren't any options or the choices had been taken from them often didn't matter. They believed there was no way out.

The change came when the person realized they still had power and the ability to change their life, even in a tiny way. Or the first of a series of tiny ways that, in the end, added up to a whole lot. In Kira's case, it was because a friend had seen what was happening and offered her a new choice. Not out of an abusive relationship, as such. Just out of a situation where she felt stuck and things weren't going well.

"Can I see?" Kira motioned to her arm.

Frankie unzipped her sweater with one hand and lowered it off her shoulder, gingerly pulling out her arm. Kira asked her a couple of questions before she palpated from Frankie's shoulder down to her wrist, noting the girl's reaction to what she was doing. Once she was done with that, she assessed what damage there might be to Frankie's shoulder and elbow. Most of the injury seemed to be in her wrist.

"I don't have my lab coat on right now, so this isn't official."

She waited for Frankie to smile just a fraction, then said, "But it would be a good idea to get an X-ray and maybe have your wrist put in a cast."

"It hurts a lot."

"I'm afraid it won't heal right if it doesn't get treated. It's something you might always have problems with."

Kind of like the festering wound of an abusive relationship that was allowed to continue, getting worse and worse. That kind of thing inclined Kira toward amputation.

She eased a little closer. "The best way to give yourself time to heal is to find a safe place to be."

Frankie tensed, and if Kira had still been holding her arm, she probably would have pulled away and hurt herself further.

"I know of a women's shelter in South Eagle. It's unregistered and unlisted, so there's no way he would be able to find it."

"He always finds me. It doesn't matter where I go." Frankie's voice quavered.

"But you can't give up. You have to keep trying." Kira kept her voice gentle. "You never know if your next choice will be the one that sets you free."

Kira shifted out of the crouch, turned, and sat on the bench so that she faced Frankie with a couple feet of space between them. "I can call you a rideshare on my account, which will take you to the house. No one will know where you've gone, and he won't be able to find you."

A tiny bit of hope lit Frankie's eyes, and Kira was glad to see it.

"If you're able to file a police report that includes your medical records from visiting the hospital the other day, that's another little safeguard. And all of them add up. Everything you do. It all gives you a little bit more protection from him than you would have without it." Kira laid her arm on the back of the bench. "You don't have to be afraid. You don't have to live like that."

Frankie hugged herself again, staring out across the path to the irrigation canal that ran along the edge of the park. A group of ducklings waddled after their mother over to the water.

Last week, Kira had been watching them when a hawk swooped down and grabbed one of the babies, momentarily startling the mother. Since then, she tried not to pay too much attention to them. Nature was a savage thing, and that was yet another reminder she shouldn't get too attached. She should do her job and stay home.

God didn't want her to live her life swallowed up in a spirit of fear, but she wasn't sure how to face the threats every day brought any other way than to just duck her head and keep going.

"What do you say, Frankie? I can get you a ride to the hospital, or I can ask the rideshare to take you to the shelter." Kira smiled. "I volunteer there once a month on a Saturday, so I'll be able to see how you're doing."

The young woman glanced over. "Shelter."

Kira nodded. "I'll order you a car." She slid the cell phone from her leggings pocket and used the Renegade rideshare app. "Someone will be here in five minutes." She glanced over at the far side of the park. "The pickup point is at the fountain."

"Thank you."

Kira smiled at her. "You deserve to feel safe and live your life without fear."

The trauma of relationships like the one Frankie was in and a life lived in a war zone weren't something the nervous system could differentiate between. A threat was a threat. Constant day-to-day trauma created similar responses in a lot of people, and Kira knew all too well the taste of fear on her tongue—and the way rest seemed like such an elusive thing when peace was hard to come by. When the next moment could be anything.

Kira walked the young woman to the car, closing the door for her. Promising to check on her the next time she was at the shelter. Aside from this small thing, there wasn't much she could do for

Frankie. If the young woman was going to change her life, then it would be up to her to make those changes.

She stood at the curb, watching the car disappear down the busy street.

A black SUV pulled up where the car had stopped. A tall man wearing a dark suit climbed out of the passenger seat and held open the back door. That was when she noticed the silver star badge on his belt. A US marshal.

He looked at Kira. "Dr. Torres would like to speak with you, if you're available."

SEVEN

L UCA KNOCKED ON THE DOOR TO KIRA'S APART-
ment, more nervous than he should be. Juggling the cardboard tray
with two kinds of juice and two coffees and the paper bag of food
he'd brought. Sure, it was five in the evening, but if she'd slept all day
like he had, she would be ready for breakfast.

He was about to knock again when the door swung open and
she stood there staring at him.

"Hey." She blinked at him, either thrown or still a little sleepy,
or both. Wearing loose blue-and-white-striped pajama pants and
a formfitting tank top that accentuated the curves of her waist,
with her hair in a messy bun on the top of her head.

"I figured you might want breakfast right about now." He tried
to keep it casual. "I just woke up an hour ago."

She said nothing.

"So can I come in?" A horrible thought crossed his mind. "Or
do you have a . . . guest."

She almost flinched. "I don't have anyone in here. I actually never invite people over. Ever."

Ah, so she was just unaccustomed to having someone in her personal space. "I can give you this and take off." He didn't want to, but he would if she asked him.

She shook her head. "It's fine."

Not super excited, but he'd take it.

She held the door open, and he didn't go too far into her space, letting her set the pace of his invasion and take the lead on where they went next. He knew she'd had a rough night last night, and it looked like she'd slept some but not much.

How she managed to still be gorgeous in pajamas, no makeup, and a thrown-together hairdo was a mystery to him. He had to fix his hair all the time, or it looked like he'd been dragged through a hedge.

"I brought passion orange guava juice and apple juice. Coffee and a bunch of pastries. Egg bites, things like that."

She led him through the apartment, past a low couch that looked like it was too nice to sit on unless you had freshly cleaned clothes. Over by the dining table and four chairs, he could see into the kitchen. The whole place gleamed spotless. Maybe she was the kind of person who stress cleaned. Or she simply hired an excellent service to keep her space tidy.

"What's your poison?" He set the bag and the drink carrier on the table.

"Unrealistic expectations." Before he could ask what that meant, she said, "But I'll take the passion orange guava. I had it on vacation last year, and I loved it. I'm more of a tea than coffee kind of person."

"Me too. But joining the military got me hooked on coffee, and now I feel like I can't live without it." He handed her the clear plastic cup and a straw and took a sip of his coffee.

She pulled out a chair on the other side of the table. "You can have a seat, if you want."

So they'd graduated from her reluctantly admitting him into her space to him actually being invited to sit. He didn't want to get ahead of himself, but that was a kind of victory on its own.

"This is a gorgeous apartment."

She sipped the juice, then lowered the cup to the table. "Basically everything was new when I moved here. I didn't have much stuff when I emigrated to the US, so I kind of overordered furniture, not really knowing what I would need. Some of the stuff I sold later, and this is everything I liked and what's functional left over."

"I rent an office a couple of streets over, and it came fully furnished. Otherwise I would've been doing the same thing." He tried to relax in the seat, like he fit here. Like she didn't have to worry about him and she could let down her guard.

Not only because he wanted to know more about who she'd been before she moved to Renegade. But also because he was the kind of person she could do that with. A safe place for her to open up.

Luca opened the bag and spread the contents across the torn paper so she could see what he had brought. He laid the napkins beside the bag while she selected a chocolate croissant.

He grabbed an egg bite and tossed it into his mouth, eating it whole.

"This is good." She wiped a thumb at the corner of her mouth. "I've had *pain au chocolat* in Paris, so in a lot of other places, they don't seem quite as good. But this isn't bad."

He absorbed the news that she had a sweet tooth and tucked that information away like a secret. "Did you sleep okay? You had a pretty rough shift."

"Kind of. After I got off work, I went for a run through the park. It usually helps me if I take some time to process what happened."

She shook her head. "And then I met the doctor who's going to be doing the procedure on the person the Marshals are protecting."

"Did you actually get any sleep today?"

She smiled, lifting her features. "We didn't talk for long. It was kind of crazy, actually. He rolls up to the curb in front of me in this SUV like they knew where I was going to be, and I get in the back of the car. If it hadn't been a marshal inviting me into the car, I wouldn't have got in." She shook her head. "Sounds way too much like the beginning of a TV special about my tragic demise."

Luca chuckled. "I'm glad that isn't what happened."

"Me too. Anyway, he wanted to talk to me in person about how we plan to treat the patient and monitor him, things to watch for. That kind of thing. He seems like he knows what he's talking about, and the procedure is cutting-edge. The patient is part of a series of trials he's doing, and he's hopeful for a positive outcome." She shrugged. "We drove around downtown for about twenty minutes, and then I had him drop me off out front here."

"So he knows where you live now?"

"I figure he already did," she said. "Considering they have to be tracking me if they knew exactly where I was going to be this morning."

"This whole operation is turning into something pretty interesting."

"I wasn't actually in the market for excitement." She wiped her lips with a napkin but missed a spot of chocolate at the corner of her mouth. "I happen to like my very calm, very ordered life that is exactly the way I want it."

"And then I showed up and threw everything for a loop."

Her eyes gleamed. "You have no idea."

He liked the sound of that a lot. "I'm not sure if I should apologize."

"I'll keep you posted."

Luca smiled, finishing up his coffee. "Trash can?" He shook the cup, so she'd know why he needed it.

"Under the sink."

He got up and headed into the kitchen, spotting a row of spices on the counter beside the oven. Ones he used often in his own kitchen. Which told him that she knew how to make some staples from her heritage and ate them often enough she needed the seasonings within reach.

At the end of the counter, a white engraved invitation caught his eye.

"Are you snooping in my mail, Mr. Private Investigator?" She appeared at the open doorway.

"I just noticed it." Luca lifted his hands. "Fancy party?"

"It's a gala for the Healing Hearts Foundation. They give needed medical supplies to kids in Africa, South America, and across other parts of the world."

"I think I've heard of it. It's based in Renegade?"

She nodded. "An acquaintance of mine runs it and wants me to join the board."

"You aren't sure?"

She frowned, as if not expecting that she'd given her feelings away. "Like I said, I like my quiet life. I do my job and I get plenty of rest. Busyness isn't actually a sign of success. It's just a way to fill your day with things you don't necessarily care about, and then I'm at work and dragging. Which puts patients' lives at risk."

"It sounds smart to be aware of your limitations like that." He smiled. "Suddenly being awake all night let me know mine."

She grinned at him. "No one asked you to pull an all-nighter at the hospital or go around interviewing my patients like they're the subject of an investigation. The people you were speaking to are actually part of this." She pointed to the invitation. "Destiny Rousseau is the one who runs the Healing Hearts Foundation. She's been my tennis partner and someone to have lunch with."

"I was talking to her husband Ralph, and they asked me if they could hire me to protect him. Destiny thinks someone is trying to kill her husband, and wants me to make sure nothing happens to him."

Kira blinked. "I had no idea. She told me she thought someone had tried to kill him, but I didn't think anything would come of it."

He shrugged. "It's good to have focus and not be swept along by everything you hear."

"Even when it means I have blinders on to the rest of the world?"

"You spent a lot of years taking care of the rest of the world. It's okay to have a season where you take care of you." And yet she was still choosing to give of herself at the hospital where she worked.

Kira leaned her hip against the counter, and Luca shifted closer.

"You understand that what you do is amazing, right?"

She glanced at him, uncertainty in her gaze. "You mean like guys who go on missions all over the world, saving people's lives when they have no idea you're even doing it? Amazing stuff like that?"

Yeah, he wanted to ask her about what she'd done with that flash drive in the refugee camp. But he was pretty sure it would ruin the moment. "Guys who go on those missions also come home and realize there are plenty of wrongs to right here. Even in a place like Renegade."

"And Ralph is part of that?"

"He was kidnapped a few months ago and mentioned something to us that we're trying to follow up on. It's actually been a frustrating investigation because Rousseau skirted out from all the legal trouble he should've been in, and beyond what he says was faked, we haven't been able to discover much so far that is real, physical evidence that there's a criminal empire at work in Renegade."

"That's what you've been working on?"

He nodded. "Almost exclusively. Signing on for this Marshals job is going to be a good distraction. It might even help me figure out things I wouldn't have been able to otherwise."

"Sometimes variety can be good. Or so I've heard."

He chuckled, and she smiled at him.

Luca said, "You have a little bit of chocolate at the corner of your mouth." He reached for it, moving slowly just in case she didn't want him to touch her.

Kira didn't move.

He wiped the corner of her mouth with his thumb, not quite shifting the chocolate.

"Thank you for breakfast."

He watched her mouth form the words.

"You're welcome." He eased a little closer. "When I saw your name on that email, I couldn't believe it was really you." Luca paused. "It was a really nice surprise to see you here in Renegade."

She had to know that. At least to start with. The rest of it? He figured they had time.

"When that guy hit you with his gun and you fell, it looked really bad. I'm glad you're okay now." He made sure not to look at the scar, since she hadn't wanted him to bring it up before.

"It took a lot of physical therapy. I was out for almost six months, healing and then dealing with headaches." She gave him a soft smile. "But I'm okay now. How about you?"

"I'm great." Considering his proximity to her and how things were going, maybe even better than expected.

She smiled wider and touched the outside of his arm, over the sleeve of his T-shirt. "I mean this."

He lifted the edge of the material, and her fingers traced the scar on the outside of his arm. "It was one way to remember you." He smiled softly. "Even if it wasn't the one I'd have chosen."

She opened her mouth, but his phone rang.

Total buzzkill.

What on earth was happening?

Kira let the phone ringing jog her out of whatever mental fog had just taken over her brain. The man came over with food and drinks, a simple breakfast, and in return, she'd gone all googly-eyed?

Luca dug out his phone and apologized. "Saxon Investigations."

Kira left him to his phone call, giving him privacy and not acting like a nitwit who needed to be as close as possible to him every second of the day.

She took the gala invitation and went to her office so she could leave it on the desk. The idea that he might want to go with her to such an occasion had crossed her mind. But the same reservation that had her turning down coffee and the chat last night held her tongue.

She should ask him though. The gala would be far better with someone by her side, helping her navigate the crowd of people and the expectations of Destiny's offer. She would be able to get an expert read on what she'd be getting into if she joined the board of the foundation.

Kira got one of the egg bites from the brown bag, not something she had ever had before. But it was tasty, and she might even be convinced to eat bacon after this.

"He did?" Luca's low voice sounded surprised. She liked the way it resonated through the room. A tall man with presence and the ring of authority in his tone. And yet, talking with her in the kitchen a second ago, he'd been soft and gentle.

It was an intriguing mix that told her he could be a threat if he wanted to, but chose to use his strength only when necessary.

"Did you just say Ralph Rousseau?" Pause. "Okay, thanks." A second later, he emerged from the kitchen. Sliding his phone back into his front pocket and shaking his head.

Kira glanced over. "Is everything okay?"

He rolled his shoulders. "More like confusing."

"Do you want to talk about it?" She took her juice cup and motioned to the living room.

Why, she had no idea. After all, it was another invitation into a part of her life where she didn't often allow other people. But then, he was already in her home. Not exactly invading her space, but definitely shifting the atmosphere in here with his strength and presence.

He stared at her for a second, then said, "I'd love to." He followed her and sat on the other end of the couch.

And immediately groaned.

Kira chuckled. "I did the same thing in the store. The second I sat on this couch, I just melted. I bought it right away."

She snuggled down into the comfy seat, bending her knees and planting her feet on the seat in front of her. Just a little bit of protection, or guardedness. But she was beginning to believe she might not need it with Luca Saxon.

He looked around the room, as if seeing things in a new light.

"Is something going on with Ralph Rousseau?"

He'd already told her the man was the subject of an investigation he was conducting. What more could there be?

"That was the old mayor, Alden Jenkins."

"The one in jail?"

"Yes, he's awaiting trial for all those charges. My teammate from the refugee camp operation? He's Jenkins's stepson. Before Christmas, Hammer was the one who figured out what Jenkins was up to. Jenkins then tried to kill Sierra and Huck, Hammer's wife and son." He shook his head. "Rowan Wallace."

She nodded. "Mack told me who was who, that Jenkins tried to burn the house down around them to inherit Hammer's land. And how you were there to save them."

"After we rescued Ralph from his captors, he told us there's a shadow syndicate operating in town and that they're the ones who kidnapped him." Luca shifted in his seat, looking like he wanted to put his boots on her coffee table. But he didn't. "I've been trying to get Jenkins to tell me who they might be, but he told me he wouldn't say anything unless Mack came to see him."

"You asked him to go see his father?"

Luca shook his head. "I didn't want him to. I told him I wasn't going to ask, no matter that was Jenkins's stipulation. I guess he did, because Jenkins just called and told me that Ralph Rousseau is the head of the Shadow Syndicate in Renegade."

"Destiny's husband is some kind of criminal mastermind?"

"You probably aren't interested in local conspiracy theories. Maybe you didn't want to hear this. We don't have to talk about it."

She waved away his concern. "The syndicate isn't the part I have a problem with. I actually totally believe there's a group in Renegade who control everything."

He blinked at her. "You do?"

She nodded. "When I first moved here, I was going to open my own private practice so I could run a business on my terms and build something that I was proud of. But I never got that far. I started to apply for permits and had so many zoning issues it was insane. When I finally got into a building, it needed renovation, because it was the only thing I could get accepted for.

"Then there were all these inspections and audits, way more than were reasonable. It seemed almost like it was coordinated. When I finally started to make progress, someone slapped me with this frivolous lawsuit about the name of my medical center." She shook her head. "It was crazy. Clearly there was someone in local government who didn't want me to open my practice here. But I thought it was just me. If there are criminals in town trying to control people or force people out, I totally believe it. After I turned down a position I didn't want, the ER was the only job

I could get, and that was only because Destiny vouched for me with the hospital."

"She did?"

Kira nodded. "She was one of the first people I met here in Renegade outside of the hospital. First at the country club, where we played tennis. Then she invited me to a charity gala. They're do-gooder types, so it doesn't really make sense if it's her husband who's behind it."

"Unless she has no idea." Luca shrugged, an easiness to his movements. Maybe trying not to betray to Kira exactly how intense the situation was.

But she'd experienced it firsthand.

Kira shrugged one shoulder. "Maybe Destiny is busy with the foundation and she doesn't really know what his business is. You talked to them both. Do you really think he's some kind of criminal mastermind? He seems like one of those down-home types—even if Destiny lives like they have crazy amounts of money."

"Definitely worth looking into." He frowned. "Not that I'd take anything Jenkins says at face value. He's probably giving me the runaround just for the sake of it. It does seem like there's a whole lot of misdirection going on. Maybe the only way Jenkins thinks he'll stay alive is by pointing a finger at Ralph. Meanwhile, Ralph is playing dumb until someone can prove he isn't innocent. I might not even put it past him to be faking the attempts on his life to make it look like the syndicate has it out for him."

"That would be frustrating, not knowing who is telling the truth and who is lying." She glanced at the windows and her sheer floor-to-ceiling drapes. Her mother would have loved those curtains. "Why can't people just say what they mean?"

"As in, be up front?"

"I don't like when people say one thing to your face, then behind your back they're telling a completely different story."

"Sounds like you've been burned."

She looked at him, expecting to see her insecurity reflected on his face. Like he thought she'd been too naive to avoid it. "I just like honesty."

"Honesty is good." Luca rested his arm along the back of the couch. "I like to dig for the truth and solve the puzzle of what's really going on."

"I do that sometimes when I'm diagnosing a patient. But it should be straightforward. It shouldn't be a challenge to work out what's wrong with someone and how to treat them." She shook her head. "Maybe I've just seen too many people who suffer from the same thing. Like a kind of shared trauma, or an outbreak."

"The kind of thing you walked away from. Working in the refugee camp."

"I didn't realize it at the time, but the truth is that it was slowly killing me." Why was she telling him this? She hadn't even admitted that to herself, despite the fact Jordan had tried to explain it more than once. "Trying to navigate people's expectations and do a job I didn't plan for, when all I ever wanted was to be a doctor."

"You got in over your head." He shifted in his seat, reaching over and squeezing the top of her foot. "But you got out."

"I didn't do it on my own. I have a friend, and she made me choose life." Kira rolled her eyes, smiling to herself. "That's what she said. She told me I couldn't keep going the way I was, that I had to choose life."

"Sounds like a good friend."

Kira nodded. "She is."

And why did he look relieved by that?

Oh, because her friend was female?

She didn't know what to think about any of this. Talk about being in over her head. She got the feeling this relationship was a whole lot different than burning out at work while trying to juggle everything—plus orders from clandestine agencies.

If she built a friendship with Luca, eventually she would have to tell him what she'd done. How her actions had led to the deaths of so many. And what was he going to think about that? Surely he would walk away from her and never look back. A guy like him, a hero, wouldn't want anything to do with someone like her.

"Too bad we can't erase what we've done." She'd certainly tried though. "Walking away from it doesn't change what happened."

"I've rebuilt my life from nothing enough times to know that who you are always stays with you," he said. "But why would that be a bad thing? Your whole life is about helping people get well."

"It has to be. I've got a lot to make up for."

He stared at her, a slight frown drawing his brows together.

"But that's another conversation." One she didn't want to have right now, in this quiet moment.

"That implies you're interested in doing this again. Or maybe we meet somewhere else, like a neutral location."

"Is that an operator's way of asking a girl out?" The question slipped from her lips before she realized what she was saying. She didn't even know if she wanted to date him. She'd been thinking only in terms of friends and how who he was just seemed to fit her. He would understand the things she told him far better than anyone else.

"If I did, would you say yes?"

She stared at him, allowing a small smile to tug on her lips. "If you're willing to take the chance, I guess we'll inevitably find out."

Luca's smile widened. "That sounded like a challenge to me." And it didn't look like he considered that to be a bad thing.

Oh boy, she might have just walked herself into being his latest mission. She needed to pivot this conversation fast. "Thanks again for breakfast."

"Off to work?"

"Not tonight." She shook her head.

"Plans?"

"The doctor gave me the impression that the patient will be

arriving tonight, unexpectedly. So I suspect we'll be called in to the hospital anyway." She shrugged. "Keeping my schedule loose."

Which made her sound like an interesting person, when in fact, having him come over was the most interesting thing that had happened to her in months. And he seemed to want to continue hanging out with her. She needed at least a week to figure out how to deal with that.

She stood. "I should get ready for the day—or night."

"Thanks for letting me in."

"Thanks again for breakfast."

They reached the front door, and he turned to her. Very slowly, he leaned down and kissed her cheek. "You're welcome."

He closed the door behind him and was gone. Leaving her standing in her entryway, trying to figure out why it felt different in here now.

As if something was missing.

EIGHT

"**H**EY." DEPUTY MARSHAL ETHAN BUTLER HELD out his hand, his dark hair damp against his forehead thanks to the rain.

Luca shook with him, and they headed inside the hospital's main building. "Everything ready?"

In the end, it had been another day before the call indicating the patient was arriving. The marshal had told him to meet up at the west wing, side door. An entrance rarely used by people coming and going from the hospital. After Luca's evaluation of the hospital, he had decided this was the best entrance to use for their patient. From here, it was straight to the elevator and up two floors.

Now that they were inside, he could see that maintenance had blocked off this entrance to keep people from using it and the closest elevator.

"Good to go." Butler nodded.

Luca spotted a scratch on the side of the man's neck. "Did you get in a fight today?"

Butler shook his head. "I went kayaking this morning and scratched myself on a branch." He touched the scratch with two fingers and winced.

"You should get a doctor to look at that."

He smelled her perfume before he realized she had approached them. "Get a doctor to look at what?" Kira reacted to her own question. "Never mind, maybe I don't want to know."

Luca smiled at her. "It's just the scratch on his neck."

She peered at the side of Butler's head. "You should clean that. Put some antibiotic cream on it." She thumbed over her shoulder. "I have some Hello Kitty bandages in my office, if you want."

Butler snorted. "I'm good, but thanks." He looked at his watch. "We have about five minutes before the detail is bringing your patient in, Dr. Yassan."

"Great."

Luca had been sent some basic details, just so he knew they were protecting the right person. Fifty-eight years old, Mexican descent. Suffering from a rare blood disorder. There hadn't been a photo included in the dossier, however. Evidently, even his appearance was being kept under wraps.

"I'm going to head outside to meet them when they get here." Butler headed for the door.

Luca turned to Kira. "Thanks for the tip about Destiny and Ralph, by the way. I just spent a couple of hours this evening digging back through their work histories, trying to see if we missed anything. We focused our search on the information we had about Rocky Mountain Land Development, but with the foundation and the other small companies, real-estate investments, and holdings they have across the city, there was more to look at than just what had been exposed regarding Rousseau and the land grab. A friend of mine, she's a tech whiz and a financial genius, took a look at the foundation's income and investments."

"I'm not sure I want to get into a real-life mystery. The book I'm reading is exciting enough."

He chuckled.

"Although, I have to admit I'm always curious if wealthy people actually have money or if they're just leveraged to the hilt and it's all about flash."

"In their case? They have a lot of liabilities, but also a serious nest egg. Ralph made a ton of money ten years ago when he set up his business. He hit the market hot and fast and ended up making a killing. Like freaky fast. Real rags-to-riches stuff."

She frowned. "That doesn't sound like it would've been entirely legal."

"All of it is totally aboveboard. It's just rare for someone to make that much money so fast."

"Almost like someone was giving them a helping hand, or they were catching breaks everywhere they went."

"I thought you said you weren't interested in a real-life mystery?"

She smiled. "Don't worry, I'm not going to quit my job to become your sidekick anytime soon."

"That's a shame."

Her smile turned to gentle laughter, lighting her eyes.

Before either of them could say anything else, the doors opened and two men in suits walked in, followed by an older man, who glanced at Kira and nodded. His eyes assessed Luca, and he followed the two men past them to the elevator.

A guy in a wheelchair was being pushed by another suited man, two more behind them. Ethan Butler, the US marshal, brought up the rear.

He nodded for them both to go in the same direction. "I already told them where to go."

The marshals were securely bringing the man to the hospital, but if they remained outside the room on duty—standing guard—for too long, it would cause too much of a commotion. People would start asking questions if there was a permanent detail of federal agents in the hospital.

That was where Luca came in, coordinating with the marshals and other people he trusted to watch out for this man. He had contracted his own team of private security and off-duty cops but would do the bulk of the protection himself.

He and Kira waited for the elevator to empty, then rode up two floors. As he stepped out, he saw them wheel the patient into the hospital room while two US marshals stayed by the door. The wing of the hospital on this floor didn't have many patients. Yesterday, a sudden leak in the HVAC system meant that hospital security needed to clear all the patients in this wing to other rooms, effectively emptying this part of the hospital.

Luca stood at the door, watching the man shift from the wheelchair to the bed with the help of the two doctors. Kira wore conservative black slacks, a cashmere sweater, and a delicate gold chain around her neck, from which hung a small cross.

As the patient settled back onto the pillows, Luca got a look at his face. Dark eyes set back in his face, heavy gray eyebrows and mustache. Matching hair, thick and wavy like he'd run his hands through it.

Luca didn't need to be told what this man's name was. After all, he kept tabs on the federal government's most-wanted criminals. Francisco Abalos had been one of Mexico's most notorious cartel leaders for nearly thirty years before his nephew tried to murder him several months back. Now his nephew, Antonio, was in charge of the cartel, and Francisco had gone underground, disappearing completely.

A guy who had murdered countless people and damaged so many others with narcotics trafficking and human trafficking operations. Now he was under the protection of the US Marshals who, in exchange for all the intel he had, would make sure he was treated for the rare disease he had. Seemed like a sweet deal, if a person could net themselves something like that.

Luca didn't think he could be a marshal. It seemed entirely too much like operating in the gray areas. Making deals. But they did catch dangerous fugitives, so he'd give them credit for that.

"Ladies and gentlemen." Francisco flashed pearly white false teeth. "Shall we begin?"

Deputy Marshal Butler said, "We'll get out of your hair. But don't worry, you're in good hands." He motioned to Luca. "This is Mr. Saxon. He's now in charge of your security."

Francisco leveled a steady gaze at Luca. A guy wrinkled with age, and clearly ill, but he had such presence that Luca wanted to shift his stance. But he didn't. He forced his body to remain still, pulling on all his training. "Nice to meet you."

Francisco barked a laugh that made Kira jump. "I'm sure it's not." He glanced at Kira. "I'm sorry if I startled you."

Kira shook her head. "Not to worry."

The doctor stood on the other side of the bed, an older man with tanned features. Dr. Torres wasn't the kind of guy you'd think spent hours of the day poring over test tubes and lab results. More like the kind of man you would find surrounded by beautiful women at a fancy resort in Monaco, under the guise of being at a medical conference. The kind of doctor it took serious money to find—and he was from right here in Renegade.

If he had created some kind of cutting-edge treatment, Luca figured it would be worth the price to get him to do this. As long as he wasn't here to kill the patient and make it look like an accident.

Francisco looked at him. "Saxon?"

"Luca Saxon." He nodded, unsure if the guy wanted him to explain the years of service and deployments he'd experienced, or the two years fighting wildfires in rough terrain, or the fact he was now licensed as a private investigator in this city. Truthfully, Luca didn't feel the need to justify himself to this guy. All he wanted was to do his job. "I'll be outside."

He looked around before he walked out. Assessing the room that he had chosen specifically for this patient. No window. Adjoining bathroom that only had one door—the one into this room. Luca wandered over to it and looked around inside, confirming it was empty.

He went to the door and stepped into the hall, where the marshals had gathered. Definitely not inconspicuous, having all these guys with silver star badges on their belts hanging around in the hospital. As if anyone wouldn't immediately guess they were protecting someone high-profile.

Butler broke off the conversation. "You're good?"

"Any idea how long they're going to be here?" The initial paperwork suggested a few days, but Luca had prepared a detail for longer than that. If this thing dragged out weeks, he would have to make some adjustments.

"I'm sure they'll let you know what their plans are." Butler hesitated. "And . . . maybe if he mentions anything about smuggling routes between Mexico and Texas, you could write it down and pass it over to us?"

"He hasn't told you anything yet?" This was definitely some kind of deal if Francisco had given them nothing so far. He tried to think back to what Judge Mullinax had said in that meeting, but all he could remember was Kira saying no to coffee.

"He refuses to say anything until the treatment is complete." Butler shrugged. "To be honest, I don't really blame the guy. He gets what he wants, and as long as he holds up his end of the bargain, then so do we."

"Do I need to worry about Kira's safety in there with Dr. Torres and the head of a cartel?"

One of the other marshals said, "*Former* head of a cartel."

As if that was the point here.

Butler said, "If he wants to finish the treatment before he's taken away and actually have a shot at kicking this, he knows he can't mess with her or hurt her. We gave him a whole lot of stipulations, and he promised to adhere to every single one. Otherwise, he doesn't get this doctor's help."

That might have to be enough to satisfy Luca, even if it still presented a risk. But he got the feeling he would be looking out for Kira as much as he was for threats against this guy while he was here. "Got it."

Butler stuck his hand out again. "We appreciate it."

The marshals took off, leaving him in the quiet hallway. Luca eased toward the door and listened for a second, hearing the low murmur of conversation. Hallway clear. His tablet was patched into hospital security, so he dug it out of his backpack and checked that everything was normal from the security guards' point of view. In addition to that, he'd added his own cameras in this hall and the room itself, as well as the closest entrance and the nearest elevator.

Things were about as covered as they could be.

Now all he had to do was stay at this post until he was relieved by Hammer for the next shift. Not the first time he had pulled an all-nighter for a mission. Maybe later, Kira would be up for hanging out a little. Like getting a drink to break the monotony of hours of observation.

He could use the time to persuade her they'd make a great team. And even though he didn't think she should do what she'd said and quit her job to become his sidekick, that would mean spending time together.

Something he was definitely interested in.

"He's a good man." Kira didn't know why she felt like she had to defend Luca, but the words were already out.

Dr. Torres stood on the opposite side of the bed, holding the patient's wrist and looking at his watch. Francisco Abalos had tanned skin, dark hair threaded with plenty of gray, and a gray shadow of beard around his mustache that was likely scratchy to the touch. A slight yellowing of the skin was the only noticeable indication that he suffered from a rare type of anemia.

Francisco's breaths were shallow. He rested his head back against the pillow. "Powerful men are often complicated."

"Speaking from experience?" She went for an easy smile, but this man was a dangerous criminal. Even if the Marshals believed he would give them what they wanted, it would never erase the pain Francisco had caused others.

Dr. Torres looked up.

She'd overstepped? That wasn't the read she got from Francisco. Kira's stomach clenched for a second, and then Francisco chuckled. The laugh turned into a cough that seemed to tax him.

"Sorry." She grabbed the water cup beside the bed and offered him the straw.

He took a sip of the cool water. "Powerful people don't apologize." He smiled at her. "It's refreshing to meet a beautiful woman who speaks her mind."

She didn't consider herself anywhere near on the same level as this man, but didn't mind being someone he considered equal to Luca. That was a nice idea. Even being in the same category made her feel good.

For all the doubts she'd had and the reasons she'd wondered if she was wrong about him, deep down, Luca was a good guy. He cared about people. She didn't believe there were any underlying motives to Luca's words or his actions.

Really, it was her own fear that kept her from trusting him.

"Dr. Torres requested you," Francisco said. "Once the Marshals provided him with a list of available doctors, he took only minutes to assess the names and declare that he wanted you to assist him."

Kira lifted her gaze to Torres, a guy who talked only about his work and took everything very seriously.

"My work requires expert assistance." Torres didn't seem in the least bit flustered to be pointed out. "There can be no mistakes."

"It's a remarkable procedure." Kira needed him to know she was impressed, but not in order to butter him up. "You've done some incredible work over the years, and to participate will be a unique experience for me."

"One that you won't be able to divulge to anyone."

Kira nodded. "I understand. Just participating and assisting will be enough."

"Markedly different from some of your other work. Hopefully the slower pace won't be a source of frustration."

"I'm looking forward to the opportunity."

Francisco said, "And the chance for us to get to know each other better."

She looked at Francisco and saw the gleam in his eyes. This wasn't a guy she worried would try to hit on her. At least, not other than just for fun. "I'm sure that will happen, considering we'll be spending a lot of time together. However, I'm here in a professional capacity first and foremost."

"A woman who lives behind a polite mask. How intriguing."

Kira smiled at him. Luca might be a guy who liked solving puzzles, but Francisco was the kind who lived for a conquest, even if it was about ruffling her feathers.

"That means you have plenty of secrets yet to be discovered." His eyes gleamed.

"When I come by later, I'll bring a deck of cards. We can find out what secrets *you* have that are yet to be discovered."

Francisco tipped his head back and laughed, causing him to gasp for breath.

Dr. Torres frowned.

"Sorry, Doctor," Kira said.

Francisco patted her hand. "Don't apologize, remember?"

She wondered if that was his philosophy concerning all the horrible things he'd done. A quick web search before she came here had yielded plenty of news articles and social media posts. Lengthy descriptions of friends or loved ones who had been caught in the web of his sins, innocent lives destroyed by the cartel.

This man, the charmer, could've fooled her if she hadn't known who he was. But she also shouldn't forget what he was capable of. He was able to turn vicious in a split second and was only here to get his treatment. If he had to tell the Marshals everything, then it was only for a ticket to better health or for the protection the Marshals offered from the current head of the cartel.

A man like this, in a position where he was vulnerable? He wouldn't want anyone to know that he was scared the procedure might not be successful. She shouldn't take anything he said at face value.

In short, he was everything she tried not to be—and hoped Luca wasn't. She wasn't anything like him, even if she was responsible for a terrible thing happening. Francisco wasn't anything like her father either.

It was a good reminder that she shouldn't judge herself too harshly. But giving in a little would lead to trusting Luca, maybe more than she should.

"There are some serious thoughts happening in that pretty head of yours," Francisco said.

She smiled politely. "It's been a long day so far. I should get some rest at home so that I'm alert when I come back."

"Too much time spent with a powerful man?" Francisco motioned to the door.

Kira said, "We met a long time ago and reconnected recently."

Francisco touched a hand to his shirtfront. "I'm heartbroken."

She laughed a little. "I apologize. That wasn't my intention."

"My illness will be listed as the cause of death, but we'll both know it was heartbreak that killed me." He winked at her.

"It was very nice to meet you," Kira said, smiling. "I'll be back later."

He reached out a hand, but Kira pretended not to notice it as she turned away. Of course, Dr. Torres saw it. Hopefully he'd respect her keeping those professional boundaries from the outset. They didn't know each other, but she needed to build a rapport quickly with the doctor so that he'd trust her when he couldn't be with the patient.

Kira eased the door closed, turned, and found herself face-to-face with Luca. "Hey." Her cheeks warmed.

"Everything go okay in there?"

"He's an interesting guy." She kept her voice low so that neither of the men in the room behind her heard their conversation. "That's for sure."

"Interesting?" Luca didn't seem to like the word she'd chosen. "He's a dangerous man who will try to charm you."

"He already did, but don't worry. Apparently, I'm a heartbreaker." Luca frowned.

"It's all good. I've got it under control."

"This is a guy who controls everyone around him, and he does it without mercy. He only plays at emotion or affection. And forget about friendship. Everything is a game to him. People are possessions."

Oh boy.

Kira touched his arms, just above his elbows. "Luca, it's *fine.*"

He led her to the two waiting chairs beside the door. "I have to know that you understand what kind of man this is. You can't let your guard down, Kira. You have to stay alert at all times. He might seem nice, but this is the kind of man who slices up little children in front of their parents."

"You think I haven't met bad guys before?" She touched the

scar on her forehead. He'd been there, he knew. But there was even more he didn't know about her and the things she'd seen or done. "I know what I'm doing." She was well aware of exactly how careful she needed to be.

"I know you've met insurgents." He took her hand and held it in his gently, as if he was trying to comfort her. "This guy? He's on a whole other level you can't even imagine. He's a mass murderer wrapped in a con artist. A good-looking guy whose job it is to get you to let your guard down so that he can be the one with all the control."

She dipped her head for a second, realizing she'd have to let him know a little something or he wouldn't believe she was all right. She should ask him to just trust that she knew what she was doing. In reality, what she needed was to guard her heart from being broken all over again. If she asked for trust, she'd have to take her own advice, or she'd be a hypocrite.

"I know what kind of man he is." She drew her hand from his and rubbed them over her knees, locking her arms straight. "Because I've met a man like him before. I know how easy it is to get sucked into their web, twisted around, then suddenly realize how far gone you are. How you've changed everything about yourself and what you want, just to align with their ideals."

"Ex-boyfriend? Or husband?"

She shook her head. "My father." Luca didn't need all the details. All he needed to know was "He wasn't a nice man. Then he was dead. End of story."

Her dad hadn't been charming or attractive like Francisco. But he had been ruthless. The way he'd been able to get everyone around him to do his bidding had been both fascinating and terrifying. People who were willing to lay down their lives for the cause he told them was absolute and the chance for a quick payout. In the end, what did that get him but death at the hands of armed police in London?

She pushed the memories away. "I know what I'm doing."

Luca tugged on her fingers, interlacing the tips of his with hers. "I'd like to hear more of the story sometime. Not right now, but eventually."

She stared at their hands, liking the way his fingers looked with hers. The warmth of his touch. The strength in him and the way he remained so gentle at the same time. She let out a breath. "I don't like talking about it, but it's part of who I am."

"I'd like to know all about you. And if you want to know about me, I'm happy to tell you anything."

She glanced at him and saw the sincerity in his gaze. "Eventually."

Someone cleared their throat.

Kira felt her cheeks flame all over again. Luca twisted around but didn't let go of her hand. "Hammer."

"You're going to introduce me as Rowan though—hold up." The big man came over to stand in front of her. "I know you."

Luca tugged her to her feet. *Eventually* meant she needed to meet his friends officially, and that time was looking like right now. "You two should probably formally meet."

She tipped her head to the side, smiling at Mr. Team Leader, and held out her hand. Everything Mack had told her about Hammer and his return to Renegade rolled through her mind. But he didn't know that she already had the whole story. "Dr. Kira Yassan."

He held it almost as gently as Luca, placing his other hand on top so that she spotted a gold wedding band on his left hand. "Rowan Wallace."

"Nice to meet you." Kira smiled politely.

"Finally." He let go of her hand and glanced at Luca. "Been holding out on me, bro."

Luca cleared his throat. "I have no idea what you're talking about."

Kira shifted away from the two of them as far as Luca's hold on her hand allowed. "Well, I should go get some rest, or I'll be worthless next time I'm on shift."

"Hmm. I'm thinking that'll probably be about the same time Luca comes back on duty."

Kira said, "Hopefully you aren't missing anything important at home." By all accounts, he was involved with his son's rodeo competitions, catching up on everything he'd missed.

Rowan shook his head. "They're having a movie night. I'm trying to convince my son I don't actually like popcorn, but he doesn't believe me."

Kira started to go and realized Luca was still holding her hand. "See you later?"

"I'll walk you to the elevator. Hammer's got this."

NINE

SHE HADN'T OBJECTED TO HIM HOLDING HER hand, but Luca only clasped her fingers loosely. Keeping it casual just in case she didn't want to be the doctor seen in the hospital hallway holding hands with a guy.

She glanced over at him. "Are you delegating the duties the Marshals gave you?"

"I can't be on duty twenty-four seven. That invites too much risk, because I need to sleep sometime. If I'm overtired, I could miss something, so I've got a couple of people switching off with me. But I'm doing the bulk of the time." He shrugged one shoulder. "Hammer is on duty for a few hours, and then I'll be back."

He couldn't stop thinking about what she'd told him about her father. Not that there had been much, just a "to be continued" type mention. There was so much about her that he didn't know. He could find out through various channels that were available to him. But in the end, he would rather she chose to tell him herself.

He didn't want to get ahead of himself, but this was going pretty well so far. Even if they had plenty they needed to get out in the open—between the two of them—he couldn't help thinking that maybe he had finally found someone worth pursuing. A woman he could actually fall for.

Don't let me mess it up.

As far as prayers went, that wasn't particularly eloquent. But he'd always considered honesty and being real as the hallmarks of a solid relationship. Including the one he had with the Lord.

Kira hit the button for the elevator. "Thanks for walking me down here." She seemed almost shy.

He squeezed her hand gently. "You're very welcome."

The elevator doors slid open, and she stepped inside. A second later, a man not quite as tall as Luca stepped inside, wearing a heavy overcoat under which he had a zippered sweater. Hood up, dirty jeans and work boots. Those weren't things that should have set off his instinct for danger, ringing alarm bells in his head. But something about this guy wasn't quite right.

Before the doors could shut, Luca slammed his hand on the side of the opening. He stepped into the elevator. "On second thought, I should grab my backpack from the truck."

He eased over and stood by Kira, keeping the guy in his peripheral vision but not making it obvious he was looking at the man. "I need to give Hammer the twenty bucks I owe him before I leave."

Kira lifted her gaze to him. Her eyes darted to the right, then back to him.

He nodded very slightly. "What are your plans for the day?"

"Apparently I'm going to have a handsome man walk me to my car."

He smiled. "Where are you parked? I'm over in the west lot."

"That's a shame. I'm not far from the edge of the east lot. You shouldn't come all the way over to my car. We can just say bye outside."

"Thanks, babe." He watched her eyes flare, liking the surprise there.

He was going to hide somewhere and follow this guy, just to make sure nothing crazy was about to happen. "Any other plans?"

The elevator settled on the ground floor.

The doors opened, and the guy said, "After you."

She turned to him. "Thank you."

Luca took her hand again, and they went a few paces out into the dark of night, where the air was chilled and lacked a breeze. Not many stars overhead, thanks to the city lights. He stopped and kissed her cheek. "I'll see you later."

"I'll be looking forward to it."

She wandered off, and he headed in a different direction, giving the parking lot where she had left her vehicle a wide berth. He supposed he would have to go toward the other lot, but he needed to ensure he kept track of where the man went. Something about the guy just made him think the man had ill intentions. Whatever those might be. Whether it was personal or by chance, it seemed as if this guy might have stepped onto the elevator intentionally because Kira had.

Luca glanced over his shoulder under the guise of watching her walk to her car and caught the man following behind her, about thirty feet.

Luca ducked between rows of cars, crouched behind the back of a Toyota, and tracked the man's progress. After a few seconds, Luca started to run, staying in a low crouch and racing down the aisle. It ran parallel to the one where Kira headed for her car. There was a good amount of space between them. If this guy was going to try something, Luca would have to run fast to cross the distance.

He stopped two-thirds of the way to the end of the row, crouched again, and waited for the man to pass him.

Luca raced between two cars and crossed a couple of rows but hid himself behind the guy, again crouching by the back end of the car. He wasn't going to pull his weapon out unless he saw one. And so far, the guy hadn't drawn a pistol or knife from somewhere.

Kira searched in her purse for her keys, slowing her pace. It allowed the other man to catch up a little. For some reason, the move made him wonder if she had a little bit of covert ops training. At least enough to know what to watch out for so that she could protect herself. Maybe it was just something a single woman had to learn in order to survive in a world like this one. He didn't want to say she'd been a terrible secret agent years ago when they met at the refugee camp, but her skills hadn't exactly been sharp when taking that flash drive from his pocket. After all, he'd caught her slipping the storage device back in.

Luca hung back still, just in case the man wasn't going to accost Kira in some way and the vibes had been for nothing. He might simply walk past her, and there would be no altercation.

Kira pulled out her keys, and they tumbled from her hands onto the asphalt. The man crouched, swiped the keys from the ground, and approached her. Her face paled as he neared.

The guy moved close, talking to her in words too quiet for Luca to hear.

He circled the back of the closest car and raced down the row, easing back between vehicles so that he could be close enough to figure out what they were saying.

"You're the one who convinced Frankie to take off." He held the keys, not handing them over to her. His voice low and full of frustrated anger. "A buddy of mine saw you talking to her in the park, so I know you're the one who took her from me."

"If Frankie wanted to go somewhere you can't find her, that's her choice. She's free to go wherever she wants."

"Frankie belongs to me." He slapped his chest.

"If she chooses to be in a relationship like that, it's up to her. But it seems like after you beat the living daylights out of her that she chose to go somewhere else and be free of you instead."

"Where is she?" He took a step toward Kira, using his physical size to intimidate her. Whether he realized it or not. This was a guy who used whatever tactics he had available to him and forced everyone to do what he wanted.

Or he was the kind of guy who had no power in one area of his life, so he took that feeling of powerlessness out on the vulnerable people he should have protected.

Either way, he wasn't going to be intimidating Kira much longer.

"I'm calling the police. You need to leave me alone." She reached into her bag and pulled out her cell phone.

The guy slapped it out of her hand. Her phone hit the asphalt and cracked, which gave Luca all the reason he needed to intervene. He strode out from between the cars, not giving the man any announcement before he grabbed the guy's arm and twisted it behind his back. "Hand over the keys."

The man shoved his upper body back, trying to slam his head back into Luca's. "I knew you were trouble when I saw you."

"And yet you still decided to do something dumb." Luca didn't let go, but he also didn't bend the man's arm back any further. He didn't want to injure the guy. "Let go of the keys."

As soon as the situation was resolved, Luca was going to call the police and file a report against this guy. Whatever was going on, the police probably needed a record of things he was doing that would add up to some serious charges. Or this guy would find a little bit of wisdom and change his plans.

The keys dropped to the asphalt.

Kira didn't bend to pick them up. "Can I have your phone, Luca? I'd like to call the authorities."

He dug his phone out with his free hand and handed it over, unlocking it for her. Which he didn't need to do in order for her to make an emergency call. But still, he needed her to know that he trusted her fully and was willing to give her access to his entire life.

Luca wished he had some kind of plastic ties, but there was

nothing in his pockets to secure the guy. He walked the assailant a few steps away from her. "I can let you go. If you aren't going to cause any more trouble."

The guy hissed out a breath between clenched teeth, his body shifting. He wanted to cause plenty of trouble but had to know that might not be the best course of action right now, when the police were going to be arriving soon.

Kira walked away a couple of steps, the phone to her ear.

"I can always tell the police that you fully cooperated and realized that what you were going to do was a bad choice."

"You mean pick up a lady's keys?" he said. "'Cause that's all I did."

"That and asking about some woman who doesn't want to be around you."

The guy let out a groan of frustration. "She knows where Frankie is." He looked at Kira. "Just tell me and I'll leave. You don't need to call the cops."

Kira looked at the man, zero remorse on her face. "I'm never telling you where she is."

Luca stared at her, this fierce and powerful woman who had so much vulnerability wrapped up in that strength. He wanted to protect her and see her in action.

Yeah, he'd found what he was looking for.

"It was over pretty quickly. That's all that happened." Kira shifted her weight from one foot to the other, ready to get out of here.

Two uniformed police officers had arrived quickly, followed by Detective Mike Martinelli, who seemed to be a friend of Luca's. He was the one who'd asked her all the questions about the incident, as he called it, while the other cops put the man in the back of their car.

"Have you ever met him before?" Detective Martinelli was a little shorter than Luca, probably five-nine. He had dark hair and Mediterranean features. Sharp, intelligent eyes. Okay, fine. He was cute.

Luca had stood by her the entire way through the questioning. He'd come to her rescue after they both realized there was something off about the man in the elevator. She hadn't realized then what would happen, assuming more that he would try to mug her or something like that. The fact he'd wanted information wasn't something she'd expected.

"We've never met before," Kira said. "But I think I know who he is."

"He had his wallet on him, so we have his name. Stuart Parker."

"I think he's the boyfriend or husband of a woman I helped. Frankie . . . Hesburgh, I think." She crossed her arms. "She came in with all kinds of cuts and bruises as well as cracked ribs. It was clear it might be a domestic-violence type of situation, so my staff would have reported it to the police."

She told the detective and Luca about seeing the woman in the park and putting her in a rideshare car to take her to the shelter. "It wasn't much, but I figured they might be able to help her."

Detective Martinelli looked up from his notepad. "Something like that might have saved her life."

"And on top of that, considering it seems like someone told him what you did, it put you in the line of fire." Luca shrugged. "Whether you were aware of it or not."

He couldn't be suggesting she should've stayed out of it. "I wasn't going to leave her there and not help her. And I can take care of myself."

Detective Martinelli glanced between them.

Luca said, "I wasn't criticizing what you did. Helping people isn't a bad thing, but something like this comes with risk."

"Then it's a risk I'm willing to take." She wasn't going to back down on that, not when it was such a small thing to book a car for the lady.

But the last thing she'd expected was this.

Maybe the fear was just coming as a delayed reaction, because her hands started to shake now. Her breaths came quick, and all she could think about were fingers around her neck. A strong grip.

His face over her, determined to squeeze the life from her.

Luca snagged her hand with his, anchoring her in the moment, here and now. Enabling her to take a full breath.

Detective Martinelli said, "We ran his name, and Stuart Parker has a record for possession. He did three years a while back and managed to get off probation before there were a couple of calls out for domestic violence. Neighbors complaining about the noise." His expression shifted. "You did what you could, and we'll take him in, but he will probably be back on the streets by tomorrow, pending a court case. If this guy bothers you again, Dr. Yassan, please call it in."

She nodded. "Thank you, Detective."

He wandered away to the patrol car, and Luca said, "I wasn't implying you did anything wrong."

"Good, because I didn't." She found her bravado, the rush of fear gone now. Out like the tide.

He gave her a small smile as if he thought she was cute.

He had to know she could protect herself if needed. Sure, she tended to avoid dangerous situations, but that didn't mean she was weak. Even if she felt weak sometimes.

"I'm going to start carrying my pepper spray again." She shook her head. "I figured a place like this wasn't a real urban big city with high crime, and maybe I could let my guard down. That might not be the case."

"Anywhere you are, it's worth being cautious and taking measures to protect yourself. That's just the world we live in." His expression shifted, and she saw an unspoken question.

She wanted him to ask. "What is it?"

"At first, I wondered if what was happening just now had to do with the case I've been working for the last few months."

"You don't think it's about the shadow syndicate you mentioned?"

He shook his head. "But now we know it's connected to a patient you helped, at least we can rule out that someone is targeting me or you for looking into crime in Renegade."

"I still can't believe that Jenkins would tell you Ralph Rousseau is the one behind all of it. Just because he was implicated doesn't mean he's the head of the whole thing." She shook her head and leaned back against the side of her car, her arms still folded. Distractions were good. Talking about something that had nothing to do with what'd just happened was even better. "It being Ralph just doesn't make any sense to me."

"I'm going to be looking into the whole case against Jenkins and everything that Ralph was accused of over the next couple of days, just to see if I can find anything amiss. Probably while I'm on protection detail for our patient."

The idea that he could dig into someone's life like that and go through all their financials was more than a little unsettling. What if he decided to look up her monetary history? Kira had done a whole lot to make sure there wasn't much to find beyond the usual smart investments if anyone went looking. But one way or another, the truth always came out eventually.

Kira pushed those fleeting thoughts from her mind. "Are you going to look into the foundation, or are you just looking at Ralph's business accounts that are connected to what he was supposed to have done?"

If she saw Destiny, she would have to employ some of her spy skills to keep the other woman from becoming aware that someone was looking into her.

"I probably should look at all of it, not just what we've gone over so far. We're past the time when we can assume something isn't connected. People who are into criminal activities usually try to hide their revenue in offshore accounts or other places they can launder the money to make it look clean. Like a nonprofit. There could easily be hidden accounts we don't know about, things only my friend would be able to find." Luca thought for a second. "For all we know, the foundation is just a cover for them. They could be using it as a way to collect the money from their illegal activity and make it look legit."

"That's what you're going to be looking for evidence of?"

He nodded. "I know she's a friend of yours, but if she's up to something . . ."

"You intend to find it?"

"Yes."

Kira looked at him. "She's an associate, but I'm not sure I would really call her a friend, even though we play tennis regularly. I don't actually have many friends at all. I've never trusted people easily. You get burned one way or another."

"You'll still feel it if it turns out she's part of this shadow syndicate." His gaze on her softened. "Even if she's someone you trust only a little, it will sting to find out she's been lying to you."

"I'll be more bothered about the fact the foundation is a sham." Kira had an idea. "Maybe I should go to that gala and find out for sure. There has to be a way to tell if it's legit when they're fundraising and showing off, giving this big presentation."

He shrugged. "She wouldn't be doing the gala if she didn't have it all buttoned up and squared away. I doubt you're going to find a hole in the operation at a public event like that."

"So come with me and we can figure out a way to dig beneath the surface while we're there." Sure, she'd invited him to be her plus-one at the event. But it wasn't exactly a date when they would only be going to dig up information and find the truth. She continued, "I don't believe Destiny has anything to do with some shadowy crime syndicate in Renegade. Even if her husband does, I doubt she's part of it. But I guess we won't know for sure unless we find out."

Otherwise, all he had were theories and accusations with no evidence. It wasn't like he could act on anything without proof, which meant there was a need to dig further.

"Do you have a suit?"

He smiled, lifting his chin a little. "Yes, I have a suit. I think you'll like it."

"Oh, really?" That sounded like a whole lot of promise from a handsome man.

"I'm guessing whatever you wear, I'm going to like a whole lot." A little boyish glint of amusement lit his eyes. Softening the warrior until he seemed to be more like a man with a serious crush—if not more than that.

She didn't like the teenage fluttering in her stomach, because it meant things were changing. Kira liked her static, comfortable life that didn't shift much. She liked it a whole lot better than the unknown. But for a guy like Luca, who had stuck around and protected her from danger today, it just might be worth the risk to see what happened.

To trust that God was doing something in her life and it would be good.

She smiled, keeping her expression placid. "I was planning on wearing a dress made out of rice bags, in honor of the occasion. It might not be stylish, but I'll be making a political point about starving people across the world. So really, it's not about looking good."

Luca chuckled. "This is where I say that you'd make anything look good."

"And I would know that you don't mean it." She shoved his shoulder playfully. "Of course I'm going to wear a fabulous dress. Any occasion is a good occasion for that. And I happen to have experience gathering intel and passing it to people who will make the world safer."

He looked at her as if he was proud of her, answering a question that had been inside her for longer than she wanted to admit.

Kira wasn't the kind of woman who needed a man to make her feel complete. That was something the Lord was supposed to do. But the missing piece of who her father should've been, and the family she should have had, was something she would always be aware of.

A family of her own would be one of the biggest blessings she might receive.

"I like this plan." He stepped closer. "I like this plan a lot."

His arms slid around her waist, and he moved into her space. She unfolded her arms and rested her hands on his shoulders.

"I figure there's potential here for us to make a pretty good team." She paused a second, then said, "You know, gathering evidence of crime in Renegade."

The skin around his eyes contracted. "Right. Investigating."

"Not that I'm going to quit my job and become your sidekick." Hadn't she already said that? This man was scrambling her brain.

"I remember." He smiled, again looking like he thought she was adorable.

"One day I'll give you the rundown of my résumé."

"Or you could come with me to the gym and we can work out. See what other kinds of skills you have."

If he wanted to test her ability to defend herself, that was fine with her. But she much preferred banter. "I think that might be more of a third date kind of activity."

He grinned, but it didn't last long. "Cards on the table, I do need to know what you can do. Then I won't be asking too much of you and putting you at risk. That's a nonnegotiable."

"And if I need that door to swing both ways?" She knew he had all that military training, but what was he prepared to do on a local level when they had no idea what they were going up against? "I might need to know how long it takes you to pick a lock or hack a computer."

"Or copy a flash drive?"

"I'll have you know I'm much better at that these days." She lifted her chin. "Well, better than I was when we first met." Kira blew out a breath. "I didn't do anything today, so maybe I'm rustier than I realized."

He should be looking at her as if he was in awe of her amazing skills, but he wasn't. "I'm glad I was here."

Me too. But she needed this conversation to swing back to banter. "If either of us had the time, I'd say we go head-to-head in a series of challenges. See who comes out on top."

"It's probably good we have this Marshals thing and the gala coming up. I wouldn't want you to be too embarrassed when I soundly beat you."

She lifted her brows, wanting to laugh. "Overconfidence. That's an interesting tactic. And a great way to trip and fall over your own ego."

"I guess we'll just have to see what happens."

She didn't plan to trip and fall. Unless this suit of his was really something.

Kira leaned forward so their faces were close enough their lips almost touched. His eyes flared. She said, "Bring it on."

TEN

L UCA TOOK THE STAIRS TWO AT A TIME, POUND-
ing up the concrete stairwell. Burning off some of the adrenaline
from what had happened last night. Thinking about Kira and
the way she'd looked at him. The last thing she'd said before she left.
Bring it on.

Right now he had to focus on work.

On the fourteenth floor of the office building across from the
hospital, he pushed out of the stairwell onto the open rooftop in
the daylight. From the west corner, anyone up here would have a
view of the window of Francisco's room, with line of sight to use
a rifle. Someone with a heat-sensing scope could shoot the patient
before anyone even realized they were here.

Luca scanned the rooftop and figured out the best angle, shifting
his backpack off his shoulders. He pulled out one of the cameras
he'd packed, and wedged it beside the air-conditioning vent, using
a piece of duct tape to secure it. The trail cameras he had were
high-end, wirelessly connected to the computer in his office that

linked to an app on his phone, and only turned on when they sensed motion.

If anyone came up here intending to use the spot to take out Francisco, Luca would know about it.

Same with the two other building roofs he'd installed cameras on after Kira left.

As he headed back down the stairwell to the ground floor, he called the detective.

"Martinelli." Mike's voice was clipped, as if he was in the middle of something.

"Did they get him booked?"

"All tucked into a cell," Mike said. "I'll go chat with him in a bit. Make sure we have it straight what happened."

Luca figured he and Kira already knew enough about the man's intentions and why he'd followed her all the way out to her car, looking for "his woman." But the cops had to ask the questions themselves.

Luca rounded the eighth floor. "I want to know the minute that guy hits the streets again."

"He'll probably go before the judge today and get bonded out."

"On a Sunday?"

"Right." Mike blew out a breath across the phone line. "And Monday's a holiday, so it'll be Tuesday then, which means he spends an extra few days in the county jail."

"Maybe he can say hi to Jenkins for us."

Mike chuckled. "Alden really told you that Ralph Rousseau is the one behind the Shadow Syndicate?"

"You don't believe it?"

"Right now, I wouldn't put it past anyone, except you and me and our nearest and dearest."

Luca smiled to himself. "Everyone is a suspect?"

"Within reason, yes," Mike said. "Outside of the land grab he and Jenkins were doing on the ranchers, Rousseau's legitimate businesses in Renegade have been making real-estate deals for years with a bunch of his buddies. Mostly business and commercial properties, and it wouldn't surprise me if any of them were dirty. Taking bribes or going around city ordinances just to make money. He's either dirty or he's planning to run for governor."

"Maybe both." With a side of stopping a doctor who was new to town from opening up her own practice.

"I'll dig up everything I can get my hands on, and maybe we could meet up tomorrow. Go over everything we know about Rousseau."

Luca couldn't do that in the evening on Monday, as he'd be attending Mrs. Rousseau's fancy foundation gala. "I have some time early."

"It'll be good to find out who he's connected to outside of hearsay."

"Catch you later." Luca hung up the phone and pushed out the exit door into the afternoon sun.

The temperature was just about perfect for a run, but that was the last thing he had time for right now. A nap might be a better idea, considering his sleep schedule was all messed up. If he wanted to line up his schedule with Kira's, he should probably switch to working nights on a regular basis the way she did.

He headed back across the street to the hospital, thinking about the way it felt so natural to have her in his arms. This woman who had seemed to be working to undermine his mission the day they met. Talk about a turnaround.

But what was it that she'd said? Giving intel to people who made the world a better place?

She must have worked for a government that was an ally of the US. Probably the British, considering her nationality. He doubted she was the kind of person who was still loyal to the place where she'd been born.

He'd grown up a refugee in the US with his brother Amir,

making sure no one ever believed they were part of the regime they'd escaped. Despite the accusations that had been leveled against his father, none of them were connected to terrorism. But his father's name hadn't been cleared before he took his own life.

Luca used his key card to enter a secure door around the back of the hospital and rode the elevator up. Hammer stood at attention beside the door, hands clasped behind his back. His mind miles away while all of his physical awareness constantly scanned for threats.

"Hey." Luca opened the door and checked on Francisco. The patient lay in the hospital bed, tucked in with blankets, his eyes closed. His doctor sat on a chair beside the bed, looking at the screen of a tablet, reading and scrolling slowly.

Luca closed the door.

"Hey." Hammer cleared his throat. "What happened?"

"What are you talking about?"

His buddy shot him a look. "You think I can't tell when you have something on your mind? You're tense. More than your usual stoic demeanor."

"Whatever that means." Luca blew out a breath and rolled his shoulders. The hallway was empty, and the normal hustle and bustle of the busy hospital seemed far away.

He told Hammer about what had happened in the parking lot and how he had taken care of Stuart Parker when the guy was intent on getting answers from Kira by whatever threats were necessary.

Hammer shook his head. "No, that isn't it."

Luca sat in the chair next to the door and leaned his head back against the wall. "It's fine. We took care of it. She helped someone, and he wanted to know where they were. The cops took the guy into custody. The woman he was looking for is safe."

Hammer scanned the hall, then looked back at Luca. "But you got a taste of what it's like when she's in danger. How it feels to know the threat is coming for her, and you realized that stopping the threat is up to you."

"I told her I need to see what she can do. That way I know in what situations she'll be able to take care of herself."

That should be somewhat reassuring, right? He would be able to breathe a little easier if he knew what she could handle.

"Maybe." Hammer shrugged. "But if something kicks off and you're not there, it's going to drive you crazy."

Luca shook his head. "There's no reason to believe that guy will come after her again."

Hammer leaned against the wall on the opposite side of the hallway, facing him. "Something will. Eventually. Maybe there isn't a real huge threat in your lives, not like what we've faced the past few years. But eventually she'll be in danger, or some other situation will arise, and you'll be too far away to help."

Luca didn't like the sound of that.

"She could get sick, and there might be nothing you can do about it." Hammer shrugged. "Or a thousand different things you won't be expecting. Ways she could have her heart broken or get injured. Or ways she might have to face death. And the fact is that you'll be facing it along with her."

Luca pressed his lips together and shook his head.

"It's a part of life, bro. Things happen that you can't control. The people you love are threatened and nearly burned to death in a house, but thankfully, you're there and able to help them."

Luca shot him a look.

"You know what I mean. As much as you want to wrap her up and keep her safe, she won't be able to live her life if you do that. This is the kind of woman who needs to feel like she's free. Not like you're dragging her down."

"I'm not trying to trap her. Just trying to get a handle on the way I feel."

Hammer said, "Literally the only thing I can guarantee you is that this won't go the way you think it will. And it's never going to be the best-case scenario. Life just isn't like that."

"You give such good pep talks."

"The point is that you have to trust. God has all of it under His control. That doesn't mean she's not at risk or that nothing will happen to her—or you. It means that both of you have to trust that He's got this in His hands, so you can rest because He'll put you where you need to be at the right time. And all of it is just another way you can learn to trust Him more."

Luca sat forward, running his hands down his face. Closing his eyes meant he saw Kira again in his mind, the way she looked—and felt—in his arms. The way she looked at *him*. Something he hadn't ever had before.

"It isn't like I've never dated before," Luca said.

"But it's different with her, isn't it?"

"You're annoying."

"Once a team leader, always a team leader."

Luca shook his head. "You're not my boss here. It's my contract."

Hammer grinned. "Just as long as I get paid. I'm gonna have four mouths to feed pretty soon, and who knows how many more babies Sierra wants to have?"

Yeah, the guy looked real disappointed about the prospect of making a big family with his wife. The difference between the man Saxon had known for years and the married guy with kids wasn't something Saxon could completely fathom. The difference between Hammer and Rowan. It really was almost like he was a different man entirely.

Which was true, wasn't it?

Not only had Hammer become a believer the way Saxon had while fighting wildfires. He'd come home and literally become Rowan once again. Hammer was the past; Rowan Wallace was the man who had married and settled down—the guy looking to the future.

Luca wasn't entirely sure he wanted to change that much. He didn't need to, right? But it just might be that the man he should become was *exactly* the kind of person who could love Kira well. The way she deserved.

"She wants me to go to the foundation gala with her. Do some snooping around in the Rousseaus' nonprofit to see what we can find out about the syndicate. If there's any connection."

Hammer grinned. "That's how it starts. You team up working on something one minute, and the next, you realize you already fell in love with her and it's too late to do anything about it."

"As long as she falls in love with me at the same time, I'm not sure I'm going to want to do anything about it."

"Good." Hammer laughed. "Then you just have to make sure she falls in love with you."

Luca wasn't entirely sure he had that skill to draw on. But he could certainly give her the chance to know him, and he wanted to see the look on her face when she saw him in his nicest suit.

"Just trust." Hammer slapped his shoulder. "God will take care of the rest."

Hammer would say that, wouldn't he? Rowan Wallace had everything he'd ever wanted.

The idea of Luca and Kira going through anything like what Sierra and Hammer had been through terrified him to his core.

But whatever happened next, his friend was right.

He needed to leave it in God's hands.

Kira scanned the patient's lab results. "This isn't good." She looked at the nurse behind the counter. She didn't work much with Barbara, but the older woman worked out so she could stay strong and outpace most of the younger nurses. She was also the kind of Christian who couldn't help but counsel the people around her. The wisdom just seemed to pour out of her. Over the course of her shift so far, Kira had told Barbara nearly everything about today—minus the syndicate parts.

Kira focused on the numbers in front of her. "Up the dosage and check on him in an hour."

"Yes, Doctor." Barbara tapped the raised counter between them. "Sounds like God is doing something in your life."

Kira smiled. "Nothing has changed for me in years. Right now it feels like everything is different, and I'm still spinning from everything that's happened in such a short period of time."

Barbara nodded. "That's when you need to cling to Him harder. It's why we go through things like this. So we can draw near to that firm foundation."

"It's not a storm or a trial though."

"It's still good practice." Barbara patted her arm. "For when it will be later and you need Him most."

It had been more than twelve hours since that man had accosted her and she'd had that sweet moment with Luca, and she was still thinking about it all. The promise, the threat, all of it mixed up in her mind. But she knew she wanted to spend more time with Luca.

Not just at the gala. She wanted to get to know him for real.

She'd tried to nap this afternoon, but it hadn't happened. She was going to feel it in the hours after midnight, that was for sure. She needed some caffeine.

The doors at the end of the hall banged open. Kira handed over the tablet and headed for the paramedics and their patient, two corrections officers following the gurney. Sure enough, the patient had on an orange jumpsuit and was handcuffed to the rail.

Kira's heart quickened, pushing away the edges of fatigue. She grabbed a pair of protective gloves and pulled them on.

"Stab wound—left side," one of the medics shouted, his voice steady but strained. Not Mack. This was one of the older paramedics. "Severe laceration, possible punctured lung. BP's dropping."

Her attention caught on the inmate's face, his dark eyes on her for a second.

Alden Jenkins.

Thank You that it wasn't Mack who responded. As an EMT, he'd have had to recuse himself if he knew the patient personally. None of them could work on someone they knew. It was far too dangerous.

Kira's training kicked in. "Bay two. Get him on the monitor."

Alden lay there, pale and gasping for breath. Blood soaked the bandage wrapped around his midsection, a dark, ominous red that contrasted sharply with his ashen skin and the orange jumpsuit.

"Sir, can you hear me?" Kira leaned closer, trying to capture his attention. His eyes fluttered open, revealing a flicker of stronger awareness, but it quickly faded. She could see the fear lurking behind his pain, a primal instinct begging for survival. "We're going to help you. Just hang in there."

Jenkins didn't respond.

She grabbed the edge of the sheet. "Ready?"

The medics, the nurse, and even one of the corrections officers mirrored her movements. "Go."

They transferred the patient to the hospital bed, and the medics wheeled out the gurney. Kira caught a glimpse of the corrections officers as her gaze darted from them to the monitors. *His heart rate is plummeting.* One of the corrections officers was a burly man with a tattoo snaking down his forearm below the dark blue of his uniform shirt. He stood with his arms crossed, his eyes scanning the room. The other officer, younger and visibly shaken, stood behind the nurse and watched the inmate with a mix of concern and detachment.

"What happened?" Kira started working on the bandage.

"Alden Jenkins," the tattooed officer replied, his tone clipped. "The former mayor. Conspiracy to commit murder, fraud and other charges I can't recall right now. I'm surprised you don't know who he is. Figured everyone did." He sniffed. "The judge deemed him a flight risk, so he's with us awaiting trial."

Kira didn't need him or anyone else here to know of her personal connection. Not that she'd ever met Jenkins. "Okay, so what happened?"

"He got stabbed."

She resisted the urge to roll her eyes at his tone and focused on the task at hand. "Let's prep him for surgery. We need to stabilize him fast before we send him upstairs." She looked at the nurse. "Call the OR. Tell them to get ready."

The nurse rushed out of the bay. Kira worked with precision, her fingers moving deftly as she inserted an IV line. Her mind calculated the next steps even as chaos swirled around her and the patient moaned.

He was barely conscious now, his eyes fluttering open.

Hammer. *Rowan.* Was he across the other side of the hospital with no idea his stepfather was here? She wanted him to be the one to tell Mack that Jenkins was here. She should contact Luca and have him pass on the information. He'd know the best way to break the news.

She touched Alden's shoulder and spoke, whether he could hear her or not. "Mr. Jenkins, we're going to take you to surgery. I need you to fight." Despite what he'd done, she believed that.

After all, everyone deserved a second chance. That meant he had to be around to accept it.

The younger corrections officer stepped forward, what remained of his bravado cracking. "Is he going to make it?"

Kira met his gaze, searching for the right words.

Barbara rushed back in. "We're doing everything we can, but he's in critical condition. We need to move quickly."

The officer nodded, the weight of his job pressing down on him.

Barbara said, "They're ready upstairs."

Kira took a deep breath and motioned for the team to roll

Jenkins to the elevator. As they wheeled him away, she knew this was more than just another trauma case. There was a story behind the blood. A life intertwined with choices that had led him here. And for the first time in a long while, she knew the people affected by the pain. The ones who would have to navigate the aftermath of what had happened.

The younger corrections officer glanced at her, and the elevator doors slid closed.

She whirled around and rushed to the locker room, digging her cell phone out and sending a text to Luca to come to the hospital if he wasn't here, and find her in the emergency department so she could tell him something important. She didn't want to tell him that Jenkins might not make it over text, but she needed him to come urgently.

He sent a text back almost immediately.

Luca

On my way.

She slipped the phone into the pocket of her lab coat and headed back to the nurses' station.

Barbara handed over the tablet. "I still need to take care of the kid in seven. The guy with the broken leg is back from X-ray. The orthopedic surgeon on call took a look, and he's on his way down for the consult."

"Thanks." Kira pushed out a breath.

"There's another ambulance incoming. They called in." Barbara's features tensed. "Their patient is coding."

The doors opened at the end of the hall, and two paramedics wheeled in the gurney. A younger medic was over the patient, performing CPR in that steady but rapid rhythm. Destiny Rousseau rushed in the doors after them, tears streaming down her face.

Kira turned to Barbara. "Call Izabella out of two."

"Yes, Doctor." She raced off to fetch the other nurse.

"Bay five!" She rushed to hold the curtain back, and the EMTs pushed the gurney into the room.

"Do I get off?" The young EMT in training didn't stop chest compressions.

Kira said, "Keep doing what you're doing. Tell me if you need to switch out."

One of the two EMTs who'd been pushing the bed moved to the head and held the Ambu bag over the patient's mouth.

It was Ralph Rousseau, back even though he'd been discharged just days ago. The EMT ran down the patient's information and what they'd done for him to try and restart his heart.

She hooked him up as she listened and scanned the monitor. The flat line stared back at her, a cruel reminder that life could end in a moment and there might be nothing she could do about it. "No pulse," she murmured, glancing at the nurse beside her. "Grab the paddles."

"Right here, Doctor."

"Hook up an IV. Give me one milligram of epinephrine."

"Yes, Doctor."

Kira patted the arm of the EMT doing chest compressions. "Hop down. Everyone clear."

She could almost hear the clock ticking, counting down the seconds they had left. The nurse moved quickly, attaching the defibrillator pads to the patient's chest.

"Ready when you are." The nurse moved into position beside Kira.

"Clear!" Kira shouted.

The EMTs stepped back. The jolt from the machine was powerful, a surge of hope that came when Ralph's chest lifted off the bed and dropped back down. Kira watched the monitor, waiting for a sign of life. *Come on.*

In the corner of the bay, Destiny cried quiet tears. The EMT closest to her put an arm around her shoulders.

The line remained flat.

"Again," Kira said, her voice unwavering. "One more time."

The nurse nodded, quickly resetting the machine. "Clear!"

Another shock coursed through the man's body, and Kira felt a flicker of desperation. She took up compressions, counting in sync with the nurse, pushing harder. Willing life back into his chest.

"Come on," she whispered, her breath quickening. "You can do this."

After what felt like an eternity, she paused to look at the monitor and check for a pulse. Nothing. She exchanged a glance with the nurse, who looked equally determined.

"Third time's the charm," Kira said, her voice steady despite the turmoil inside. "Let's go."

"Clear!"

The shock hit, and this time, a jagged blip appeared on the monitor. Kira held her breath as the line started to rise, a fluttering heartbeat where before, there hadn't been one. *Thank You.*

"Pulse!" The nurse smiled, her eyes wide with relief.

"Good work." Kira felt a wave of triumph wash over her. "Keep monitoring him so we can ensure he's going to remain stable." She blew out a breath and removed the gloves she had pulled on. The battle was far from over, but they had won this round.

The EMTs pushed their gurney from the bay, and Kira crossed to Destiny. "Back so soon?"

The other woman whimpered and rushed into Kira's offered hug.

"It's safe to say he has a fighting chance."

Destiny put her hands to her cheeks. "Why is someone doing this to him? Why can't they leave us alone?"

"What do you mean?" Kira shook her head.

Sure, Jenkins—currently in surgery—had told Luca that Ralph was head of the Shadow Syndicate, but that didn't explain why someone wanted him dead. It was more likely the reason Jenkins had been targeted. For telling Luca anything at all.

Ralph had more of a motive to see Jenkins dead than the other way around. This only made sense if someone was trying to get rid of both of them.

Fatigue washed over Kira like a wave. It would retreat shortly, but until then, she couldn't let it drag her under. She had patients counting on her to be alert and do her job to the best of her ability.

"Someone tried to kill him again, I just know it." Destiny gasped. "It's because they didn't succeed the first time!"

Kira held the woman's hands. "I'm going to call the police. Can you tell them everything? They're the ones who can find out who is doing this and stop—"

Destiny rushed to her husband's bedside. "Ralph!"

His eyes fluttered.

"If he wakes up, it may only be for a minute," Kira said. "He needs to rest as much as possible." She looked at the nurse. "Let's take blood for a full panel. Find out what's going on."

"Yes, Doctor." The nurse left the room for the supplies she'd need to do that.

"Destiny, will you speak to the police?"

The other woman didn't look at her. "As if it will do any good."

"It's worth a try, isn't it?"

"Fine. Call them."

Kira frowned. She spotted Luca at the edge of her peripheral vision and told Destiny, "I'll be back to check on Ralph shortly." She passed the nurse on her way out and walked toward Luca. The words got stuck in her throat.

He looked at Ralph, then back at her. "What did you need to tell me?"

"Someone tried to kill Jenkins. He's in surgery upstairs." She blew out a breath. "It doesn't look good."

Luca tugged her toward him and kissed her forehead. "I'll call Mack."

ELEVEN

LUCA REACHED OVER AND TAPPED THE DASH screen, answering the call from Detective Mike Martinelli. He hadn't heard an update about Jenkins since early this morning, when it had been touch and go.

"Hey." Luca sat back in the seat, his hands in his lap, watching out the windshield where two men had entered a bar that hadn't opened for the day.

"Ready for an update?" Mike said. "Everything is quiet here at the hospital."

"I'm on surveillance with Hammer. He's in the car with me. I appreciate you helping me out on your day off."

The clock on the dash read 4:30 p.m.

He would sleep at some point, but it hadn't happened in more than twenty-four hours. Kira would be even more exhausted than him. She was the one who'd worked an entire shift at the hospital last night.

Hammer said nothing, probably still deep in his thoughts about Jenkins and his brother Mack.

"Alden is out of surgery and stable. You guys told Mack what happened to his father, right?"

Luca watched a car pull into the bar parking lot and stop at the far side beside a lamppost. The occupant didn't get out. "I told him, and Rowan went to pick him up."

The fact Kira had passed it on so quickly impressed him. She was the kind of woman who knew that someone was going to be upset by news and made sure they got the information as fast as possible, not waiting for the police to trickle information down from the jail.

"Ralph Rousseau lapsed into a coma."

Luca hissed out a breath.

Mike continued, "The tox screen came back with something called silent lily. It's from a rare plant called moonshade lily that originates in Guatemala. It can be distilled into a clear liquid that's tasteless. Kira explained the whole thing to me when she showed up to take over for Dr. Torres. It's lethal, so Ralph must not have ingested that much. They have no idea when he's going to wake up, or if he even will."

"Makes you wonder if Destiny is going to go ahead with this gala, given the condition her husband is in right now."

"I haven't heard anything," Mike said.

"And Kira is okay?"

"She looks like she needs a nap. But she's currently reading the newspaper to Francisco and drinking coffee."

Luca said, "Did they do the procedure on him?"

"They need his lab results to look a certain way before that. Apparently they're hoping for tomorrow or the day after."

"Heads up." Hammer motioned to the entrance of the bar, where the two men they had been following emerged and headed to their car.

A third vehicle came in, pulling alongside the car that had parked by the lamppost. Something was exchanged between two open windows, and then both drove off. "Drug deal."

But nothing to do with them.

"What's that?" Mike asked.

"Don't worry, we'll report it," Luca said. But right now, they had other issues to worry about. "Who are these guys Homeland told the Marshals about?"

All the information Saxon had was that both men were connected to Francisco's cartel. He had received two headshots and a description of their car.

"It came in as a BOLO. The whole PD has been on the lookout for these dudes, and thankfully, one of our patrol cars spotted them quickly," Mike said. "The two of them are mid-level enforcers for Francisco's cartel, the one his nephew forced him out of. If they're suddenly in town, it's because the cartel found out that Francisco is here and they want to kill him before he's able to testify."

"Copy that."

The car the two men had climbed into pulled out, and Luca gave it a few seconds before he eased into traffic behind them. There was an art to hanging back far enough that they wouldn't be spotted as a pursuing vehicle, but remaining close enough they didn't lose the other car. Being in an old truck wasn't exactly inconspicuous in the city, but this part of Colorado was rural enough that there were plenty of other Ford trucks on the road.

"We have eyes on them." Luca gripped the wheel. "If they approach the hospital, we'll let you know."

Mike said, "I'll keep an eye out just in case they're decoys. Any movement on your cameras?"

"I haven't had any notifications." Luca trusted his system, but he still activated the cameras and checked they were operating well regularly. Just to be double covered.

"Gotta go." Mike hung up the phone.

Luca glanced at Hammer. "That's good that Jenkins is out of surgery."

"If he dies, it would solve a lot of problems."

Luca winced. There wasn't a lot of love lost between the two men, considering the way Alden Jenkins had treated Hammer as an adolescent—using him as a punching bag. But the guy was Mack's father, and no one wanted Hammer's half brother to be torn up with grief or regret over what he might've done differently.

The bottom line was that Jenkins had treated Mack not so differently from Hammer in the end. But hope always longed for a better outcome. Like the restoration of a relationship, even when the worst kind of hurt had been dished out.

God was able to save people out of even the most wretched of situations.

After all, He offered salvation to everyone. Not just supposedly good people or those who cleaned themselves up before they came to Him.

Everyone.

"But he's still Mack's father," Hammer said.

Luca was relieved to hear that. "If he does recover, maybe there's still a chance he can repent and ask both of you for forgiveness." Then he added, "I contacted Deputy Marshal Butler and asked him to transfer my brother to the Renegade Correctional Facility so that there's at least someone in the prison who can look out for Jenkins and keep this from happening again."

He turned a corner in Southwold, an area south of downtown that had some rough neighborhoods.

"Thanks." Hammer shifted in his seat. "I appreciate you doing that. And I'd love to believe that Jenkins can change, but I'll be waiting for some fruit before I trust that he's become a different man."

"No one's asking you to do anything other than that."

The car they were pursuing pulled over, sliding into a space at the curb in front of a row of storefront restaurants. The kind with awnings and tables outside. Where late at night, the lively evening crowd spilled onto the street. A place where the restaurants were authentic and never had enough seats for their customers.

"I didn't know there was a Middle Eastern restaurant over here."

Hammer said, "It's good. I took Sierra there last week. She's not a big fan of spicy food, but she gave a couple of things a try. You should take Kira when you guys get a night off."

"Right now, that doesn't seem like it will happen for a while. Both of us need sleep more than a night on the town."

Hammer glanced at him.

"Separately, in our own beds."

"Just checking." Hammer grinned. "Anyway, I showed Sierra a picture of her, and she said that Kira goes to Redeemer Community Church over in North Eagle with us. She just goes to the early service, and we're always at the later one. So I never saw her there."

"That would've been a surprise." Luca had been shocked enough to see her name on the email for that Marshals meeting in Judge Mullinax's chambers.

Hammer chuckled. "I'd have probably thought she was there to assassinate us at church and freaked out."

"Good thing you didn't, then." Again, the protectiveness he felt toward Kira welled up in him. Not that she couldn't take care of herself. The point was that he wanted to be there as backup. A partner. Or someone to stand in front of her and take the hit on her behalf.

Not only that, but he needed the chance to prove to her that he was the kind of guy who would pitch in with dishes and laundry. Housecleaning and home repairs. Even getting a tall ladder to change the battery in the smoke alarm on the vaulted ceiling in her apartment.

To get her to take a chance on him, because he would always try to make it worth it. So she'd never regret choosing him.

"You're gone for her."

Luca didn't need to tell Hammer that he was right. "Can we just do our jobs here?"

"You're the one the Marshals asked for. I'm just here for the entertainment value."

"And gas money."

"If you make it worth my while, I could take my family to Florida in the winter. Get some sun."

"We'll see."

Hammer chuckled again. The easy laughter from this family man was a welcome change from the guy Luca had lived with for the past few years. The same kind of change he wanted to happen within himself.

The front door of a tapas restaurant opened, and a man emerged from under the red-and-white-striped awning. He wore a suit and had a familiar face. "That's Dr. Torres. He's the one doing the procedure on Francisco."

"So they're going after the doctor to get to Francisco?"

"Maybe." He watched the two men emerge from the vehicle and follow Dr. Torres along the street, away from where Luca had parked. "Let's go."

Dr. Torres turned the corner into an alley between two red brick buildings. The man would be around the corner in seconds.

"Drive over there," Hammer said. "It'll be faster."

Whatever these two men from the cartel were going to do to Dr. Torres, Luca had to stop it from happening. He threw the truck into Reverse and peeled out of the space, slammed it into Drive, and hit the gas. Not concerned with how much attention he was drawing to himself. He checked there were no pedestrians and bumped the curb into the alley.

The two men had Dr. Torres backed up against the side of the brick building, both of them in his face. Luca spotted a knife at the doctor's throat. Not going for any tactics with finesse. Apparently, these two men had chosen a bolder approach to getting what they wanted.

Usually, he would have called it in to the police and reported someone being mugged, but he needed to make sure Dr. Torres wasn't killed first. Luca hit the brakes and put the truck in Park, threw his door open, and raced over. "Hey!"

The guy with the knife broke away from Torres and started to run.

Hammer said, "I've got him!" and raced after the fleeing man.

Luca pulled his weapon but kept it at a low angle. "Hands up. Drop your weapons."

"You some kind of cop?"

The guy hadn't run, but he might at any moment. Or he might try for the same bold tactics and go after Luca before he raced away.

Dr. Torres didn't move, his back still to the wall and his face pale.

"I'm not a cop." Luca shook his head. The guy flung a knife through the air and narrowly missed Luca's shoulder. He brought his gun up. "Hands."

The guy rushed Luca, tackling him to the ground. As soon as his back landed on the asphalt, Luca swung with his gun and slammed the butt into the man's head. He rolled them both, then levered up enough to pull the guy's hands behind his back.

He holstered his weapon, one knee holding the man down, and pulled out some plastic ties, which he used to secure the man's hands behind his back. When he looked over at Dr. Torres, the man had vacated his position. He wasn't anywhere around that Luca could see.

Hammer raced toward him from the other end of the alley, breathing hard. "He got away. Where's the doc?"

"He must've run off."

"At least we still have this guy." Hammer motioned to the man under Luca.

"I guess he's the one who's going to give us some answers."

Kira lifted the hem of her long silver gown just enough that she didn't trip on it, walking up the steps to the stately house set back in the mountains on the west side of the city. A place that could be rented for events like this gala, or weddings. Something she definitely hadn't contemplated before. Much. Debating, probably as most women did, between a big wedding and the kind of small, intimate gathering she might prefer.

The whole place was lit up, bustling with people. A valet took her keys and gave her a ticket, which she slipped into the tiny clutch.

The party didn't start for another half an hour, but she wanted to have a few minutes with Destiny just to check in with her.

Kira showed her invitation to the young woman behind the table, who was wearing a white button-down shirt and black waistcoat, her hair tied behind her head and slicked down with gel. "I have a plus-one, but he will be here shortly." She gave Luca's name, and the woman indicated it on her paper.

"Enjoy the party."

"Thank you very much." Kira scanned the lobby of the event center, checking all their faces for Destiny Rousseau. Waitstaff wandered around with small trays of finger foods or glasses half filled with champagne.

Kira asked for a soda water and located Destiny in the corner, chatting with an older woman wearing a long green gown. Destiny wore a floor-length black velvet dress, her hair pinned on top of her head. Despite the attention to her appearance, Destiny had dark circles under her eyes and the edge of grief in her expression.

Kira had left her hair long and curled it, since that was a style Luca hadn't seen on her before. Not that she had dressed up for him. But the fact she knew he was coming shortly had her making doubly sure that her curls would stay in place for the whole evening.

Destiny glanced her way as she approached, smiling at Kira. "I'm so glad you came." She gave Kira a kiss on the cheek.

"I am as well." Kira held the other woman's hands. "How are you doing with everything? I'm surprised you didn't cancel the event after everything that has happened this week."

"There's nothing I can do for Ralph tonight. And he would be so disappointed if he found out I canceled the event."

The woman had been sitting at her husband's bedside for days now, holding vigil, hoping that he would wake up. Destiny was right that there wasn't much she could do. Taking a break from the hospital might be a good thing, if this was the kind of event that was planned to the level that there wasn't much left to do except show up.

Destiny squeezed her hands, then let go. "The show must go on and all that."

"Did the police have any idea who it might've been that tried to hurt Ralph?" She didn't want to mention attempted murder or shadowy crime syndicates, just in case someone overheard. Plus, she wanted to know what Destiny knew—or was willing to admit she knew.

Destiny shook her head. "I'm so grateful that you figured out what he'd been given. You might have saved his life."

Such as it was. "I do regret that I didn't manage to do that before he lapsed into a coma." They had no idea when, or if, Ralph would wake up. "I'll be praying for him to make a full recovery."

Destiny's brow crinkled. "I'm not really the praying kind."

"Then it's good that you have someone like me in your life to do that for you."

However Destiny felt about prayer or faith in a loving God, Kira could ask for favor in the situation. For God to heal Ralph and for Destiny's heart to be softened toward the Lord.

When there wasn't much else for her to do that would help in this situation, she could at least do that.

"If there's anything you need tonight, please don't hesitate to ask."

Destiny smiled. "Does that mean you're agreeing to come on the board of the foundation?"

"I'm still making my decision. I have a busy schedule at the hospital, and I want to ensure I have the time it requires to devote to it. But I'm here to help if you need it."

"You're so sweet." Destiny's attention snagged on something over Kira's shoulder. "I have to go check on something with the staff. If you'll excuse me?"

"Of course." Kira nodded.

Destiny wandered off, and the server brought Kira's soda water to her. She watched the other woman chat with people. Exchanging pleasantries as she made her way to the young woman in the gray suit, holding a tablet, an earpiece in her ear.

As the two talked, Kira decided it was silly to investigate at this point. After everything that had happened this week, and the fact someone had tried to murder Ralph twice, it was obvious that they weren't the ones in charge of the Shadow Syndicate. Otherwise, they would be far too powerful for people to come after them.

Anyone in charge of the criminal organization was going to take steps to protect themselves. Destiny and Ralph just seemed far too vulnerable.

What Kira should be doing was encouraging Luca to figure out who was trying to kill Ralph. More likely *that* person was the head of the Shadow Syndicate. Trying to take out a threat to their business: Ralph. And maybe Jenkins also. For whatever reason, whoever was in charge of the Shadow Syndicate wanted them both silenced—permanently.

After all, pointing the finger at Ralph and setting him up as the one behind the land grab and then murdering both men wrote a specific narrative. If they were implicated and dead, then in the end, no one would ever learn the truth. The people behind the Shadow Syndicate would remain anonymous.

"Kira?" The voice was low and rough.

She knew that voice.

She glanced over her shoulder, then turned to Luca. And yes, she made sure that the move looked good.

His eyes flared.

She caught a glance of his suit and the way it fit him. Definitely a custom fit. Something Italian for sure. Her cheeks heated, and she was pretty certain her eyes flared as well. "You were right about the suit."

She hadn't imagined anyone could be this handsome. The guy was gorgeous, with his dark hair tied back neatly and his beard trim. He could be a movie star. But Luca chose instead to live a humble life, not drawing attention to himself. Working to make the world safer for the people he loved.

She stepped toward him, and he closed the distance between them.

"You look beautiful."

She wanted to make a crack about the dress being some old rag she found in her closet, but the words stuck in her throat.

He held out his hand, and she placed hers in it.

He kissed her knuckles. "Thank you for inviting me. It was worth it just to see you in this dress."

"And here I thought this was just a work thing."

"Too bad I just forgot what I do for a living. It's gone," he said. "Completely slipped my mind. What's my name again?"

She laughed softly, and he touched her waist.

"I just need to check something." He was closer now, close enough he could kiss her. His hand slid to the small of her back, where he touched her bare skin.

She touched the lapel of his suit jacket. "Careful now."

He winked at her, and his hand slid back to her waist. "What was I saying?"

"I have no idea." She smiled at him.

He shifted and held out his elbow. "I think that means it's time for us to dance."

"You know how to dance?" She slid her arm through his, glancing back but not seeing Destiny.

"I believe I have some skill. How about you?"

"It depends if the goal is to draw attention to us or fade into the crowd. While I happen to know how to tango, this isn't one of those operations where we show off in front of everyone so that they all see—and remember—our faces."

"Good to know." He glanced at her, a smile lighting his eyes.

They crossed the threshold between the expansive lobby and the main ballroom, which had been decorated with candlelight. A band played quietly in one corner, giving the room some background noise so that people could still talk to each other. A stage had been set up beside them with a podium and microphone.

All around the room were huge posterboards and banners with images of children from overseas who had received treatment thanks to the foundation. Illnesses that could easily be cured with modern medicine often went untreated in places where people lived in poverty, with little access to sanitation and medical supplies.

Luca led her around the exterior of the room while they danced so they could look at some of the posters, and she realized he had done so because he'd seen her notice them.

They lingered in front of a poster of several children from the Sudan.

"Do you miss it?" he asked her.

"Sometimes." She leaned against Luca, just a little. "People here don't realize how good they have it. When you live in a place where war is a daily reality and poverty is the only thing you know, it's hard to imagine any other way to be. Those are the people who need help. Because there's no one to pull them out of it and show them that they can find peace."

"Do you want to go back?"

"I don't have any plans to leave Renegade anytime soon." Just in case he needed to hear that. "Being there for so long, working in the refugee camps, it sucked me under. Then I was the one who had to be reminded that I can find peace."

"That's why we only deploy for a predetermined period of time, so that we can come back stateside and recoup. No one can work for years on end and not end up crushed under the weight of it. You have to take a break at some point."

"I tried to keep going," she said. "I thought I could do it in my own strength, but I had to remember that God is the one who sustains me. I just didn't until it was too late. I had to let Him give me this sabbatical, but it's been a few years, and I don't know if I want to go back. Those places will always have a huge part of my heart. But unless He leads me back there, I'm going to stay here."

"You can do valuable things here as well. I already know you are."

She squeezed his arm, about to respond, when the band quieted down their music.

Destiny stepped up to the podium. "Ladies and gentlemen, the Healing Hearts Foundation is so very glad you are here tonight to celebrate with us the work that we do across the world. Around the room, you can see love in action. The donations that you so generously offer to us save lives every single day."

Luca led Kira to a table and pulled out a chair for her.

Destiny continued, "Here with me tonight is my son Roger, who we adopted from Guatemala. He will be sharing later about his experience and the journey that brought him to us. In this trying time, the best thing for us to do is remember the good things we have in our lives."

Kira leaned over and whispered in Luca's ear. "Did you know Destiny and Ralph have a son?"

He shook his head.

"She never said anything about him to me."

"Maybe it's a new thing. Or an old thing, so it's not news."

Kira frowned, not sure what to make of it. Maybe Roger had been gone when they met, on a long trip or away for a while. Or Destiny was embarrassed by him. Kira had no idea.

"The auction is about to begin. This is your last chance to get bids in for our array of amazing experiences and items you don't want to miss." She leaned toward the microphone. "Thank you all for coming."

"Is it just me," Kira said to Luca, "or is this whole thing really weird?"

He nodded. "Something isn't right here."

TWELVE

L UCA LOOKED AT THE TEXT MESSAGE ON HIS watch.

<u>Jamie</u>

Done.

"Anything I should know about?"

He glanced at Kira, sitting beside him at the table. White tablecloth. A glass vase in the center had been filled with cut flowers and little twinkly lights. Even with how the space had been decorated for this event, she was still the most beautiful thing here.

The kind of woman who took his breath away.

"When I was in Alaska last year, one of the firefighters started dating this woman, Jamie Winters. She's the CEO of a finance company and pretty amazing with numbers." He left out how she had grown her business from nothing to the point she was in fact worth billions. "I asked her to make a donation to the foundation so she could track where the money went. It's something she's done before, so I figured it didn't hurt to ask."

"And she agreed?"

He nodded. "She jumped at the chance to help us figure this out. She was actually part of rescuing Hammer's wife and son just a few months ago. She tracked Sierra's cell phone, and Hammer was able to get there in time to save them both."

"Wow, that's pretty amazing."

"I'm a lucky guy, considering there are so many amazing women in my life." Enough that he had never given up the idea he might one day meet someone like that. A woman who would be his one and only.

Not every guy was wired to find the one person God had saved just for them. But he had always been traditional like that. Even before he became a believer, Luca had known that there was someone out there for him. It seemed as if the minute he met Kira, his heart already knew what she would mean to him, even if it had taken the rest of him a while to catch up.

"It shouldn't take her long to figure out what's behind the scenes of this foundation."

Kira took a sip of her drink. "As long as the money actually moves. If Destiny and her people leave it where it is for a while, there's not going to be anything to find."

"So let's hope they've got this thing on automatic and the money shifts accounts right away."

Several of the items had already been auctioned off, and Destiny had told them all there would be a short reprieve before the winners of the next batch of items were announced.

An older couple came over to their table, striking up a conversation with Kira. She introduced them as being board members for the hospital. The husband just wanted to talk about an upcoming budget meeting while the wife stared into space, so when Luca's phone rang and he saw the name *Butler* on the screen, he touched Kira's shoulder.

When she turned to him, he kissed her cheek. "I should take this. I'll be back in a second."

She nodded. "Of course."

Luca found a quiet corner of the room, away from where most of the crowd gathered. "Saxon."

"Figured you might want an update. Busy?"

"Hit me with it."

The marshal said, "The person who stabbed Jenkins in lockup is the same guy who attacked Dr. Yassan outside the hospital. Stuart Parker. He was being kept for the weekend and took the opportunity to try and kill Jenkins. Now there's no way they're letting him out. Judge Mullinax set bail at one million, and the DA wants Parker to tell the police who hired him to do it."

"Any update on Jenkins's status?" Luca glanced around to make sure no one was listening to him.

"I haven't heard anything since he came out of surgery. The knife nicked his spleen and they had to take it out, so he's still touch and go."

That was as much as Luca already knew from talking to Mack on the way here. It wasn't a surprise that the kid had mixed feelings about his father's condition. He was also wrestling with the idea of forgiving Jenkins, something Hammer had told him they both needed to do in order to move on with their lives.

"What about the cartel guy the police brought in? Have you discovered anything about why he and his buddy were tailing Dr. Torres earlier?"

Ethan said, "Our techs are still trying to get in his phone, but at this point, if he doesn't voluntarily unlock it for us, we might not be able to get anything from it."

"How is that possible, with all the technology you guys have? Can't you just compel him to unlock it for you?"

"Usually we'd be in it by now. But this phone isn't like anything our techs have seen before. It's like it runs on a whole different network." Ethan paused. "If this is the future of unregistered phones, it doesn't bode well for us getting intel. We can't locate a phone company that runs the operating system on this device. The techs tell me it seems to be some kind of proprietary operating system."

"Like a criminal phone network?"

Ethan said, "I hope not."

Luca shook his head, his gaze catching on the corner of one of the posters. An image of two Afghan girls smiling, clutching books. "Has he said anything?"

"We ran his prints. The file that Homeland had on him matches up with what we found. Plus a couple of extras they weren't aware of," Ethan said. "The US Attorney is going to pressure him on the two missing persons cases we have in Arizona. Young girls who never turned up, but his fingerprints were found on their cell phones. Looks like he took them and left the phones behind in both cases."

"It's a good thing this guy is off the streets." Not that it entirely solved the problem. "His friend is still out there."

"Has Dr. Torres shown up?"

"Not according to Detective Martinelli. He's the one watching the patient right now. I'll be back there later tonight to check on things, and first thing tomorrow, I'll be on the door for the day."

He wasn't sure what Kira's plans were and wanted to ask. But they would get there. Maybe she'd want to go to dinner tomorrow night.

"Sounds good," Ethan said. "Martinelli is a solid cop."

Luca wasn't going to reaffirm that he knew what he was doing. The proof would come when Francisco was done with his treatment and could be back in the Marshals' custody.

All because Judge Mullinax wouldn't allow the Marshals to protect the witness before he testified. He would only authorize the detail once Francisco had given the Marshals what they needed to know. A deal with some significant strings attached.

And those strings were getting tangled, considering members of the cartel were here to cause trouble. The doctor had run off, as had another man.

Right now, Luca didn't even know if the doctor was alive. The other man might've caught up to him, and anything could've happened after that. But the patient, Francisco, would be safe either way. Kira could administer the treatment, if it came to that, and the deal could be salvaged.

"That's all I have right now."

Luca said, "I appreciate the update."

"I appreciate you doing this job for us. It's a regular lovefest over here." Ethan chuckled. "We're thinking about privatizing the entire agency. Contracting all our work out to guys like you so we can stay in the office all the time eating our admin assistant's brownies and cookies." Ethan hung up the phone, still laughing to himself.

Luca's gaze snagged on the corner of the poster. A slight discoloration that shouldn't be there on the image, given the rest of the picture didn't contain that color. It almost looked like the edge of a watermark. Had the foundation used stock photography instead of an original image one of their people had taken showing real people they had helped?

He could understand if every single one of the images they used might not be their own. But still, he wondered if it was an indication that things about the foundation weren't quite honest below the surface.

As soon as the money moved, Jamie would see where it went and track her funds—how they were distributed, the kinds of accounts they landed in. It was just another way to untangle the web of what was going on. If Destiny and her nonprofit were legit, then great. But if it was somehow connected to the Shadow Syndicate, then Luca needed to know.

He saw Roger Rousseau duck out of a side door of the main hall, checking first that no one saw him by looking around. Then he disappeared out of sight. Luca knew that look on the man's face, and it didn't bode well. He was up to something. Even if that something was only that he needed to duck out and smoke where his mother wouldn't see.

The son of Ralph and Destiny was older than Luca. Someone who had been around Renegade for a while.

Luca glanced across the ballroom to see Kira now talking to a different couple that he didn't recognize. She chuckled at something the woman said.

He took the opportunity and ducked into the hall, glancing to the end to where Roger had gone.

The younger man turned the corner at the far side of the hall, the walls all lined with wallpaper that looked like fabric. A giant vase of fresh flowers sat on a tiny table halfway down.

Luca followed Roger, picking up his pace to catch up and then stopping before the end of the hall. He peered around the corner and saw Roger in an intense conversation with another man in street clothes. Not dressed for the foundation gala. No, this was the man that had gone after Torres today.

Luca gave it a second, assessing the conversation and both men's body language. Seeing that Roger wasn't in any danger let him relax a little. In fact, it seemed more like he was giving the other man orders.

They broke off their conversation, and the man who had come after Torres turned away. He headed for the exit at the end. Roger watched him for a second, then headed back toward Luca.

Luca stepped around the corner.

Roger spotted him coming.

Luca lifted his chin. "Is the restroom down here?"

"How should I know?" The guy's tone dripped with disdain.

They passed each other, and Luca waited for Roger to step out of sight before he took off after the other man. Racing toward the exit door before it could swing closed. He caught it a second before it clicked, and eased out of the door into the night air, behind the building.

His shoes crunched on the gravel, and he looked around for the other man, finally spotting him heading toward the west corner of the building, a phone to his ear. Luca headed to the grass so he could pursue the man with quieter steps.

As he raced after him, he heard the man speak.

"That's what he said. At the hospital." The cartel guy paused. "We're going to take him out tonight."

Luca forgot all about the need to be quiet and remain undiscovered and raced over to the man, tackling him around the midsection. They both hit the ground, and he punched the guy in the side of the head just hard enough to knock him out. He scrambled for the cartel guy's phone so he could make sure it didn't lock.

Then he pulled out his phone and called Mike Martinelli to warn him that someone was coming to the hospital with plans for assassination.

Mike didn't answer.

Luca hung up. "Let's go."

Kira hung on to the handle, gripping tight while Luca parked his truck in front of the side entrance to the hospital. As soon as he came to a stop, she jumped out—a little tricky, considering she still had heels on. She wobbled but got her balance and slammed the door shut. Kira raced around the front of the truck and met him at the entrance right as he pulled it open.

Just inside the door, Kira stopped to remove her shoes, continuing on bare feet toward the elevator. It felt like it took far too long.

Luca hurried ahead of her just as the doors opened, drawing his weapon as they approached the corner. He peered around first and visibly relaxed. "Martinelli!"

She got there in time to see the police detective turn to them.

"What's going on?" Mike's hand drifted to the butt of his weapon, but he didn't pull it from the holster on his belt.

Luca raced to him. Kira stopped beside him, breathing hard. She put her hands on her hips, trying to steady her heart rate. After Luca had rushed into the gala and told her what happened outside, they'd both run to the valet station, where the staff had already pulled his truck around.

He hadn't asked her to go with him, necessarily. Rather, she had chosen to climb into the truck—more difficult than it looked in this outfit—and make sure her patient was all right. Technically, he was under the care of Dr. Torres, but that didn't mean Kira felt no responsibility for him.

If there was a threat to his life, anything could happen.

Driving over here, worrying about the same thing and having the same aim, had felt a whole lot like she and Luca were a team. She liked it more than the idea of gathering information together. Even though that seemed exciting, the push to save a life, which had them both running out of the gala, was far more important.

As if being together with him healed a little bit of what was inside her.

She could do good things and save lives in more than just the work she did as a doctor. Her whole life could be about making the world a better place. Something she hadn't acknowledged before, thinking that had only been part of her life when she was overseas.

Maybe she could do it here as well. In some fashion.

Luca said, "I overheard one of those cartel guys Homeland sent us after, talking about a hit at the hospital." He pushed out a breath. "I called you, but you didn't pick up."

"I just got off a call with one of my sisters. I was about to call you back."

"I'm glad you're all right." Kira nodded to Mike and squeezed Luca's triceps. She went to the door and knocked quietly before she eased it open.

Francisco lay in the hospital bed, his face pale. Eyes closed. Torres sat in the chair beside his bed, quietly reading a worn paperback novel. Her brows rose. Luca had told her that he'd disappeared earlier, and yet, here he was.

She eased the door closed again without going in. "Everything looks okay in there."

Luca bent forward, breathing hard. "Okay, so it either hasn't happened yet, or Francisco wasn't the target."

"That's a good thing, isn't it?" she asked them both.

Luca holstered his gun. "I'd rather have caught someone in the act. But yes, finding nothing happening is better than bloodshed." He glanced at Mike. "I'm glad everything is okay here."

"Why don't you run down for me what happened?" the detective said.

Luca told him about seeing Roger Rousseau talking to one of the men who'd been after Dr. Torres earlier, and how he'd followed the man outside to overhear his phone conversation. "He's in police custody now, so hopefully we can get some information from him."

"We?"

Luca said, "You know what I mean. We need to find out who these guys are taking orders from and why the one just now was talking to Roger. We still have too many random pieces to this puzzle and no idea what any of it is supposed to look like."

"You guys were over at Wiltmore House, right?"

Kira nodded. "That's where the gala was."

"That's in the jurisdiction. The station I work out of. I'll call over there and find out what's happening with the guy that was just brought in."

Luca said, "And the one from earlier. Butler said he isn't giving up anything, and they can't get into his phone. Maybe if we pit them against each other, they'll talk."

"Anything is worth a try at this point." Martinelli pulled out his phone.

"What about the doctor?" Kira glanced between them. "He's the one who was talking to these guys. Maybe he has something to say."

Luca turned to her. "Good idea. We should ask him why he ran off after he saw me tackle that guy."

Kira put her hands on her hips. "That's twice today you've tussled with a gunman. Should I be worried that you're the kind of person who is itching to get in a fight?"

Mike grinned at her.

"Seems to me like I might not be the one itching for a fight right now." Luca lifted his chin, humor in his gaze.

"You've ruined my evening." And the fact nobody had been hurt was a huge relief. "You're going to have to make it up to me."

Mike wandered away a couple of steps, waving his hand and focusing on his phone. "I'm staying out of this. Whatever it is."

Luca pinned her with a stare. "You want me to make it up to you?"

Kira stood her ground. "That depends on whether you plan to run out and tackle someone in the middle of it."

He touched her waist, his fingers easing back and forth over the curve of her hip. "If you don't want that to happen, I think it can be arranged."

"Good." She stepped toward the door. "I'm going to interrogate the doctor for you. You're welcome."

She heard Mike let out a bark of laughter and slipped into the room.

Luca had plenty to keep him busy, with the men they had in custody and everything else that was going on now. If anyone could disarm the doctor and find out why he was being targeted specifically, it was her.

Either those men Luca had seen earlier intended to force the doctor to tell them where Francisco was, or they wanted him to mess up the treatment protocol. Whichever one it was, the patient's life was in danger from men associated with the very cartel that had been stolen from him. Nothing but a bunch of infighting between bad guys, one of whom was protecting his own behind by making a deal with the US government.

Not a situation she ever would want to be in. But criminals like Francisco might feel they had no choice but to take whatever deal they could be offered, in order to save their own skin.

The doctor looked up from his novel, and Kira gave him a little wave.

"That's a very fancy dress."

"I was at an event tonight, but we heard that there might be an attack on the patient here, so we rushed back over to make sure everything was all right."

The doctor set aside his book, using a piece of paper as a bookmark, and kept his voice low when he said, "And is it?"

"As far as I know." She brought the second chair over and set it down beside him as quietly as she could, then settled into it. "How is the patient doing?"

"Everything looks good right now. We should be able to begin the procedure first thing tomorrow morning."

She nodded, even though that completely upended her usual sleep schedule. She'd explained it to him, but he must've forgotten. Still, Kira wasn't going to delay Francisco's treatment just because she normally worked nights and slept during the day.

"That's great news." She gave it a second, smoothing her dress over her knees. "And how was your day? Did you do anything interesting while I was here?"

She had no idea if he was aware that she knew what'd happened with Luca and the two men earlier. He might be completely un-aware that Luca had filled her in on nearly everything about the investigation and this assignment.

"I had lunch with a friend of mine at this tapas place not far from here."

She tried to keep her facial expression neutral. "I know you're a local, but did you know the patient before he made this agreement with the Marshals?"

"Francisco and I have been friends for a long time."

That sounded like a serious security threat to her. It might not take much for someone from the cartel to look up Francisco's old friend and discover he was capable of treating the former boss. "Isn't it risky to do the procedure on him here in Renegade?"

"We didn't have another choice. The judge refused to authorize the Marshals taking Francisco and me out of town for the time being." He shifted in the seat, as if nervous.

"Is anyone harassing you about what's going on? Maybe asking you to tell them where he is?"

"It wouldn't be the first time the cartel has approached me about giving them information, or even working for them." The doctor shrugged. "I wouldn't be doing this if it wasn't Francisco. I owe him a lot."

"What do you mean?"

"Just that if I do this, then not only do I repay an outstanding debt from a long time ago, but Francisco is going to work it into his deal that I also get protection." Torres didn't seem fearful. "We all have enemies, and it's up to us to take steps to protect ourselves. After all, no one else is going to do it." He nodded to the door. "At least, not beyond the short term."

"I'm sure the Marshals will be able to keep both of you safe." She tried to figure out how to word it. "If you pass what you know to the police, or the man who is in charge of your security here, they can work to eliminate the threat against you. Then you'd be free to live your life."

"Francisco might be prepared to hand over what he knows to the US government, but I haven't reached the point where I'm willing to do the same. There's far too much water under that bridge for me to trust any deal the government is going to give me."

Kira said, "But you trust what they are giving Francisco?"

He shrugged. "That's different."

She wasn't sure how that could be true, but he seemed to believe what he was saying. This wasn't a man who was trying to do an end run around her concerns. "I'm sure the procedure tomorrow will go well. Then there will be one less thing to worry about, and the two of you can move on with your lives."

"I'm looking forward to it." He didn't smile. It seemed more like he felt nothing, which was odd for a man who was working to get a different life or some kind of fresh start.

"You've built a good life here with all that real estate I see your name on the side of." She thought back to the first time he had rolled up in that car and the marshal had told her that Dr. Torres wanted to speak to her. "You have a lot to leave behind."

"Sometimes, cutting ties is the only way to get what you want."

The door swung open. Kira turned to it as Luca stuck his head in. He didn't have to say anything for her to get up and step outside with him.

She hadn't been getting much information from the doctor. It would take a longer conversation for her to dig enough to let him know that she knew he wasn't telling her everything. Then she would ask him to give her what those men had said to him in that alley, before the altercation with Luca.

But at that point, he might not trust her as his assistant, and this whole plan would be thrown for a loop.

She closed the door behind her. "What is it?"

"Mike went upstairs to check on Ralph Rousseau." Luca winced. "He's dead."

THIRTEEN

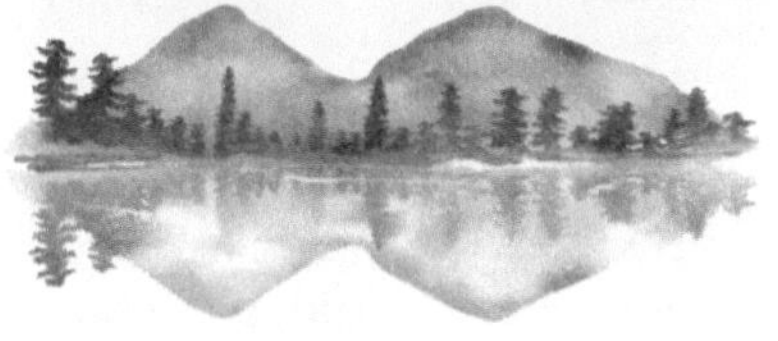

LUCA SIPPED FROM THE PAPER CUP OF COFFEE and stared through the one-way glass into the interrogation room the morning after the gala. He wasn't supposed to be here, technically. But after Detective Martinelli had explained to Deputy Marshal Butler his connection with the syndicate investigation, he'd been allowed to stay. It didn't seem that Ethan even really believed their theory that the city was being controlled by some kind of shadowy syndicate. Or at least, he might not be ready to believe it.

On the other side of the glass, Detective Martinelli stood by the wall with his arms folded across his chest. Deputy Marshal Butler sat at the table, the cartel muscle that Luca had tackled across from him.

Ethan tapped his first two fingers on the table. Beating out a steady rhythm that might drive some people crazy.

Luca had withstood a whole lot worse than incessant tapping. Going through Army boot camp and then Delta Force training on top of that had pitted him against the worst things his trainers could come up with. Then he'd gone out in the field and met the real nightmares.

The cartel guy at the interrogation room table seemed a whole lot more bothered by Butler's tapping. Shifting in his seat, darting glances at the two men. Gearing up to start talking—which was probably the marshal's intention.

None of them said anything.

The door to the interrogation room opened, and a uniformed sergeant stuck his head in. He handed Detective Martinelli a file folder.

"Thank you, Sarge."

The door shut and Martinelli opened the file. "Hector Carlos Ramirez. Twenty-seven years old, two counts of accessory to armed robbery. Four years in prison in San Diego before you were kicked back across the border. Now we find you here in Renegade, Colorado." Martinelli paused. "What was the reason for your visit to the US this time?"

The guy sounded like he was auditioning for a job at Immigration and Customs Enforcement.

Hector muttered something in Spanish.

"I'm sorry, I didn't catch that," Martinelli said. "Is there something you'd like to tell us?"

So far, the guy had waived his right to an attorney. Probably a good idea, as the court would assign him someone for free. Who knew what kind of lawyer would show up to represent him?

Luca had his own lawyer on retainer even though he had no reason to require representation. Definitely not a risk he was willing to take.

Hector just stared at the two cops.

Luca's coffee cup flexed in his hand, spilling a little of the hot drink on his skin. He winced. They might be closer than ever to real answers on the investigation, but if this guy didn't start talking, they would only have as much as they had yesterday. Not a whole lot.

Despite the doctor's insistence that someone must have given Ralph Rousseau the overdose of the drug that stopped his heart, there had been nothing on surveillance when they'd gone over the footage. Kira had watched the hallway and told them it was all normal, just medical staff doing their jobs—nothing and no one out of the ordinary.

Now someone was going to have to tell Destiny that her husband was dead. Kira would probably want to be there. They might even be doing that now. Sure, he could text her, but it was also in the early hours of the morning, and she might be trying to get some sleep.

Ethan shifted and placed an evidence bag with the suspect's phone in it on the table. "This is an interesting device, Mr. Ramirez. How did you come by it?"

Hector said, "That's not mine."

"Sure. That's why you were talking on it when you were detained."

"That guy isn't even a cop. I can't be arrested by a guy who isn't even a cop." Hector's expression turned deadly. "You can't pin this on me."

Ethan shrugged. "Pin what on you?"

Luca wasn't a huge fan of the back-and-forth that went into interrogations. Or the subtext. He was much more into getting to the point—not allowing Hector to imply that Luca had planted the phone on him. Though, his preferred tactics meant he'd probably already have the suspect up against the wall and he'd be punching him to get answers. So maybe Luca should leave the interrogation business to the police.

Ethan pointed to the phone. "You were overheard talking on this. We know what you were saying, and we have the number of the person you were talking to. What you don't know is that your friend, the one you left a message for, is in our custody. After the two of you followed Dr. Torres out of that restaurant earlier in the day, you ran off and your friend was arrested."

Ethan set a photo on the table.

"Never seen him before in my life."

None of them were going to buy that.

Ethan said, "You were talking to him on the phone, leaving him a message. Now both of you will be charged with the aggravated assault of Dr. Torres and the murder of Ralph Rousseau." Ethan didn't even wait for him to respond to that. "Unless you can tell me what business your cartel has with two men in Renegade."

A tendon in Hector's jaw flexed. He didn't like that at all. "You can't pin this on me. I don't even know that Rousseau guy."

"Tell us what we want to know before your friend does. Otherwise, we'll persuade him to talk first, and when he's done, you'll be the one who goes down for all of it."

"Did I kill someone?" The man shrugged. "Or was I in a cell at the time? Pretty good alibi, right?"

He wasn't wrong, considering the murder had happened after the man was detained by Luca at the gala. The cops had taken him to the station before Rousseau died.

Martinelli came over to the table and pulled out the other chair to sit. "Who did the job at the hospital? Unless you want to go down for Rousseau's death."

"Guy like you," Ethan said, "I figure you do as you're told and you either get paid well or you get unpleasant consequences because you failed. Maybe it's time you're the boss of your own life for once. Give us what we want."

Luca didn't like the idea of any lowlife making a deal, but it was how the cops often chose to flip someone lower in the ranks in order to work their way up the chain and eventually get the boss in custody. Cutting off the head of the snake. That would get all the other parts of their operation to scatter with no leader.

Was that going to be the case with the Shadow Syndicate?

He would love to find the person at the top of the food chain, take them down, and see the whole thing dismantled. But if the syndicate was making deals with the cartel to kill the competition, then they were strengthening their operation. Luca was going to find it a whole lot less vulnerable to being broken apart.

"What do you say?" Butler shrugged. "I don't really care if you go to federal prison for the rest of your life, but you might want to think about making a deal. Otherwise, you take the fall when someone else does exactly that."

"I don't talk."

Ethan opened the file folder in front of him and pulled out a photo of Francisco. He set the image in front of the man.

Hector leaned forward and spat on the picture. He said the word *traitor* in Spanish. One of the few words Luca understood. But even if he hadn't known what the word meant, he would understand the gist of how Hector felt about his former boss.

"Talk to me about this guy." Ethan wasn't about to admit they had Francisco under their protection, was he?

Before Luca could wonder what else was about to happen, Ethan motioned to the picture. "You don't like him, so help me find him. Nobody just disappears. Tell me what you know so that I can pick him up."

Hector muttered something in Spanish.

Martinelli ignored it. "Tell us what you wanted with Dr. Torres."

"Prescription." Hector smirked. "I have a bad back."

Ethan shook his head. "It's time to start talking, Hector. You aren't doing yourself any favors pretending to be stupid when we all know you're up to your neck in this." The marshal sat back in his chair. "Or I continue to have the techs go through your phone, and we dig out everything it can tell us about who you work for. Maybe your buddy Pablo will make a deal, and I'll get what I need from him."

Hector stared at the two cops across the table. "Lawyer."

Ethan said, "What was that?"

"I want a lawyer now." Hector folded his arms across his chest. "I'm not saying anything else."

In the viewing room, Luca rolled his eyes and tossed the paper cup into the trash. He left the room, went into the hallway, and checked his phone.

Mike stepped out of the interrogation room. "Anything?"

Luca conveyed the contents of the message. "Hammer said Jenkins is being transferred back to jail so he can recuperate in their medical wing and the hospital can have their bed back."

Mike nodded. "The attacker, Stuart Parker, is in solitary. He'll go before Mullinax again tomorrow, and the judge won't go easy on him."

Ethan eased up to their huddle. "No one wants Jenkins to skate out from under justice, so you don't have to worry that the corrections officers will allow anything else to happen to him. One of the guys who works at the prison? His dad was forced off his land. It wasn't Jenkins that did it, but none of them have any sympathy for a guy who did that to so many people."

Luca reached over his shoulder and squeezed the back of his neck, trying to ease some of the tension of this long day. "So what do we do with Hector now?"

Ethan said, "That's up to whatever his lawyer convinces him is the wisest choice."

"I'm more inclined to cut him loose and follow him. See where he goes and who he talks to." Martinelli glanced between them. "We might get way more from doing that than whatever it is he gives us once a deal has been signed."

Luca didn't like that idea. "Just let him go? Put him back on the streets?"

"What did he actually do?" Martinelli shrugged. "His lawyer, if he's good, is going to argue that twice you saw him talking to somebody, and that you were the one who attacked him, not the other way around."

Luca lifted his hands. "Maybe don't arrest me."

Martinelli said, "Maybe don't tackle anyone else before they commit a crime."

Luca shot him a look.

"As entertaining as this comedy routine is, I need to get back to the lab so the techs can look at this phone." Ethan shook the evidence bag in front of him. "If anything happens, give me a holler." He walked away.

Luca turned to Martinelli. "Did you really have to say that?"

Mike snorted. "What are you going to do now? Hammer is watching out for Francisco."

"I'm feeling the need to tear apart Dr. Torres's life and find out what he's hiding."

"Hang on one second, Jordan." Kira pulled her car into Destiny's neighborhood just two days after the gala—the night Destiny's husband had died—and was waved through by the guard in the small structure at the entrance. "Okay, you're good."

She hadn't wanted Jordan to say anything potentially sensitive or for their relationship to be exposed, even if it was only in front of the neighborhood security guard.

Jordan's voice came through the car speakers. "So Luca just ditched you?"

"He had to take a business call." She slowed her speed to match the neighborhood restrictions. "And I got the chance to speak with some of the hospital's biggest donors. I didn't have a problem with it."

"Hmm." Apparently Jordan didn't agree. "But he came back

to tell you that he'd detained someone and found out there was going to be a hit at the hospital?"

"I missed all the fun."

"That doesn't sound like a bad thing. I thought you enjoyed your quiet life," Jordan said. "That was the point of you moving back to Renegade. So you could get some peace and perspective."

Kira looked at the giant houses, set back from the street behind expansive front lawns. Talk about perspective. All of the landscaping was mature and perfectly manicured by someone the homeowner paid to take care of it. Staring out at someone else's hard work wasn't the kind of perspective she was interested in—or what Jordan was talking about.

Did she miss the excitement of her former extracurricular activities?

She'd never been officially employed as a covert agent. Just a contractor on top of her duties as a doctor.

"I don't miss it. I like my life here." It even sounded like she believed it this time.

"And it wasn't the patient that someone tried to kill, it was another guy who died?" Jordan knew the name of the man the Marshals were protecting. But for the sake of security, it was better not to mention his name over the phone.

"Apparently the hit was for Ralph Rousseau. How that connects back to his and Destiny's son, I have no idea, and we wouldn't have known they were connected if Luca hadn't seen them talking. Maybe Luca and Detective Martinelli figured it out. It could be that this Roger guy knew nothing about it, considering all he did was talk to the man. It was only after the guy went outside that Luca heard him talking about it on the phone."

She turned the corner onto Destiny's street and saw that cars lined both sides of the road.

"If he's behind it, that's a pretty spectacular alibi."

Kira said, "I was as surprised as anyone that Ralph was the target. We really thought the patient was in danger."

"Could be he was killed as a test, all so they could ascertain what kind of security surrounds the patient."

"You really think they killed a guy across the other side of the hospital just to find out our response time?"

Jordan said, "It's possible."

"Only because we don't have enough information. At this point, anything is possible."

"Maybe you can find out at this memorial service you're going to," Jordan said. "Why is Destiny having it so quickly after her husband died? His body isn't even cold yet."

"Actually, she already had him cremated, so temperature isn't really a factor."

"Are you serious? Who gets that done so fast?"

The first open parking space Kira found was way down the street from the house. "Maybe she was following his wishes. Or she just wanted to do it quickly so it didn't drag out."

"Seems suspicious to me, that's all I'm saying."

"People don't always do things that make sense when they're grieving."

"I suppose."

Kira said, "Hang on a second. I'm going to turn off my car, so the phone will disconnect from Bluetooth." She shut it off and lifted her phone to her ear, gathering up her purse and climbing out of the car. Her body clock was so far off, she wouldn't have been able to say what the time was without looking at a clock. The dreary cloud cover wasn't helping.

Kira had taken a nap this afternoon that lasted a few hours, and woke up confused about where she was—or who she was—until it came rushing back. She figured she'd slept hard and rested well.

"I'm sure Destiny is just trying to get things done so she doesn't have to worry about any of it." Kira closed the car door. "Then she can take some time and grieve in private."

It's what Kira would do. But she didn't have anyone in her life except for Jordan that she felt that deeply about. Sure, she had hoped that by now she would be married and have kids. But life never seemed to work out the way she planned.

Meeting Luca again after all this time had sparked something in her. It had made her realize that he might be the person she needed. The one God had brought here for her—a blessing she was grateful for and hadn't been expecting.

Jordan said, "How is the patient?"

"The doctor conducted the procedure this morning, and he's been stable since then. All of his levels are coming up to normal." Kira stepped onto the sidewalk and headed toward Destiny's house, feeling awkward in this black dress she rarely wore. "It's really a remarkable thing he's come up with. If everything works out, it will open up plenty of research into all kinds of lifesaving measures for the disorder we're dealing with."

"I've been looking into him and his background a little more," Jordan said. "This Dr. Torres has a few thriving businesses in Renegade. On top of his research, he seems to have his fingers in a lot of pies." Jordan was quiet for a moment, then said, "Nothing has happened that makes you believe he's part of this shadow syndicate, right?"

"I think he knows more than he's saying." Kira spotted a couple on the side of the house, as if the party had spilled from the yard all the way to the front. "But it's going to take time to get him to trust me with all of that, whether he is part of it or just knows who is."

"Are you going to keep pushing it?"

"We won't be with the patient at the same time. Not for the most part," Kira said. "And if we are, the patient is going to overhear everything we say."

"Once the job is done, maybe you could keep things going with Torres. Build up a professional relationship."

"If I can find out anything, it will probably help Luca's investigation."

Jordan said, "Just as long as it doesn't put you in any danger, it might at least scratch the itch you still have to do some of that work."

Her friend sounded frustrated, probably because of the lack of information she'd found on the syndicate. Plus, she probably had real CIA work to do. There was no way for Jordan to discern if Torres was connected to the Shadow Syndicate on paper, even if she could connect the doctor to Rousseau's legitimate businesses. Things would be too clean. This was something that needed to be discovered in person.

Kira said, "How do you know that I miss it?"

"Why else would you be hanging out with Luca Saxon? He isn't your type."

"I'm not sure that's true."

"Oh, come on. A guy like that? You'd never be able to keep your secrets from him."

At a certain point, she'd always assumed that there would be no secrets between her and whoever she ended up in a long-term relationship with. "He could be the guy I don't keep any secrets from."

"Not a good idea," Jordan said. "There aren't many people who would actually understand your history. All of it. Probably better to keep your business private, like I do."

Kira needed to think about that. "I should go. I'm outside the front door."

"I know. I can see you on my screen," Jordan said. "Be careful. Do what you need to do to keep yourself safe."

Jordan hung up. Kira stowed the phone in her purse and stepped inside, trying to wrestle with the idea of not being honest with Luca. That probably wasn't what Jordan meant. She was just looking out for Kira and not wanting any guy to toss her aside after she told him the truth about her family or the things that'd happened before she quit.

But what bearing did her father's criminal activity have on her?

Kira didn't want to deceive Luca. Which was the one thing that actually told her how serious her feelings were. Otherwise, she would have no problem withholding the truth from a guy.

Luca was the one who deserved her honesty. He was a good man who did the right thing and worked tirelessly to make Renegade a better place to live for the people he loved. If she told him the truth and he ended things between them, then he wasn't the man she thought she knew. And the fact that she'd been burned by her expectations before when it came to that man was another thing that told her how serious her feelings were. She wasn't putting him on a pedestal, this warrior hero. She was choosing instead to have a more take-it-or-leave-it approach.

Did she want to open up and spill all of her secrets? No, she would rather hide from the fear of being rejected and say nothing. But that didn't seem like the thing the Lord wanted her to do.

Perfect love casts out fear.

Barbara quoted that verse all the time, and she was right to keep it at the front of her mind. Kira needed more of God's love in her heart to banish the fear. She needed to give and receive that kind of love every day to keep it at bay. All so she didn't get swallowed up by the things trying to press in on her all the time.

As the door eased shut behind her, Destiny appeared in the entryway. Kira had been here before a few times and was always in awe of the massive chandelier that hung down over the two-story entryway.

The stairs swept up in an arc, starting from the left side and rising over to the right at the top of the stairs, where a wall of bookshelves stared down. Inviting her to go up and peruse the titles on the shelves.

"Destiny." Kira opened her arms. "I'm so sorry for your loss."

The other woman swallowed back a sob. "It's all been so very difficult."

They embraced and Destiny stepped back. Despite the circumstances, her makeup remained perfect. Whatever products she bought had to be waterproof—and she reapplied frequently. There was no way Kira would be this put-together if her husband had just died. But she would likely have the same red eyes of a grieving widow.

Kira needed to stop trying to look for reasons to distrust this woman when God had put them in each other's lives as acquaintances they could rely on. There was no reason to believe anything underhanded had happened, especially not originating from Destiny.

Kira had taken a look at the medical chart and spoken with the doctor in charge of Ralph Rousseau's care. She had no reason to believe that this was a hit or murder. All the information in the chart indicated that Ralph had simply taken a turn for the worse after he was administered medication, and the weak state of his body meant that he hadn't been able to recover from it. He'd simply had no fight left.

If there had been poison or the dosage had been too high, the coroner should be able to discern as much from an autopsy. But the results of that could take days or even weeks, and there would need to be an investigation within the hospital.

"Whatever you need," Kira said. "I'm here for you."

"Thank you so much," Destiny said. "There is something. Could you check for Roger in his room? He's supposed to be down here helping me with the guests and everything, but he seems to have disappeared."

"Of course." She squeezed Destiny's arm.

"His room is the second door on the left. I'll be on the patio with the rest of the guests."

Kira nodded and headed for the stairs, where her shoes made no sound on the carpet. At the top, she could see all the way down the upstairs hall, doors on either side and a set of double doors at the end that likely led to the main bedroom.

She approached the second door and heard muffled voices.

Kira knocked. "Roger, are you in there? Your mother sent me to check that you're all right." She eased the door open, her senses on alert. Not just from everything that had happened recently but also because of her own experiences.

Someone grabbed the door from her grip and pulled it all the way open, but didn't grab her. She wobbled on her heels.

Luca stood there holding the door. Roger sat beyond him in a chair, his face red and the beginning of a bruise on his cheekbone. Luca had clearly been questioning him, and Roger didn't want to answer.

On the day of his father's memorial? Talk about insensitive. This wasn't the time or the place to question a man's involvement in the incident that killed his father.

She looked at Luca. "What are you doing?"

FOURTEEN

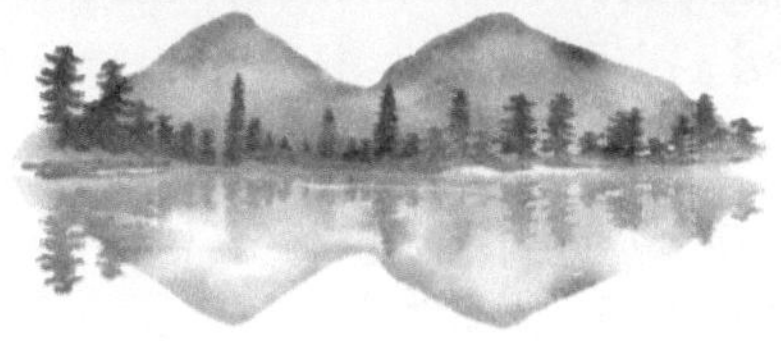

LUCA STARED AT HER, WATCHING KIRA SASHAY into the room in a dress that wasn't quite flattering—but maybe that was the point, considering this was a memorial service. At least, that's what was happening downstairs. Up here, they were doing something different.

Or he'd been trying to, anyway.

She glanced at him. "Close the door."

Luca's brows rose.

As he had with Detective Martinelli and Deputy Marshal Butler in that interview room, he wondered if she had quickly read the situation she'd wandered into and, between opening the door and entering, decided to change things up. Use the time-honored good-cop–bad-cop tactic.

Did that mean she was on board here to help him?

Luca didn't know, but it might prove more effective than the questions he'd been asking since he got here.

"What is going on here?" She put one hand on the curve of her hip, her elbow bent out. "And somebody talk fast, because Destiny wants to know where Roger is. We can't send him downstairs looking like that now, can we."

Did she think he was the one who had punched Roger in the face?

"Roger and I are getting to know each other." Luca folded his arms, because she either trusted him or believed he had come in here and punched the guy on the day of his father's memorial.

He'd snuck in for the memorial, hence the fact he was wearing his best jeans and a black button-down shirt, and seen Roger up here in the second-floor hallway for a second. No point in wasting the opportunity of talking to Roger just to make small talk with people he didn't need to speak to.

Turned out, Roger had been in a fight, and Luca thought he might need someone to unload on. He could play the part of friend. It didn't seem like this guy had many of those.

This was supposedly his room, but the place was decorated like a model-home showroom and made Luca wonder if the guy crashed elsewhere most of the time. He was nearly forty. Luca hoped he didn't still live with his parents.

Roger wore a suit today, but likely only in deference to his mother's wishes. The material hung on him in a way that suggested it had fit better before ten pounds of weight gain. Something he didn't wear often but pulled out for special occasions like this.

Between the buttons of his shirt, Luca could see the white T-shirt underneath. Roger had removed his suit jacket, and if there had been a tie, it was nowhere to be seen now. A drop of blood on the collar of his shirt was the only indication that he had been in the altercation since getting dressed.

Someone had punched this man in the cheek. Maybe not here in this house, but certainly sometime today.

"I believe he was about to tell me who hit him." What Luca

actually needed to know was whether there was a connection between the Shadow Syndicate and the cartel.

He wasn't sure there were many other viable explanations for what had been happening.

Kira turned to Roger, still sitting in that chair Luca had pulled over for him when he'd seen how much Roger was weaving and about to fall over. Given the smell on the man's breath, it was clear he'd drunk too much alcohol today.

"Well?" Kira turned the full force of her attention on the younger man. "Who hit you?"

"Doesn't matter." Roger shook his head.

"It might matter. So why don't you try us?"

But the expression on Roger's face didn't change. Luca hadn't been getting anywhere in the few minutes before Kira showed up. He doubted they would actually gain answers before someone else came looking for them.

The fact no one connected to this case wanted to tell Luca anything was becoming irritating. Hopefully Jamie could come up with answers now that she'd told him the money was moving through foundation accounts.

"We are not talking about that." Roger looked at Luca. "You said this was about my dad."

Kira glanced at him, but Luca didn't know why. He said, "I'm investigating your father's connection to the shadow syndicate operating in town." Luca shrugged. "That's the bottom line here. I'm sorry, but if you didn't know, someone pointed their finger at your dad as the head of the syndicate." He watched Roger's face for any indication as to how he felt about that or the fact Luca knew. "That doesn't surprise you?"

Roger shrugged. Maybe he just didn't care. A guy staring down the barrel of turning forty, adopted into money so that he didn't have to work. Luca wondered what drove him to do anything when whatever he wanted was handed over on a silver tray.

"Was your father the head of the Shadow Syndicate?"

"Can't say I know what you're talking about," Roger said.

Kira shifted her stance, dropping her hands from her hips. "What is it that you do for a living, Roger?"

"I am an ambassador for the foundation my mother runs. I enjoy helping other people the way I was helped." That sounded a little too rehearsed.

"And your father?" Luca watched the other man's reactions. "You never visited him in the hospital. Is that right?"

Roger sniffed. "We didn't get along that well. He said I was a mama's boy."

"There's nothing wrong with having a close relationship with one of your parents," Kira said. "It's a natural part of life that we get along with some people more than others."

From where Luca stood, it seemed more like the beginning of a theory that had Roger and Ralph at odds. Even to the point where Roger might have believed he had a reason to kill the older man.

But was that what had happened? It was possible Roger had contracted the cartel to take out his father. Was this man colder and more calculating than he came across? Luca wasn't willing to let the other man pull the wool over his eyes—not in the biggest investigation he'd ever undertaken.

Luca shifted and leaned against the wall beside the dresser. If he opened the drawer, would it be empty or full of Roger's clothes?

Luca said, "Did your father ever hurt you?"

"He's dead," Roger said. "It doesn't matter now."

Kira's body language softened. "Does your mother know?"

Roger started to chuckle. "Are you going to save me? I think she picked the right person for the vacant position on the board. Seems like you're a real bleeding-heart type, which means you'll fit right in, because she can have you all twisted around trying to help people. Doing all the work for her."

"Your mother has built an incredible organization that helps a lot of people." Kira sounded like she believed that, whether the statement was made to get Roger to argue with her or not.

"That's the point."

Luca frowned, unsure if the *point* was that Destiny worked to help people, or that everyone believed it was true. "Is there something going on with the foundation that we need to know?"

When Roger didn't say anything for a few seconds, Kira chimed in. "I need to know what you know about the foundation. You're one of their success stories, right? If you don't think it's a good nonprofit, then I'm not going to choose to be part of it."

"I would never do anything to jeopardize the foundation." Roger glanced between them. "Is that what you're here to do? Undermine my mother's life's work?"

"No, we're here to honor the memory of your father." Kira didn't let his words bother her.

Luca said, "If you're in some kind of trouble, we can help you."

Someone had punched this young man in the face. That and the fact he'd been talking to the cartel guy, the one who'd mentioned the hit they now knew was on Roger's father, all added up to a whole lot of suspicion.

Roger didn't look at him.

Luca tried again. "I saw you in the hallway outside the gala. You were talking to a man I know was involved with the death of your father. I should call the police and tell them my suspicion that you're involved in your dad's death. After all, you probably have reason to hate him enough to order someone to kill him."

The young man glanced at him, those dark eyes staring at Luca. "I'm not the one who ordered him killed."

"But you're going to benefit from his death, aren't you? Surely he left something to his son."

It was a bold accusation, but only by guessing wildly did he have a shot at getting Roger to argue with him and explain the truth, just for the sake of correcting what Luca "thought." Kira moved in a way that suggested she didn't like what he'd just said, but she didn't argue aloud.

"None of that is any of your business." Roger lifted his chin. "I don't even know you."

"You aren't worried about me going to the police about you?"

Roger shrugged. "Do whatever you want."

Either he wasn't worried about guilt, or he had protected himself enough that he believed he was insulated. Or him being hit had nothing to do with crime.

Maybe Destiny had hit him.

Luca said, "Is there anyone in your father's life who might've wanted him dead?"

"Obviously, otherwise he'd be alive."

Luca wasn't sure that was a helpful answer to his question. "Are you aware that Alden Jenkins recently pointed your father out as the head of the Shadow Syndicate? Then soon after that, Alden was nearly killed in prison and your father was targeted."

Kira looked at Luca. "The medical files don't support murder."

"There are plenty of ways to kill someone that don't look like a crime. It took someone more than one attempt to end Ralph's life." Whatever had happened in the hospital that led to his death needed to be investigated. Someone might have snuck into his room and done something to him. Only, what evidence would there be when Destiny had already had her husband cremated?

The whole thing was more than suspicious.

Roger said, "How would I know anything about some shadow syndicate in town? I don't have anything to do with my father's business."

"No one is accusing you of anything." Kira lifted her hands. "I'm sure there's no reason for anyone to call the police about this conversation either. It was just a friendly chat, right?" She glanced at Luca, then back at Roger. "Maybe we could all go our separate ways and pretend this never happened."

Luca wondered if she thought Roger might press charges against him for storming in here. Was she trying to save him from getting into trouble?

"You're exactly right, Dr. Yassan. This was just a friendly chat." He motioned to Roger's cheek. "Although you might want to report whoever punched you to the police. They shouldn't get away with hurting you."

"Who cares?" Roger got up and crossed to the door. Not the first time he'd been hit, and maybe Roger thought it wasn't going to be the last. In fact, he didn't seem bothered by what'd happened at all.

But Luca had to try. "I'm a private investigator. If you tell me who did this to you, I could go and talk to them. Maybe smooth things out."

Roger opened the door and held it. "I don't need your help. Either of you. My father is dead, and that's the end of it."

One way or another, Luca needed to get answers still. Whether that was by finding a way to get information about Roger without him knowing, or tracking down the guy's friends and associates and getting what he needed from them.

Maybe Jamie could hack Roger's phone. Or his home computer.

She probably drew the line somewhere with illegal activity, but he figured it didn't hurt to ask. If she didn't want to do it, he could figure out a way to get enough probable cause that Detective Martinelli would be able to get a warrant for the same thing. Keep it all above board.

But all that did was tip off the bad guys that they were being investigated.

Kira stepped into the hallway first. Luca walked with her downstairs, his hand on the small of her back. She wore heeled boots that came up high enough they disappeared under the hem of the skirt below her knees.

When he glanced back, Roger had moved out of sight.

"Guess he's not coming down with us to placate his mother."

She turned to him at the bottom of the stairs, a look on her face he'd never seen before.

Luca shrugged. "What?"

"Are you serious?" She couldn't even elaborate enough to verbalize the problem. Did he really not know what the issue was? "This is a memorial service. Roger is processing his father's death. Even if you think he's in on it, this isn't the time or the place to talk to him."

Luca didn't seem the least bit repentant. Or he had schooled his features enough that she couldn't tell what he was feeling. "I took the opportunity I was given. Maybe even the one God gave me."

"And you aren't the one who hit him in the face?"

Both of them could have been lying to her about that. She wouldn't put it past a guy like Roger to go along with what was said. The charisma of a man like Luca would sweep along a certain type of person in his wake. He was the kind of guy who drew people to him, whether he liked it or not. They trusted him, and some even wanted to impress him.

"I didn't hit him, Kira."

Not that he wouldn't. Just that he didn't this time.

She sighed. "That's good. Because he could have called the police and had you arrested for it."

Luca shrugged. "I'm not worried about Roger. He probably knows more than he's saying, but he goes along with far too much to make waves. If he files a police report, they're going to show up here asking a whole lot of questions. Digging into his life and his family. So either he wants to protect himself or them. But whichever it is, the police won't get called."

"It's only Destiny now. His mother is all he has left, and Roger needs to be down here helping her."

"You realize the two of them could be behind this entire shadow syndicate?"

She wanted to laugh at the ridiculousness of that idea. But the somber occasion and something else stopped her.

In the end, she said nothing. The note of disquiet inside her made her worry that there was something to his suggestion. They genuinely *could* be behind the Shadow Syndicate. For all she knew, that might be exactly what was going on.

But the idea that Destiny might be the one who'd arranged her own husband's death or that someone else had taken him out because they were all involved in the syndicate just opened up a whole new can of worms.

"I don't think she's part of it."

Luca said, "Of course you don't want to think she's involved in something like this."

"Okay, but she could be a target of whoever is involved now. If they took out Ralph and tried to take out Jenkins, then maybe they're going to come after Destiny next?" How were they even supposed to figure out if that was the case? "Did Roger say anything to you before I came in?"

"You mean before you barged in to accuse me of smacking him around?"

And why did he look like he thought that was amusing?

Kira blew out a breath. "You think I should have been completely convinced you'd never do something like that?"

"No, because I have done something like that. Many times."

She lifted her hands. "Well then, what's the problem with me asking?"

"Maybe you should tell Destiny you have to go, and we can find somewhere quiet to talk."

Why did she get the feeling he was going to end things between them when they had barely started? "I probably do need to leave. I'm not in the right frame of mind for this, or for a conversation about 'us.'"

Maybe it was because Jordan had put all that other stuff in her head. Added to the exhaustion and having her focus split between the foundation, the emergency department, and Francisco's medical treatment, she got the feeling she wasn't dealing very well with this.

She said, "I had a quiet life before you came along. Everything was fine, and I wasn't this mixed around trying to figure it all out."

He touched her shoulders, a soft smile on his face. "It's okay to need time to process it. I didn't tell you I was coming here, and talking to Roger was a surprise to me. I just jumped on the opportunity when I spotted him."

"I think I need about two months. Does that work for you?"

He squeezed her shoulders gently. "As long as those two months involve coffee dates, movies, and dinner out."

That didn't sound like breaking up at all. That sounded like dating the way normal people did, rather than two people thrown together by circumstances and tackling some dangerous situations.

"Before we leave, you should come with me and talk to Destiny." She lifted her chin. "That way you can get a read on whether or not you think she's a criminal mastermind."

"I never said I thought she was. Right now, there are a lot of possibilities," Luca said.

"Then let's rule one out." She shifted and his hands dropped.

Kira grabbed one, not only because she needed to lead him out to the patio where Destiny was, but also because she liked holding his hand. Working this as a team would be a lot more effective than operating separately.

Surprising each other with a sudden appearance.

Getting the wrong impression.

Jordan's words rolled through her mind again. Her friend had been the person who stood by her in all kinds of tough times. Who convinced her to finally cut ties with the world of covert operations. But Jordan seemed to think that Kira was only in this with Luca to scratch an itch, like she needed to relive the glory days.

She'd even said that Luca wasn't Kira's type.

Maybe Jordan just needed to see for herself how well Kira and Luca fit together. But the comment had taken root in Kira's mind anyway, and when she had seen Luca with Roger, she'd assumed the worst. That he might be everything she'd walked away from.

The kind of person who did whatever it took to get the results, even hurting other people.

She tugged on his hand halfway down the hallway, turned to him, and stopped in one move.

He frowned. "What is it?"

"There isn't really an easy way to tell you this, so I should probably say it. Maybe I should've said it days ago before things got to this point." She ducked her head, not entirely sure how to explain. "I don't like it when people hurt others just to get what they want."

"It's not okay to jump to conclusions rather than trusting someone you already know you can trust." Luca touched his warm palm to the side of her neck, his thumb on her cheek. "But it is okay to apologize for getting the wrong idea, and it's also okay to be a human being with faults and things that trigger you into acting without thinking."

It sounded like he knew what he was talking about, which gave her the courage to explain. "There was a CIA agent who showed up at the refugee camp I was working at. Just after January. It must be nearly four years ago now."

"Just before you quit and came here?"

She nodded, continuing to speak quietly, hoping no one was listening to them. "He said a shipment of medicines was coming in and he needed to look inside the crate in order to intercept it. One of the vials was apparently not the medicine but the prototype for a deadly disease that someone was going to use to destroy a lot of people. I think he was stopping it from being sold to dangerous people."

"Was he legit?"

She nodded. "Yes, but he was also the kind of person who was willing to condemn an entire camp of people with polio to die just so that he could stop one vial from getting through to the bad guys who were buying it."

"In exchange, he might have saved millions of lives."

"We don't know that." She lifted her chin. "What we know is that I was facing a massive outbreak and thousands of people were going to die within a few days. But his mission was more important than their lives, and he was going to delay the shipment until he had orders as to where his vial was going next."

Luca's expression hardened. "What happened?"

"I refused to let him look in the containers before I took the medicine out so that I could begin distributing it. He didn't like that, and we fought about it. In the end, I was on my back and he was strangling me." She closed her eyes, still able to see his face above hers. Those eyes so set on killing her. "I managed to reach a knife, and I stabbed him before he could kill me."

"He died?"

"I murdered a foreign agent and then completed his mission for him—but it was too late for a lot of the people. Some were saved, but far too many didn't make it."

"So you quit and came here?"

She nodded, swallowing against the lump in her throat. "I can't work with people who are willing to trade others' lives like that."

"He would have killed you to complete his mission."

"And I had to kill him to complete mine." To do the job she was there to do—as a doctor.

"But in the end, you did both of your jobs."

Kira nodded.

"He knew what he was getting into. He went there prepared to die and also prepared to kill to get it done. I'm glad it was him and not you." Luca winced. "Maybe that makes me a terrible person, but you saved more lives with your actions than he would have. I'm guessing he wasn't going to listen to an agreement where you both got what you wanted."

"I tried." She shook her head, tears gathering in her eyes. "He didn't want to listen. He didn't care about those people at all."

"So you gave up covert work and started over."

She said, "I don't want to start doing it again. But I know it's what you do."

"Seems to me like if you work with me for a little while, you'll realize my tactics are a whole lot different than that guy's. Not just because this is local investigations and if I break the law, I'll go to jail. But I'm not going to ask you to do it if you don't want to."

She wanted to trust this. To get to know him better so that she had evidence for her belief in him. Not just blind faith. "Maybe I should take a couple of weeks off from the emergency department and do that."

"If you're going to take a vacation, we should go somewhere more exciting than wherever I'm working." He leaned in and kissed her cheek. "But thank you for telling me."

She nodded, exhausted from having to relive the memories again. Even if it was only a quick conversation, the whole thing seemed to weigh down her heart all over again. Making her feel heavy in ways she didn't like. But God had asked her to carry these things.

It wasn't as if she could just forget them all or watch them get washed away.

"I still think you should meet Destiny."

Luca said, "We can give her our regards and then go somewhere else. Maybe get some dinner and talk through everything."

She wasn't sure she was ready to talk about *everything*, but she understood what he meant. "Dinner sounds good, as long as we can check on my patient before we go."

He squeezed her hand, taking it and leading her through the doorway into the expansive dining room filled with people here to remember Ralph Rousseau.

It seemed as if any of them could be a suspect. In fact, everyone involved in the Shadow Syndicate might be here in this house right now.

And she had no idea who they were.

The idea made her want to go home, get under the covers, and hide away from the world until it was all over. When she had become a complete coward, she didn't know. Or maybe it was a completely normal reaction to the life she'd lived.

Jordan was wrong. Kira wasn't looking to relive her glory days—unless it involved sneaking into an office and copying files on a computer.

And Luca was exactly her type.

FIFTEEN

WELL? DO YOU THINK DESTINY IS A CRIMINAL mastermind?"

Luca didn't look at her. There was a loaded question if ever he'd heard one.

Luca figured it had a whole lot to do with the story she'd felt the need to share with him. Plus other parts of her background that she hadn't mentioned. Things he needed to discover as they got closer.

When he added it all up, they hadn't actually spent that much time together over the past week or so since they'd met again. There would be more to discover about her. Good and bad. Same with him. What would tell him their relationship could stand the test of time was how they both dealt with those things they'd rather change about the other person, and the ways they agreed to grow together. To always keep striving to make the best of themselves and the relationship.

From what he'd been taught since he'd become a believer, the goal of a Christian was to be more like Christ. Doing that meant he couldn't stay the way he was for the rest of his life. He needed to find ways to allow God to change him and grow him.

Human relationships were the same. Marriages, especially.

No one wanted to wake up forty years later and realize they were married to the exact same person they'd said I do to all those years ago. Life would change who they were in unexpected ways as they shared the losses and everything gained in living together for years. Spending those years with each other meant they wouldn't—or shouldn't—stay the same person.

"Is this a trick question?" He held open the side door of the hospital and she stepped through.

She glanced at him. "Maybe I'm being defensive, but if I'm wrong about her, then maybe I'm a terrible judge of character about everyone."

Luca said, "Then I have to argue that you're actually an excellent judge of character." Because otherwise, she might be wrong about him.

"And that would mean Destiny isn't involved in any of this." Kira seemed satisfied by that logic.

Luca decided then that she didn't need to know everything he was working on or who he was investigating. This sweet woman with her high-stress job and her quiet personal life didn't need to know all the dark secrets this city had to offer.

Again, he felt that protectiveness in him surge up.

Not that he wanted to secure her somewhere, wrapped up in layers of protection—or cotton wool—but he did want to keep her safe. To protect her from anything dangerous in the world.

She had faced down some of the worst kinds of people and gone head-to-head with them, even though he got the feeling it wasn't in her nature. Whatever had made her agree to pass information back to her government in the first place hadn't lasted through an entire career. She'd done what it took to protect her heart from that life and got out.

Walking away from the Army had been one of the best things for his team. They had grown so much closer through the handful of years since, when everyone in their lives thought they were dead.

She had done it while living here all alone.

They stepped off the elevator and turned the corner into the hallway, where Hammer sat outside Francisco's room. His friend looked up, unsurprised, as Luca had texted him so he knew to expect them. As soon as they were done here, they were going to Kira's home so she could change. After that, he wanted to show her his cabin in the foothills of the mountains to the west of the city. Maybe cook her a steak over the grill. Sit on the back deck and watch the sunset, forgetting about all the danger and intrigue in town. Or this shadow syndicate that was working behind the scenes.

He wanted some time with Kira. No stress, no bad guys. Just the two of them, relaxing and eating dinner together.

He should tell her about his father and his brother. Maybe she would tell him about her family.

"It's been all quiet here," Hammer said.

Luca held out his hand and they shook. "I appreciate you doing this."

"As if you had to ask."

Kira stayed beside Luca rather than going into the hospital room. "Why do you say that?"

Luca shifted, turning toward her and trying to formulate an answer that wouldn't sound like tooting his own horn.

Before he could explain, Hammer said, "Because Saxon has saved my life more times than I can count. It was high time I repaid the favor."

As if it wasn't a paying gig. "And you'll get to take your wife and son on vacation."

Hammer grinned. "That's a bonus. She's pretty excited about it, actually."

Kira smiled at him.

Hammer said, "She asked me to tell the two of you she wants to have you over for dinner. Nothing fancy, probably just a nice home-cooked meal. Whenever the two of you have a break in your schedule and we can get it on the calendar."

"I would love that." Kira glanced at Luca. "What do you say?"

The idea of Kira coming over and spending time with him at the Wallace household made the relationship between them sound far more settled than it was. A whole lot more real.

"You look scared." Kira glanced at Hammer. "I scared him off."

Hammer said, "He should be scared. It keeps a man honest."

Kira frowned.

Luca shook his head at this ridiculous conversation. "I'm not scared. I'm just trying to figure out when on earth I'll have a break in my calendar."

"You have to do this thing called 'taking a break.'" Hammer made quote marks with his fingers.

"Maybe you need to explain it to both of us." She pointed over her shoulder with her thumb. "But I'm going to check on the patient first."

"Sounds good." Hammer nodded. "It's been quiet around here since Dr. Torres headed out."

She flinched. "He's not supposed to leave."

Kira whirled to the door and flung it open. She rushed to Francisco's bedside and started talking to him in a soothing tone. But Luca couldn't hear what she was saying to the patient. A second later, the door clicked shut.

Luca turned to Hammer. "How long ago did he take off?"

Hammer shrugged. "Maybe half an hour. He told me he'd cleared it with you guys."

"He didn't say anything to us." Luca scratched his jaw. "Did he say where he was going?"

"Nope." Hammer looked up and down the hallway, assessing for threats. "What do we do?"

"Maybe the Marshals can find his GPS location from his phone. I'll call Butler, and if they don't have access, I'll head over to his home." Luca needed ideas. And leads.

The doctor may have just rushed out for an appointment. Or run home to take a shower. There could be any number of explanations, but there could also be one that would prove to be the worst-case scenario. At least Francisco was alive in that hospital bed, because this was a serious breach of security.

Luca paced down the hall and called Butler, but the guy didn't pick up. He left a message explaining what'd happened and asking for the guy to run Torres's location and call Luca back.

As he hung up, Kira emerged from the room.

"Is Francisco okay?"

She nodded. "He's actually doing remarkably well following the procedure. If he stays like this, there will be no need for him to be here after tomorrow morning. He even said I don't need to stay, and I'm inclined to agree. But not for long."

"Okay." Luca blew out a breath. "Let's go track down Dr. Torres and find out why he left. I don't like this at all."

"Me neither," Kira said. "But we should swing by my place so I can change first. It's close by, and I don't want to be wearing a dress and heels if something happens."

Luca nodded. "That might give Deputy Marshal Butler time to call me back."

But he didn't.

The call came from Renegade Correctional Facility, and Luca had to agree to accept the charges.

He disconnected the Bluetooth from his phone and put the

cell to his ear, knowing exactly who was calling. "How do you like your new place?"

"Are you kidding me?" Amir huffed over the phone line. "Care to tell me why I'm suddenly in Colorado?"

"I needed a favor, and I figured you could use some goodwill for the parole board."

Kira had told him her dark secret—the reason why she'd quit the work she'd been doing overseas. It was past time for him to tell her about his family. The reason he hadn't settled down before with someone else. And, until he'd met her, hadn't had any plans to.

"What's the favor?"

He explained who Jenkins was and the connection to Hammer. "Someone tried to kill him."

"Does he want protection?"

"No," Luca said. "But he needs it."

"Great. So protect him but don't make it look like I'm looking out for him?"

"The guy who tried to kill him is in solitary. Just keep an eye out for anyone else who might have been persuaded to try and take his life."

Kira glanced over at him but didn't say anything.

"And this is going to help me with the parole board how?"

"It's called a good deed. The police here know what's going on. I know a detective who can put in a good word for you if you help us with the investigation."

"I think I just graduated to snitch."

"That's not what I'm asking from you. Just try and keep the guy safe."

"I'm so glad you're worried about my well-being. Sure, I'll keep this lowlife who beats on his family safe. No problem." Amir hung up the phone.

Luca tossed his cell in the cupholder. "My brother. The newest inmate in Renegade Correctional Facility." He pulled over to the curb outside Dr. Torres's house and turned to her. "He was in jail the weekend I graduated high school. No one I knew showed up to the ceremony."

But he wasn't telling her this sob story to get her sympathy. It was what it was.

"I never met my mom and don't have the first clue how to find her, if I even wanted to. Which I don't." The words were coming out quickly now that he'd started talking. "Amir's three years older, and he got into the wrong crowd. I saw everything he was doing and tried to make better choices, but life is life. The day after I graduated, I walked into the Army recruiting office. The rest, as they say, is history."

But it wasn't all of it.

"I'm sorry you had to do that alone. It should be a celebration with your family."

Luca shrugged. "My father died two years before I finished high school, and Amir got custody of me after. For all the good it did. In that community? We were pegged as terrorists by everyone, all because of a war going on in a country we'd never been to. A war that had nothing to do with us."

She nodded. "I understand."

"It was the middle of the night. The FBI kicked the door in and raided our apartment. Someone had put money in an account that had my father's name on it, but he swore he had no idea where it came from. The funds had come from accounts connected to ISIS, and they said my father had researched training camps on the computer. They let him go a couple of weeks later, but he was never the same." Luca had to swallow so he could continue. "He lost his business. No one in the neighborhood would speak to him. He killed himself about a month after."

A tear spilled from the corner of Kira's eye. Luca swiped it away with his thumb.

"I'm so sorry."

He tried to smile. "Thank you."

He looked out her window at the house, wanting to get to work rather than dwell on a past he couldn't change. "This place looks like it belongs in Destiny's neighborhood."

"South Eagle is a little older, but it isn't any less glamorous than North Eagle." She pushed the door open, swiping her cheeks like she was trying to hide her reaction from him. "There are a lot of houses over a million dollars in both areas."

"Probably because they all have this incredible view of the mountains." He glanced at her across the hood of his truck and saw her nod. Then he spotted what was wrong. "The front door is open. Maybe you should stay in the truck."

"If he's hurt, you'll want me with you inside the house."

"Fine," Luca said. "You can stay behind me."

"Because of what I said at Destiny's? Because that guy nearly killed me and so I might not be able to defend myself? Is that what you think?" She looked ready to cry again, but it had been an emotional day, and she was in need of rest.

"It's so that I can point my gun at the bad guys instead of you."

"Oh."

Luca touched his lips to hers quickly, wanting to linger but knowing they didn't have time. He wasn't even sure they were safe right here. He turned back to the house, and she squeezed his side from behind him. That was all the reassurance she gave him that she understood what he'd said.

He stepped into the house first, easing the front door open with his gun.

"Should we call 911?" Kira whispered.

"We will. But I want to look around first."

The issue of whether or not he believed the police in Renegade were corrupt didn't need to come up now. But they weren't in Detective Martinelli's jurisdiction here. This part of the city was covered by a different police station, and the responding officers would come from there. Detective Martinelli might not be able to smooth out any issues they ran into—or stop another officer from implicating them.

Because the fact was that with all the investigation and snooping they'd been doing into the syndicate, there was no way Luca and Kira could remain under the radar. Eventually someone would come gunning for them because they got too close to the truth.

Luca had her wait by the door while he searched the house.

When he came back to her, he said, "Torres isn't here, but you should take a look at what I found."

"In here." Luca led her to a small study, an interior door open at the far end. He walked her to the door and stood to the side to let her go in.

"You were going to show me this office? It looks like everything Dr. Torres owns has been tossed from its place and onto the floor."

The entire house looked like this. It was one of the few things that could have distracted her from the fact that she'd told Luca the worst part of her history. In response, he had absorbed the news, deciding that getting to know each other better and spending even more time together was obviously the answer.

Maybe she hadn't expected him to dump her then and there, but it was like her actions didn't even faze him.

Then he'd reciprocated by telling her the darkest part of *his* story.

She couldn't believe the racial profiling he'd endured.

Okay, so maybe she *could* believe it. But the idea they'd been falsely accused of a connection to terrorists that had his father seeing no other way out but taking his own life was beyond tragic. It had torn their family apart.

"Someone definitely broke in and tossed the place looking for something." Luca waved her over to the open doorway. "But maybe they didn't realize what they'd found."

She frowned and stepped into the smaller room, barely bigger than a closet. Someone had drawn all over the walls in permanent marker. To anyone else it would've probably looked like the scribbles of somebody who might need the benefit of a ninety-day psych hold.

"Do you know what this is?"

She looked around, scanning the formulas and notes. Tracking the progression of Torres's work to the inevitable breakthrough. "If they were looking for this, they probably just took pictures of it."

"Maybe they just took him." Luca stayed by the door. "I know there are people in the world who will traffic someone with this kind of skill. A person who can come up with a unique formula they can exploit, and then they sell whoever it is to the highest bidder. Someone who will force them to create another drug or biological weapon for them."

That was incredibly specific, leading her to believe this wasn't just knowledge but something he had experienced personally. "If Dr. Torres isn't here, that doesn't mean he's in danger. Or that he got kidnapped. Maybe he saw them coming and ran."

"Unless he's already at the police station telling them what happened, we have to assume that he's in danger. At the very least, he might be on the run." Luca shifted away from the door. "I need to look around some more and check to make sure he doesn't have security cameras we can take a look at."

Kira looked back at the walls. "This isn't what he was working on for Francisco. It's something else entirely. But I would need some time to figure out precisely what everything means."

It almost looked like a kind of chemical formula. But she didn't know what he was using for the code that kept the substances a secret from her. Considering someone had broken in and ransacked his house, Torres might have been clever to keep his work a secret by making the compounds a code only he knew.

She shook her head and muttered to herself, "What on earth was he doing?"

"I'd love to know who he was doing it for," Luca said. "Or who he might've sold this formula to."

He ducked out of the room. Kira spent a few more minutes looking at the equations on the walls, catching places where Torres had run into a block that meant his formula wouldn't work. On more than one occasion, he'd backtracked and chosen a different direction. Some of them involving radical leaps she wasn't sure she would have made.

Whatever he was working on, it was far beyond her scope of practice as the head of an emergency department. So much of what she did was routine illnesses and injuries. Broken arms and stomach bugs. She'd considered that to be a good thing as well as bad, but this wasn't the kind of break from monotony that she was looking for. Kira had no desire to get into creating new drugs or chemical compounds.

If she'd known about this when she'd been trying to get information from Dr. Torres, she could have asked him about it. The fact the man kept so much to himself didn't bode well in a city where anything could be going on.

She went back to the study, looking around at the papers. Whoever had been searching here would have taken all of this if it were relevant. But still . . . She crouched and lifted a paper from the floor. Who printed out their cell phone bill these days?

"Find something?"

She shook her head and dropped the paper. "Do I need to wipe my prints from all of this?" She hadn't touched much, but it would be clear that she'd been here.

"When the police get here, I'm going to inform them that we

looked around. It's natural to come inside and walk through the house when you're trying to find someone you believe is in danger."

"Okay." That made sense.

She didn't want to feel out of her depth, but this was Luca's world, not hers. Kira had spent years avoiding anything about her past. Now that it was standing in front of her, she was having a hard time knitting their worlds together. Things were colliding inside her heart and mind in ways she hadn't expected, leading her to almost take out her frustration on him.

And yet he'd made no attempt to separate himself from her.

"I didn't even realize until now . . ." She stopped, unsure she even wanted to say it. Hadn't been planning to.

"What didn't you realize?" He had his phone out, probably ready to call the police and inform them what had happened.

"That I've been avoiding everything I was for the past few years. Working here and having a quiet life. Maybe I was just burying my head in the sand and trying to forget who I was."

"I can tell you over and over that you didn't do anything wrong, but you're the one who's going to have to believe it."

This was probably something that would be far better to unpack with a psychologist rather than the guy she liked a whole lot.

"Change is always an upset to your life, no matter if it's good or bad. Some people love when change happens, and others are surprised by it." Luca eased closer and touched his lips to hers in a sweet, quick kiss. "I happen to like surprises."

"I don't think I like surprises, but I did like you bringing over breakfast." She didn't want to make it sound like he always had to do things for her, so she said, "Next time, I'll bring the food. I should make you my chana masala."

"It's a date." He smiled gently. "I'm going to call the cops and report this. Someone needs to be looking for Dr. Torres."

Kira wandered through the house, confirming there was no one inside. It seemed strange to move through someone else's personal space when they hadn't invited her to be here. She wouldn't want someone walking like this through her house, but taking a moment to process her thoughts was something she needed right now.

As she walked back down the stairs, her phone rang, and Jordan's name showed up on the screen. "What's up?"

Two phone calls in one day was more than unusual.

"Figured you'd want a heads-up. Someone is snooping around in your bank accounts, probably trying to dig up information on you."

Kira frowned. "Luca's friend is supposed to be doing that on the foundation."

"Well, someone is checking out everyone, and you're included." Jordan went quiet for a second. "I've gotta go. The boss is headed this way."

The call ended.

She headed down the stairs and found Luca by the door. Before she could ask him why Jamie was looking through her bank accounts, he said, "The police are on their way, and Hammer just called me. The Marshals showed up and whisked Francisco away. He said Butler heard that Torres was gone, and told him what you said about Francisco's condition being good." Luca shrugged. "I guess they decided to pull the plug on the operation."

"Francisco wasn't nearly strong enough to be moved." She shook her head. "They should have called me and asked for permission to do that."

"They're the federal government." He shrugged. "Do they ask for permission?"

Given his history, she figured that was a loaded question.

"Maybe not, but a little professional courtesy wouldn't go amiss. Kind of like not informing someone you're snooping through their bank accounts. I'm guessing you're probably trying to find out if I'm connected to any of this?"

Luca said, "How did you find out someone is looking through your bank accounts?"

"Isn't that what your friend does?"

"She's looking into the foundation. She'd only be looking at your accounts if that's where her donation money went."

"I'm not trying to jump to conclusions. It might not be your friend doing it, but someone is rooting around in my personal business." She had worked hard to secure herself a nest egg. And the way the world was these days made it hard to trust that any of it was completely secure. "Jordan just told me. She keeps an eye on all my stuff from her CIA computer."

"Could she tell who's doing it?"

"She had to go. But hopefully I'll find out more later." Kira sent her a text. "I'm sure she'll get back to me when she's able to."

"How about you stick with me right now? Then you'll know for sure that there's at least someone in your life that you can trust a hundred percent."

Kira wasn't sure she needed more evidence to be convinced that was true. She already believed it. But if she was with him, then she wouldn't be at home alone, worrying that, at any moment, someone was going to break the door down and toss her stuff all over the place . . .

Then kidnap *her*.

"Okay," Kira said. "It seems like it's probably safe for me if I'm standing next to you."

"I can't promise nothing's going to happen. But we're going to look for Dr. Torres, and if anything does happen, you can be certain I'll do what it takes to keep you safe."

"Nothing about any of this makes any sense. Least of all you."

Luca slid his arms around her and tugged her to him, hugging her in a way that made her feel safer than she'd felt in a long time. Smiling at her.

That was how the two uniformed officers found them.

SIXTEEN

LUCA LAID HIS BELONGINGS IN THE PLASTIC TRAY and pushed it into the scanner just before nine a.m. The first time they'd been allowed to speak with Jenkins, and they'd had to wait two days for permission.

He walked through the metal detector at Renegade Correctional, and the officer waved him forward.

"You're good."

Luca nodded to him. "Thanks."

The officer on the other side of the scanner took Luca's bin of personal belongings and slid them onto a wire shelving unit behind him.

Most of the police department was on the lookout for Dr. Torres, as well as still debating the issue of whether he'd been kidnapped or was simply missing. No one at the police department wanted to punt the case to the FBI office in town, but if there had been a kidnapping, that might prove necessary.

He turned to Kira, who had just been waved through the scanner. She watched her belongings get transferred to the shelf.

Luca said, "You get them back when you leave."

He had explained a little bit about how it worked to go into the prison and the restrictions on what they could take with them. Since they were only here to speak with Jenkins, they didn't need any files or personal items.

"I've never been in here before." She glanced around, assessing the white-walled lobby and the handful of corrections officers mingling outside the security office to the left.

Ahead of them was a long hallway sectioned off by gates that could only be opened by somebody in the security office releasing the lock.

"Are you nervous?"

She smiled at him, looking a little tentative. "It's just new."

"You've faced worse than this."

"And lived to tell about it. Except not, because it was classified."

Put the woman in the middle of a refugee camp under fire, in the middle of disease outbreaks, or in the hospital in Renegade, and she rose to the occasion. With medicine, she knew what she was doing. She could take charge, and everything she did was with confidence.

Outside of her work in the emergency department, it seemed like she wasn't convinced she could handle much else. Luca didn't know if that was true. He figured she could withstand a whole lot more than she knew. But maybe she simply didn't want to.

A highly trained covert operative had nearly killed her. Kira had ended his life in self-defense and saved a lot of people in the process. That wasn't the work of a woman who couldn't handle a dangerous job.

He understood the need to take a break, recharge, and heal from burnout. It seemed more like someone had convinced her that she had to keep everything small and not step out of her comfort zone in order to be safe. Trusting herself would go a long way to proving what she could do. Luca could only do so much to convince her that she was stronger than she knew. It seemed more like God needed to take the fear and change her heart for her to live with boldness.

"This way." One of the officers waved them to the door. "Jenkins is already waiting for you."

They were buzzed through the gate and entered the hallway, going all the way to the last interview room. But Luca could still see the door to the security office at the end of the hall. Not to mention all the cameras and other measures to keep visitors safe and inmates from escaping.

The officer pulled the door open. "I'll be out here."

Jenkins sat at the table, wearing the same orange jumpsuit and shackled to the floor. He was upright, but seriously pale. The former mayor glanced between the two of them as if nothing was wrong, like he hadn't been stabbed a week ago. "You brought me a friend?"

Kira tried to pull out one of the chairs, but it was bolted to the floor. "There's no call for being disgusting."

Luca sat beside her. "We needed to talk to you. If you give us the answers we want, we'll get out of your hair and you can go back to . . . whatever it was you were doing."

"Stay as long as you like." Jenkins sat back in the chair. "My social calendar is wide open."

"What do you know about Dr. Torres?"

Jenkins shrugged. "Who's that?"

"You know who he is," Luca said. "The guy has been prominent in Renegade society for years, and he's well known for his medical research."

"I was in real estate. Not all that hospital stuff."

"Turns out he's also in real estate. The guy has property all over the city, commercial and residential. I'm really surprised you didn't bump into each other."

Kira laced her fingers together in her lap. "I'm surprised they didn't bid against each other."

Jenkins's expression shifted, his lips curling into a sneer for a second, then it was gone. "Fine, I hated the guy with the fire of a thousand suns. So what?"

Luca rested one forearm on the table. "Someone ransacked his house, and now he's missing."

"Well, I didn't do it. I've been in here the whole time." Jenkins seemed to find that hilarious.

"But you haven't been here the whole time," Kira pointed out. "You were in the hospital after you got injured."

Jenkins leaned forward slightly. "You mean after someone tried to kill me?"

"Stuart Parker is in solitary, and you're back here acting like nothing ever happened," Luca said. "Why don't you tell me who would pay someone to try and kill you? Then we can put a stop to it."

"You want to keep me safe. That's so nice of you."

"I don't want Mack to lose his father," Luca said. "What happens between the two of you is up to you."

"Don't hold your breath waiting for me to see the light."

Luca's brother had told him that exact thing, but the truth was, he would always want the best for Amir. Not just his help. Now that Luca had found the peace that came from a relationship with Jesus, he wanted that for his brother as well. Amir would still have to serve out his sentence, but redemption happened in the heart, and freedom came in all kinds of ways.

"Why'd you tell me that Ralph Rousseau was the head of the Shadow Syndicate?"

Jenkins said, "Because he is."

"Then it's *was,* because he's dead now." Luca gave him a second to absorb that, then said, "Someone tried to kill you, and they succeeded in killing Ralph. It doesn't make any sense that he would be targeted if he's the head of the Shadow Syndicate."

Jenkins just stared at them. Probably trying to figure out what was going on as much as Luca.

"Who targeted you?"

"If I knew that," Jenkins said, "they'd be dead."

"This is bigger than you. It's bigger than your scheme that you had going on, trying to grab up land for the mineral rights."

Kira shifted in her seat and glanced at him. "Minerals like lithium."

"What is it?" Luca asked her.

She shook her head. "I'll tell you later." Then she looked at Jenkins. "What do you want with all that lithium? Where was it going?"

The skin around Jenkins's eyes contracted.

Luca said, "Who wanted to buy it from you?"

Jenkins leaned forward. "Ralph Rousseau."

"Is that the truth?" Was this guy purposely misleading him, or did he really believe what he was saying?

If their business about mineral rights was the basis for Jenkins's assumption that Ralph was the head of the Shadow Syndicate, then he could be wrong about that. Ralph was far more likely just another middleman doing their bidding. Maybe neither of them knew who was in charge of the syndicate.

This entire thing could be nothing but hearsay, pointing fingers.

Meanwhile, it felt like whoever was in charge of the Shadow Syndicate was laughing, thinking they were safe from the investigation.

"Doesn't matter now. He's dead. I'll be dead pretty soon." Jenkins shrugged.

"The police and corrections officers are doing what they can to keep you safe." Luca wasn't sure they could do more than that. No one was going to leave Jenkins unprotected, but the truth was that he was living with the consequences of his choices.

Jenkins shook his head. "Whatever."

"It would help if you knew who was calling the shots. I could pass that information to the police, and they can help you."

"I told you what I know, and I was nearly killed for it. I'm not about to tell you anything else, or I'm likely to end up hanging by a noose in my cell."

Luca leaned forward a little. "Mack deserves to have a father who is alive and at least trying to do the right thing for once."

"Sounds like work. Better to die a martyr and let the kid move on with his life."

"That's what you want?" Kira said. "I know Mack well enough that he's told me stories about Hammer and the rest of the Trouble Boys. All the adventures they got up to, fighting wildfires and saving the world. But do you know what? He didn't once mention you."

Mack hadn't mentioned his father because he didn't want to face the reality of who his dad was. Or so Luca presumed. The kid didn't want to deal with the fact that he loved his father but the old man continually hurt all of them. Emotionally and physically.

In a lot of ways, Mack was similar to Kira. Instead of facing the fear, he'd hidden away and buried his head in the sand. Now he was having to face the reality of who his father was. But in the middle of that, he'd chosen to make a life for himself and find a career he could love. Focusing on work seemed to be a common tactic between Kira and Mack, which was probably why they got along.

Luca's tendency was to do whatever job was in front of him, and it had worked for him for a long time. Going from occupation to occupation. From the military to fighting wildfires. Sure, there was a theme, but he appreciated change more than he liked one particular type of work. He enjoyed being an investigator but wasn't sure he wanted to do that forever. Once they took down the syndicate, he would probably find something new to do.

"My family," Jenkins said, "my business. Not yours."

"Tell me what the lithium was for," Kira said.

Luca waited for an answer, proud of her that she seemed to have figured something out—maybe the formulas on the walls at Dr. Torres's house.

Before Jenkins could say anything, a commotion erupted in the hallway. Through the window in the door, he saw the officer outside their room collapse.

Another officer raced toward him from down the hall. "Get a medic!" The yell sounded muffled and faraway, barely audible through the thick door and reinforced glass.

Kira jumped up and opened the door. "I'm a doctor. What is it?"

The door clicked closed, plunging the room back into quiet. Luca got up to watch for a second through the window, then turned back and faced Jenkins. "The operation you were running wasn't just about you. It was about providing the Shadow Syndicate with minerals they needed to make something. What was it? A drug, or some other kind of substance?"

"I told you everything I know. There's nothing more for me to say."

Luca stared at him, realizing from Jenkins's expression that he wasn't going to get anything else. If the man knew who might've taken Torres, he certainly wasn't going to share. "One day I hope you can find it in you to give Mack what he's looking for."

"And what is that?"

"I can't answer that question for you," Luca said, "but I can tell you that it's worth your time to figure it out."

He turned to the door and looked through the window to find the hallway empty.

Luca grabbed the handle, and the door clicked. No, everything around him clicked, and the room plunged into darkness.

He pulled down the handle, but it was locked.

———————

All the lights in the infirmary went out. Kira had seen enough when they entered to know it was empty and there were maybe two steps to the closest bed. "Let's lay him down."

Despite the fact it was almost pitch black, with only an emergency exit light above the door in one corner still lit up, she found her way. She and the man who'd been helping her carry the downed officer laid him onto the hospital bed.

"We need lights." Without electricity, there wasn't much she could do for a man who had suddenly suffered a heart attack. She searched for the man's pulse with her fingertips. "Do you know how to do CPR?"

Right now, she didn't even know where the other officer had gone or if he was standing right next to her. It was too dark to see.

A flashlight flicked on over on the other side of the bed, then swung down at the man on the bed. The metal casing cracked against his skull.

Kira screamed. "What are you doing?"

Someone's arms snaked around her, grasping her tight across her hips and across her shoulders. A bigger person, wider and stronger. An inmate she hadn't seen. And there was nothing she could do.

Except kick her legs and scream.

She let the worst sound she could conjure up escape from her mouth and caught his shin with the heel of her shoe, wishing she wasn't wearing canvas shoes and jeans right now. But she'd dressed for a trip to the prison, unsure what it was going to be like here. She'd decided the goal was to keep from drawing attention to herself. But somehow, that had completely backfired.

"Shut up." The man holding her breathed against her ear.

She didn't stop squirming.

He took a step back and to the side, then swung her around and slammed her into a metal storage cabinet. Her head glanced off the door—and left a dent behind, she was pretty sure. Only in the light would she be able to tell what damage had been done. He didn't let go.

Then he tossed her onto the floor.

Her knee slammed down on the floor first, and she managed to catch herself with her hands. Pain ricocheted through her. But this wasn't the time to be distracted by anything. She had to keep her wits about her.

Kira tried to sound steady. "What are you doing?"

The officer. He'd killed that man—his colleague.

She could still barely see, what with most of the room in darkness. Just that murderous flashlight in the hand of a prison guard. The kind of person who attempted murder in the dark so that no one could ever prove it was he who'd done the deed.

Just moments ago, she'd been riding the high of figuring out Torres's formula. Her organic chemistry was a little rusty, but she'd worked out that lithium could be used in the way his formula had indicated. The one he'd written all over the walls of that room in his house.

Combining elements to create recreational drugs.

The lights flickered and came back on.

Two inmates stood to the left, a prison guard on the other side of the bed. It was the guard who held the heavy flashlight in his hand.

She gasped, lifting her chin and trying to sound tough. "You killed him."

The officer who had collapsed when his heart suddenly stopped beating lay on the bed with a deadly head wound. From the blunt force trauma of being hit by a man who was supposed to be his colleague. The murderer said nothing. The guy had to be about forty and wore a wedding ring. His hair was receding, giving him a high forehead and making his eyes look tiny.

He held the now dented flashlight in his hand still.

The inmates turned to her, and one said, "Looks like everything is going according to plan."

It was the cartel guy they had arrested after Rousseau was killed in the hospital—the man Roger had been speaking with at the gala, who claimed to know nothing about what was going on. If he was still here awaiting trial, then he hadn't been granted bail at his arraignment. The judge must have thought he was a flight risk.

Unfortunately for her, it turned out this man came with a lot of risk. The kind where a prison dissolved into chaos.

Kira curled her legs up in front of her, trying to protect herself. But what could she do against these men?

The other man turned, his orange jumpsuit too tight around his stomach.

She gasped again. "You."

Frankie's boyfriend, Stuart Parker.

He was supposed to be in solitary. How was he . . . ? Right, the murderous prison guard.

This man had made Frankie's life a misery until she needed to seek shelter where she could be safe. Then Stuart had followed Kira to her car and demanded to know where Frankie was. In prison, he'd stabbed Jenkins and put him in the hospital.

So had he been in all of this from the beginning, or did he get paid for that attempt on Jenkins?

He came toward her and crouched, a deadly smile on his face. "Welcome to the party." His brows rose. "I didn't know you were here, but when I saw you? Surprise." He muttered a curse. "Now you get to be part of all the fun."

Kira shivered.

"The system will be rebooting in a second," the guard who had killed his colleague said. "That means we only have a few minutes."

Stuart whirled around to him. "I know what that means. This whole thing was *my* plan."

"Just so long as I get paid."

Stuart motioned to the dead man on the hospital bed. "You ain't getting his share. So you can forget about that. You did one job, you get one split."

Kira glanced at the cartel guy, trying to keep an eye on all of them at the same time. He had a calculating look on his face. Dark hair and dark eyes, far too many tattoos on his arms that might have deadly meaning. Not that she had anything against tattoos. But on him, they were menacing. Almost like another weapon.

The fear she'd felt when that covert agent was on top of her, his hands around her neck, squeezing the life out of her, rushed back up to swallow her like a king tide. There was nothing she could do about it, and in the end, she would drown under the weight of it. Fear would keep her from moving. Keep her from saying anything.

Fear would keep her from living if she let it.

God, help me. She was so out of her depth that she had no idea what to do.

Stuart said, "Let's go." He grabbed her arm and hauled her to her feet. "Jenkins needs to be dead before the system comes back online."

He'd said this was his plan, and it must have taken some coordination to get the cartel guy and the officer to cooperate. They must have given the officer something to cause his heart to stop—possibly as a result of an underlying condition. Maybe they'd done something to his medication.

Her mind wanted to assess all the symptoms like she was trying to diagnose a disease. But how did that help her figure out what to do? She would be left floundering with no way to protect herself. Swept along by more of that fear and the tide of their intentions.

The cartel guy opened the door and peered out, looking both ways. "I see someone. It's that new guy."

Stuart shook her arm. "Maybe you know him. He's one of your people."

She had no idea what he was talking about. "Excuse me?"

"You know, Middle Eastern or whatever."

She hissed a breath in through her teeth.

"I'm sorry, did you find that offensive?" He laughed. "Maybe you shouldn't be so sensitive all the time. It's not like I meant anything by it." He was still laughing.

Kira kept her thoughts to herself. Even asking him who had paid them to do this likely wouldn't yield any results. They might be planning to kill her, and she wouldn't have anyone to tell what she knew. Or she was going to be used as leverage. Traded for their freedom after talks with some kind of hostage negotiator. Either way, she didn't figure she had much time left.

Luca was in the prison as well, back in that room with Jenkins. Would they kill him too? There were officers on staff whose job it was to respond to incidents like this. Surely they were gearing up right now, having realized what had happened—that the staff was no longer in control of this section of the facility.

Any minute now, they would rush in and take these guys down, sweeping her to safety. That, or Luca would show up and overpower them.

If no one came to rescue her, then she didn't like her chances of survival.

It might be up to her.

Hope was a flighty thing, disappearing before she could grasp hold of it. For so long, she'd only had herself to rely on. In the end, that might have saved her life, but she had taken one as well. She hadn't been able to do her job as a doctor the way she wanted to because she'd been working covert ops for the government. In the end, everything had melded together, and she'd realized she needed a simple life.

A job. Margins in her life for relationships and hobbies.

But she'd come here and retreated from everything except her occupation. At the hospital, she was the doctor she needed to be, but outside that, she hadn't filled her spare time with much of anything.

She'd lived a Christian life, someone saved from her sins.

But not saved from herself.

From the guilt and shame she carried. As if she didn't believe that God could wash *all* of it away. That she had to carry the burden, even after He'd taken her sin.

Around the same time she'd been offered a board position with the foundation, she had met Luca. Even if Destiny's foundation didn't turn out to be a total sham, Kira would still rather spend her time with Luca.

Who else in the world would understand who she was to the extent that he did?

It wasn't even really about their shared skin color. They weren't from the same country, but he had seen the places she'd lived. He had walked through those same situations and done it trying to help people live free and save lives.

He was even doing it here, something she was immensely proud of him for.

Kira wanted the chance to be proud of herself for facing her fear and choosing to act anyway. To live her life to the fullest. But she didn't know how to reach out and grab it. To accept that God had washed away everything and she didn't have to carry the past around like a burden anymore.

Did she wait for rescue, or figure out how to fight back?

"Okay, let's go." The cartel guy ducked out of the room.

Stuart followed him, holding tight to her arm so that she discovered a new way she could empathize with the victims of domestic violence. She'd understood the pain involved before. But now she knew exactly what it felt like.

"You're hurting me." She looked at him. "Just leave me back there in the infirmary and do what you need to do. I won't say anything."

He didn't stop dragging her down the hall, the four of them making short work of the distance. She needed to find a way to slow them down.

He grinned, and his rank breath brushed her face. "You won't wanna be in there when we let everyone loose."

Her stomach flipped over in her midsection. "What do you mean—"

"Shut it."

The officer rushed ahead of them. "Stay right here. Wait till I say." He ducked around the corner, and Kira heard his boots squeak on the floor. He was running.

The cartel guy looked at the reflective circle up high in the corner of the wall. She did the same and watched the officer wave his arms.

The murderous guard yelled, "They're out! Cellblock three! They're all out!"

A buzzer sounded and the door swung open. The officer ran through it. Seconds later, she heard a man scream.

Kira turned to Stuart. "What are you doing?"

This was about Jenkins. So why were they hurting others?

He flashed his teeth at her. "We're taking over the prison."

SEVENTEEN

LUCA PEERED THROUGH THE WINDOW, TRYING to see the security office.

"What's going on?" Jenkins was still shackled to the floor, and even if Luca wanted to free the man, he didn't have any way to do that.

"The guard went into the security office." Since he'd seen the officer rush past, he hadn't heard anything, so he had no idea what was going on in there. Thanks to the reinforced glass that was likely here to protect them and offer some privacy, there wasn't much they could hear.

Until the muffled gunshots.

"Someone is shooting."

Jenkins said, "So that guard is shooting other people, or they are shooting him?"

"I can't see how we would tell either way." Luca tried the handle again. Since the lights had come back on, it was a whole lot easier to see. Not that there had been much to give him an indication of what was going on. Not until that guy ran past the window.

None of the other officers had come down here in response to the guy going for help, which was what Luca had thought he was doing. What was going on?

Much like her fear and her need to trust that God had everything in His hands, worry for Kira settled on him. He had no idea where Kira was, but had to pray that she'd been able to help the officer with the medical emergency. There was nothing else he could do except pray. Thankfully, it was also the best thing he could do right now.

The corrections officer emerged from the security office with a gun in one hand. As he approached, Luca slammed both palms on the window. "Hey, let us out of here!"

The guy looked at him, and Luca realized it was the one who'd run over and yelled for medical assistance. But the question was, had he drawn Kira out of this room on purpose? Where was she?

No, he couldn't think like that.

There was no way anyone could have targeted them intentionally. But the thought that they had been purposely separated left him cold and desperately in need of information.

Not only did he recognize the guy, but the officer had blood spray down the side of his face. He was the one who had fired the gun in his hand and killed people inside the security office.

Did that mean help wasn't coming?

Luca slammed his hands on the window again, as if he hadn't realized that this man posed more of a threat than Jenkins right now. "Hey! I'm talkin' to you!"

The guy slowed not far past the window, ignoring Luca.

A group turned the corner. Two men. Hector and Stuart, who was dragging Kira with him.

Luca flexed his fingers on the window. As if he could reach through it and grab these guys—take them down.

This isn't what I meant. He prayed the words, even though he hadn't meant to be that blunt.

Sure, he'd been thinking earlier that Kira needed to trust her own strength. To believe that she could face more than she thought she could handle. To not shy away from life because she was scared to embrace the parts that were hard or painful—the parts she couldn't tackle with medical care.

But he didn't want her to have to face a dangerous situation where she was forced to be stronger than she believed she was. That wasn't what he'd meant.

She didn't need to learn strength all at once while fighting for her life, just to have circumstances prove to her that she was strong.

He wanted to protect her no matter what.

Lord, keep her safe.

His deal was making Renegade safe for the people he cared about. Generally speaking—the way he had operated in the military. Not protecting a specific person who was in danger. Luca had spent years purposely not forming relationships like that. After all, Kira could get killed or walk away from him. And then where would he be? He would have nothing.

He would be just like his father.

Loving a woman will destroy you. That was what the old man had said before he proceeded to try and drink himself to death like there was no other reason to live. In the end, it had taken intensive questioning from federal agents and a self-inflicted bullet to the brain to finish it.

Part of him wondered if the FBI's accusations had been true and his father had killed himself out of guilt. Or if it was simply a sad end to a sad life.

Luca had loved a woman during the second year of his military service. When Bridget left him, he'd been crushed. He had sworn off all relationships as a result, sticking with close friends who had become family to him. Now that Kira had crept into his heart, he knew that if something happened to her, there was no way he would be able to continue.

Kind of like there was no way out of here. He had zero ability to keep Kira safe from in here, which meant Luca had to leave her fate entirely in the Lord's hands. Another thing he wanted to learn, but not all at once.

The whole thing was like a kick to the stomach that left him breathless.

I don't want to lose her.

The man who held on to Kira came to the door, dragging her in front of him. Stuart Parker had his hand around her neck. Behind him was Hector, the cartel guy Luca had heard talking about the hit at the hospital. Were these guys really working together, or was this a crime of convenience?

Stuart called out loudly, "You're going to set Jenkins free, and then we're going to trade. Send him out and you can have her back in one piece."

Kira winced, but he didn't see tears in her eyes. And as far as he could see, she didn't have any injuries either. Luca wanted to communicate with her. Reassure her somehow. But what could he say when there was no way to get out of the room?

"So open the door," he told Stuart. "I need a key to set Jenkins free."

They knew he cared about Kira, but they didn't know how much he cared about Jenkins. Unless they thought Luca's association with Hammer meant that he wouldn't want Jenkins to be killed. There were ways to play this that meant minimal carnage. Especially to anyone in this situation who was innocent.

Not the first time he'd been in a face-off with a bad guy. But it was the first time it'd happened when he didn't have any weapons on him. Neither did Stuart, but that wouldn't stop him from snapping Kira's neck at any second.

Stuart looked at the officer. "We need this door open."

Luca managed to make out the words "We need an admin password to get any of the doors open."

Stuart leaned over toward him, deadliness in his body language. "Figure it out."

Hector said something and followed the officer to the security office.

Luca glanced back at Stuart. The guy was watching him, trying to read how he felt about Kira. How far he could push this and terrorize her while Luca watched, just to get as much sick satisfaction out of this as he possibly could.

Luca turned away.

She wasn't going to understand why he gave them his back. But doing so took all the power from Stuart. Luca wouldn't be able to see what he was doing, and he couldn't object to something he didn't hear. With his back to them so they wouldn't know, he said to Jenkins, "What is he doing?"

"Staring at you." Jenkins glanced over. "You ticked him off with that move."

"Is he hurting her?"

"She's scared, but he's just holding her too tight."

Luca said, "Those other guys had better hurry up and get this door open."

"As soon as they do, I'm a dead man."

"And you think my priority here is keeping you alive?"

"It had better be if you want to know anything else about the Shadow Syndicate."

Luca glanced at him. "Really? Right now you're going to pretend like you have more information about this?"

"I guess you'd better keep me alive, and we'll find out exactly how much I know about what's going on in this city."

"I'm getting Kira, and I'm getting out of here. That is literally my only priority."

"Be sure to explain to Mack how you hung me out to dry and let me die just so that you could survive." Jenkins's attention drifted past Luca's shoulder.

Luca turned around just as the cartel guy and the officer raced back. The officer ran a key card through the reader next to the door, and it clicked. Luca grabbed the handle and pulled it open, needing to be on the same side of the door as Kira. Otherwise, there was nothing he could do to help her.

Stuart backed up, pulling Kira with him.

The officer lifted the gun and pointed it at Luca, aiming at his face. "Keys."

Hector tossed a set of keys to Luca.

The officer said, "Unlock his cuffs."

Luca didn't move. An alarm sounded down the hallway, followed by the words "Lockdown initiated" in a robotic voice through the speakers overhead.

The officer whirled around, swearing a blue streak.

Stuart yelled, "What is that? What did you do?"

"I thought I shut it off! Someone elsewhere in the prison must have turned it back on. The police department will have been notified."

Stuart said, "We're going to have company?"

"Armed SWAT in full gear." The officer looked at his watch. "We don't have long to get this done."

Stuart motioned to the gun. "Let me see that."

The officer handed it over.

Luca didn't know whether to step out of the room and let the door lock again, securing Jenkins inside, or figure out how to grab Kira and get her in there with them.

Stuart swung the gun up and pointed it at the officer, squeezed the trigger. He didn't even flinch when the man fell to the ground.

Kira screamed.

The cartel guy said, "Now kill Jenkins. If he isn't dead, then we don't get paid."

"How can you get paid when you're in prison?" Jenkins yelled from inside the room. "They're never going to let you out for this."

Luca lifted his hands. "Everyone, calm down." He focused on Stuart. "Let Kira go, or things will be so much worse for you when that SWAT team arrives. I don't really care what you do to Jenkins, but you need to let us go."

Stuart said, "I've got the gun. Seems to me like she's leverage. Which means she and I should go."

"Go where?" Luca didn't think the guy would get far.

Probably the moment he stepped outside, guards in high towers would take him out. Luca just prayed Kira didn't get caught in the crossfire.

Luca said, "You have to know that you aren't getting out of here. Just put the gun down and let her go. She doesn't have anything to do with this."

"I say she and I find a quiet corner and wait out the police." Stuart sneered. "After I kill Jenkins, we'll have time for some fun before I get thrown back in solitary."

Luca moved just enough to let the door shut behind him before either of them could do anything about it, locking Jenkins in the room again.

Hector came at him, swinging his fists and forcing Luca to defend himself. Kira screamed, and he was aware of Stuart dragging her away down the hall, but there was nothing he could do about it until he dealt with this guy.

Hector grabbed his arm and twisted it back painfully. Luca turned into the twist and punched the guy with his other hand. Hector let go of his arm and came back at him, swinging his head forward. Luca dodged the headbutt and punched the guy in the stomach, grabbing his shoulders and then kneeing him in the middle. Hector fell to the floor.

Luca raced away down the hall after Stuart and Kira.

Kira gritted her teeth. Stuart dragged her with that punishing grip on her arm, through the door back into the infirmary.

"Lock that door." He swung her toward the far door. "If anyone tries to get in, I guess you'll just have to deal with it." His laughter followed her across the room.

Before she could shove the door closed, a tall man with a full beard shoved against it and came in. She froze, backing up from him. The guy turned and threw the lock over. Broad-shouldered, tanned skin.

A second later, three guys appeared in the window, which was crisscrossed with wire, rendering it almost unbreakable. They hammered on the glass and fought against the handle, the looks on their faces feral. They wanted to get in here with a desperation that drove them almost to insanity.

She shivered, backing up.

The big man with Middle Eastern coloring looked through her and said to Stuart, "I can take her off your hands."

"Don't think I need any favors from you, Sax," Stuart said. "Barricade the door."

The Middle Eastern guy seemed unbothered by that comment but did as the man asked. Sax?

Did that mean . . .

She kept her thoughts to herself. If this was Luca's brother, the one he'd told her about, she should be safe with him. Right?

But there was nothing safe about this guy.

She whirled around to look at Stuart. "No more shooting." She held up her hands, trying to come across as desperate—which didn't take much with the dead body on the hospital bed on the other side of the room. "No more blood. Just *stop*."

Stuart waved the gun around. "I'll shoot whoever I want."

Sax said, "You want someone on your side, I'm your guy." He

slammed a hand against his own chest, over the white tank that showed off powerful arms. He'd taken his orange jumpsuit and tied the arms around his waist. She saw a lot of similarities with Luca, but also so many ways this man was remarkably different.

And far more dangerous.

She couldn't let on that she knew this Sax guy was Luca's older brother, Amir. Stuart would use anything against her, and she didn't know if this other inmate would protect her. He might be here to do whatever he wanted while she had no way to fight back.

Kira huddled against the wall, thinking of Luca. Wondering if that guy from the cartel had killed him. Tears gathered in her eyes, the last thing she needed. These men would take any vulnerability she showed and exploit it for maximum carnage.

The phone started to ring.

"Check the window," Stuart ordered.

For a second, she thought he was talking to her, but Sax strode to one of the tiny windows in a row on the far wall. Moving between two empty hospital beds, stepping on gauze packets that had been strewn across the floor. He looked out the window.

Kira glanced around. The pharmacy cabinet was open, and the padlock discarded on the floor. Stuart stood between her and the supplies. She could use any one of those meds to incapacitate him if she could get over there and prep a syringe.

The whole thing looked like it had been picked over. No doubt there was a group of inmates somewhere in the prison mixing meds and getting high on narcotics.

She bit her lip.

What they wanted to use for evil, she needed to use to save her own life. Maybe even Luca's as well. Could she get over there?

Lord, show me when to move. How to do this fast so I can take him down before he shoots me or anyone else.

It felt so natural to cry out to the Lord in the heat of the moment, when she was facing death with no way to fight back. But did she do that on ordinary days when there was no peril, or with a patient whose condition she didn't know how to treat? Even then, she relied more on her knowledge and less on the God-given wisdom that the Bible told her to ask for.

Give me that wisdom now, Lord.

When she got out of this, which she had to trust would happen, she was going to quit treating God like a friend she only called when she was in a jam and needed help. Kira would start fresh and work on having a real relationship with the Lord. One where she was in more constant communication with Him, about anything happening or nothing at all. Especially about her fear.

She had to cultivate a closeness with Him that she'd never had before, or she would be calling herself a Christian when, in reality, she was missing something huge about what her relationship with God *could* be.

Sax turned back from the window. "Hate to break it to you, bro, but the cops are here. SWAT teams. There are all kinds of flashing red and blue lights out there."

"So they know something is going on." Stuart shrugged, but Kira wasn't all the way convinced he didn't care that the police were here. "It was gonna happen. And now I can ask for what I want."

"You think this is a situation where you have any leverage?" Sax pulled back the shoulder of his tank top to reveal an angry scar below his right collarbone. A gunshot wound from a long time ago. "What do you think happens when they're done talking and they decide you need to be taken out? Good luck. I'm not part of that." He shook his head. "I'm not here to get shot again."

"Too bad, because I guess I don't need you." Stuart leveled the gun at him.

"What if you do?" Desperation tumbled the words from her mouth, and Kira suddenly had to find a plausible reason Stuart should care about this random inmate—or so he thought.

She cleared her throat. "He has family, right? I mean, everyone does." She tried to shrug. "Maybe they're important and you can negotiate with them. They might even be rich enough they can give you money. You never know. This guy could be somebody."

"He's new. No one knows much about him."

"See?" Kira didn't know what else to say.

"I kill him, it'll just be for pleasure. Not for the paycheck."

Sax reacted to that. "Someone's paying you? Bro, get me in on that action."

"I don't need any more help. This is a solo operation now."

Kira could see that. He'd killed the guard who'd helped him breach the prison in the first place and kick off this whole situation. The cartel guy was out in the hallway still, where he'd attacked Luca.

She couldn't see through the window in that door, off to her right.

Was he out there? Was he hurt?

She sniffed back tears.

The phone on the desk beside the pharmacy cabinet rang again. Stuart swept his arm back and forth, aiming the gun at her and then Sax in turn. He backed up and used his free hand to hit a button on the phone. "What?"

"This is Lieutenant Rutherford with the Renegade Police Department. State your name."

Stuart said, "I don't gotta tell you nothin'."

"I'd like to find a way to resolve this situation peacefully."

Sax lifted one hand and tapped his shoulder, ostensibly reminding Stuart of the police's idea of "resolving" situations. Kira wasn't sure that was necessary. Why did he feel the need to warn Stuart? She would much rather he was taken down—and quickly—so they could get out of here.

Rutherford said, "Can you tell me who is in the infirmary with you?"

"I'm sure you'd like to know that, Lieutenant." Stuart sneered the last word as if it was a slur. "I got a live one right here." He looked at her. "Get over here."

She didn't move.

"Now!"

Kira stumbled, caught herself, and walked to him. Stuart grabbed the back of her neck, his fingers tangling painfully in her hair. She gasped.

"Say your name for the police."

She swallowed. "Kira. Kira Yassan."

"The *doctor* here will die if I don't get Alden Jenkins in here in the next ten minutes."

"It's going to take more time tha—"

Stuart set the gun down and jabbed at the button on the display to hang up the phone. What he didn't do was let go of her—or check that the call had ended—all while he maintained his punishing grip on her.

Kira grabbed for the gun.

He saw what she was doing.

Oh no.

He slammed down on her hand, his grip on the back of her neck tightening so that she cried out. White spots flashed at the edges of her vision.

He lifted the gun, her hand wrapped around the grip. His finger crushing hers on the hard metal of the weapon.

She gasped, tears running down her face. *Think.* But her mind refused to recall any kind of self-defense with all the pain swelling like bookends around her, pressing in and threatening to crush her.

"Stuart Parker, this is Rutherford." His voice rang through the phone speaker. "Do not kill that woman. If you end her life, we will not hesitate to breach that room and take you out."

His grip on her didn't relax, not even slightly.

Kira gasped, and it sounded like a muffled cry.

"Let her go, Parker."

He shifted, then kicked her away. Her fingers slid from under his around the gun, and she fell to the floor.

"Get me Jenkins." He hung up the phone.

Kira took the chance to look at the door, but from the floor, she couldn't see if anyone was in the hall. She stood and turned so her back wasn't to Stuart. Not that it made her any less vulnerable to face him rather than have her back to him. But at least this way, whatever it was, she'd be able to see it coming.

She straightened, pain making itself known in her hand and on the back of her head. "Why do you want him?" Her voice shook and she sounded scared. Small. Kira cleared her throat. "What do you want with Jenkins?"

Stuart looked at her like she was something smeared on the bottom of his shoe. "I wanna kill him. What do you think?"

As soon as he did that, he was going to kill her. That's what she thought. But she said, "I thought you wanted Frankie."

"Oh, she'll suffer. Don't worry."

"You can't hurt her if you're in prison for the rest of your life."

That's what he would get if he carried on with this. A judge wasn't ever going to let him out. How could he think this would end well for him? It sounded to her like the plan had a lot of issues. And yet, he seemed convinced it was a sure thing.

"It isn't me that's gonna pay her a visit. That's the deal."

She frowned. "Who did you make a deal with?"

He rolled his eyes. "So many questions."

"You're going to kill me." She saw the other guy look at her, but didn't lose focus on Stuart. Amir just stood there, watching everything. "What does it matter if I know why or if you explain what is going on? I think I deserve to know."

He chuckled. "Good one."

The low regard he had for women was distressing, to say the least. Stuart thought anyone who wasn't male didn't get respect or deserve to have an opinion or be considered.

"Who is paying you?" She had to ask, needed to know.

If the worst was about to happen, would Amir step in to save her?

"How should I know?" He looked bored more than anything. "It was anonymous."

And he'd taken that deal? Getting paid to commit a crime in exchange for revenge. He would spend his life in prison, so how did that make accepting money a good idea? It wasn't like he could spend the funds.

Unless Stuart was figuring he could spend the money when he got out. Eventually. He'd be old and gray by then, but it could be his plan.

The question was whether Kira would be alive.

EIGHTEEN

"DON'T MOVE." THE UNIFORMED SWAT OFFICER dragged the cartel guy's hands behind his back, and Luca heard the metal snick of the cuffs around Hector's wrists.

He peered around the corner of the wall, trying to get a look at Kira in the infirmary, but wasn't able to see her. If he got closer, he might, but that meant potentially letting Stuart know he was out here.

"Let's go."

Luca realized the cop was talking to him and shook his head. "I'm staying here."

"Wasn't a question." The cop waited.

Luca didn't want to, but he followed the guy back to the entrance on the secure side of the security scanners. Past the office, where the corrections officer had murdered three of his colleagues in cold blood. Hector might've helped, but in the end, it was the dead officer who had betrayed his oath and put this entire facility at risk.

"I'm going back in there." Luca announced it, unsure who he was talking to. Didn't matter.

He spotted Mike Martinelli coming over to him, wearing a bulletproof vest with POLICE on it over his dress shirt. The detective passed through the scanner and set off the alarm.

"Someone shut that off." A man with a white-shirted uniform that had bars on his shoulders turned to Luca. A lieutenant and African American, his name badge said Rutherford. "You're Saxon?"

Luca nodded.

"Any relative of Amir Saxon, one of the inmates?"

"My brother. I asked the Marshals to transfer him in so he could protect Jenkins."

Lieutenant Rutherford frowned. "If he's in the middle of this, I can't guarantee his safety. Got that?"

Luca nodded, and Detective Martinelli didn't argue.

"A snitch!" Jenkins had been uncuffed from the table, and one of the SWAT guys walked him into the entrance lobby. The guy looked like he was about to pass out from the pain. "You put a snitch in here!"

Rutherford said, "Makes good company for you."

Luca pressed his lips together. "I say we send in Jenkins and trade him for Dr. Yassan. Get her out." He folded his arms, unwilling to debate the issue.

"You think our intention is to leave her in there with those wolves?" Rutherford turned to one of his guys. "Get ready to breach."

Mike turned to Luca. "The other cellblocks are locked down. Most of the inmates in this one are behind doors. They're contained, but it's kicking off back there. We need to get this situation under control *now*."

Rutherford picked up where he left off. "Means we need everyone to go in at once. We'll get the doctor out, but the priority has to be containment. There are corrections officers shut in with the inmates beyond the infirmary, and we need to get them out as well."

Right. Luca nodded. "Understood."

Even if that was the last thing he wanted to say. What Luca *wanted* was to rush into that room and rescue Kira. Which would, of course, get him killed, since Stuart had a gun. But everything in him was pushing him to sweep her up into his arms and get her out of there.

He loved her.

Maybe he'd have felt this way if it was any other innocent in there at the mercy of a dangerous man with a gun. But Kira was under his skin. Without him realizing, he'd fallen for her.

He wanted her in his life. Wanted to take her to dinner, to a movie—all those things he'd said to her. But not just so they could be dating.

He wanted more.

He wanted it all.

Lord, I need her back. You're the one who needs to rescue her. If not me, then someone else You use. But use me, Lord. Help me bring justice to this situation. Your justice.

His thoughts rambled through some more of the prayer, and he let it keep going. Circling around thoughts and ideas, interceding on her behalf with the One who had the power to resolve this situation without any more bloodshed.

That was the key here, wasn't it?

No one else had to die.

Luca cleared his throat. "Stuart has information."

Mike and Rutherford both glanced at him.

He continued, "He was probably paid, or he made a deal, and that's the reason he tried to kill Jenkins before. He's doing this now for the same reason. So he can finish the job. We need him alive so he can tell us who it is that hired him or forced him to do this."

Rutherford frowned. "We have no idea how this is going to go down. You can't make demands on how it shakes out."

"But you're going to do your utmost to keep Kira safe."

The guy's eyes flared, reacting to how Luca used her name. "Of course."

"Then at least try and do the same with Stuart," he said. "That's all I'm asking."

A couple of officers in SWAT gear came through the scanner. It flashed, but the audible alarm didn't sound. "Ready, Lieutenant."

Mike said to him, "We'll do what we can."

Luca nodded, not wanting to talk about this anymore when they were about to breach. He prayed silently while they made their way down the hall, and tagged on the end of the group. No one needed to worry about him. He still wasn't armed.

He just wanted to be there when they brought out Kira.

Up at the front of the line, one of the SWAT guys nodded to another. They hammered once over the handle, the blow taking out a chunk of the door that included the lock. The officer tossed a canister into the room.

A deafening bang and the brightest light Luca had seen exploded in the space. The line of cops rushed into the room, yelling over the ringing in Luca's ears.

He thought he heard a gunshot, but wasn't sure.

Luca followed them and saw Stuart get thrown to the ground and subdued. His brother had his hands on his head, his fingers laced together.

The officer pushed the back of his knees, and Amir went down to a kneeling position.

Kira stood with her back to the wall, her face far too pale and her eyes dark and wide. She glanced around, her gaze not quite settling on anything. Shock suffused her features.

Luca went to her, gathering her up in his arms.

She didn't resist. Her arms snaked around his waist. Luca held her close and looked at Amir, watching as his brother was cuffed. Stuart yelled at them, resisting, so that it took multiple officers to hold him down.

Amir nodded. He'd been here, and he knew Kira meant something to Luca. He knew and he'd come into the infirmary to protect her. Luca returned the nod, mouthing *Thank you* to his brother. The officer saw it, but still Mike took over handling Amir's arrest.

"Come on." Luca led Kira to the door and out into the hall. "Let's get out of here."

He held on to her, one arm around her waist and the other holding her arm.

She sniffed, and he heard her audibly exhale on a groan.

"Let's find the EMTs and get you checked out." There should be some outside. "Do you want me to carry you?"

She shook her head. "I want to walk out of here."

"All right." He didn't let go of her. If she wanted to do this on her own two feet, he wasn't going to object. She needed those moments to feel capable, even strong. Luca had to ask, "Did he hurt you?"

"Only some bruises." She reached up and touched the back of her head. "And my hand. But I'm okay."

"Hey!" They passed Jenkins.

Luca didn't slow down, and they kept moving, going through the scanner toward the exit doors that would take them outside. He paused a second and gathered their things, figuring they wouldn't want to come back anytime soon. He didn't look at his phone, just slid it into his pocket. "Come on."

"Saxon! I'm talkin' to you!"

Luca glanced over his shoulder at Jenkins. "You have something to say to me?"

Kira slowed and the cops in the room quieted, everyone wanting to know what the former mayor had to say.

"Maybe the names of who is in the syndicate?" Luca was willing to give the guy a second to talk. But after that, he was getting Kira out of here. "Who are they, Alden?"

"Guess you'll never know."

Luca shook his head, walking Kira outside. "That was a waste of time."

They'd come here trying to find out where Torres might have been taken, if he was even the victim of a kidnapping. This whole situation had been chaotic, not to mention terrifying for Kira, that he'd almost forgotten the reason they'd come.

"That was your brother, wasn't it?"

He headed toward the ambulance, where two EMTs waited for them. Luca lifted his chin as they approached the uniformed first responders, both women. "This is Kira. She has some bruises, and her hand is hurt."

Both EMTs grinned. One said, "Hey, Doc."

"Laura." Kira sounded like she was smiling. She glanced at the other. "Becky."

"Barbara's in the ER today. She's worried sick about you, girl. Said she hasn't stopped praying since she heard the news you were in there." Laura took Kira's arm, and they walked her the last few steps to the ambulance. "We can radio in so she knows you're safe now."

"Sounds good." Kira settled onto the stretcher. "I don't need to go to the hospital, though I could use an ice pack for the back of my head and a couple of ibuprofen."

The EMT said, "Let's get you checked out."

Someone yelled, "Luca!"

He turned and spotted Mike jogging toward him. "What's up?"

Mike glanced in the ambulance, then focused on Luca. "They're working their way through the prison, getting the guards who are trapped out and securing all the inmates. I just wanted to let you know that your brother is good. He's back in his cell."

"Thanks." Luca shook the other man's hand, not sure why he

was grateful for the fact his brother had been trapped back in that place. Going in there . . . seeing Amir in there . . . all of it was a reminder he hadn't wanted that Amir wasn't getting out for a couple of years.

His brother needed to make better choices next time. Stick to the rules of his parole and not go back to prison.

Luca didn't want him to be another sad statistic.

"I appreciate you taking care of him."

Mike shrugged. "He's your brother. A lot of cops like to draw that clear black-and-white line between bad guys and them, but there's a verse that says 'and such were some of you' that's there to remind us that we aren't any better than any other sinner. We're all the same at the foot of the cross, no matter what we've done."

Luca nodded. "Then there's guys like Jenkins, who don't think they need redemption. Kind of like I didn't think I needed it. Not for years."

"Me either. Took a lot of hits to make me take a hard look at myself and admit I couldn't do this on my own." Mike clapped him on the shoulder. "Glad everything today turned out all right."

"It will have after we locate Dr. Torres. Make sure he's good."

Mike frowned.

"He was missing from his house. It would be good to locate him and check he's safe."

"I'll call the station and get an update." Mike jogged off again.

Luca turned back to see Kira slide off the stretcher, holding something to the back of her head. The ice pack she'd asked for.

The EMT frowned. "I really think you should go in and get checked out, Dr. Yassan."

"I'm okay," Kira said. "Just give me something to sign."

Luca wasn't sure what the big hurry was. Before he could ask if she was certain, she said, "We need the police to go to the shelter. Seeing Mike reminded me." She shook her head, which made her wince. "Stuart told me the deal was that he killed Jenkins while someone else took out his revenge on Frankie."

"The woman you helped get to the shelter?"

She nodded. "It might've been compromised. They could all be in danger."

"I'll tell Mike."

Kira touched his arm, clinging to his biceps. "I want to go there and make sure they're okay."

He stared at the woman he loved and found he had a hard time telling her no. The police could take care of it. Luca and Kira didn't necessarily need to see for themselves. But still . . . "Okay."

She lifted onto the balls of her feet and touched her lips to his. "Thank you."

Kira made it about a mile away from the prison before she bent forward in the passenger seat and had to take deep breaths. Luca's hand touched her back, and she took solace in the smooth strength of it, anchoring herself to the feeling so she didn't flip out more than necessary.

You protected me.

Yet again, God had proven Himself. She didn't need Him to do that in order for her to believe He would show up in her life, but looking back and seeing it built her faith. She never had to be sufficient on her own, strong enough or brave enough. God was always with her, even in the craziest situations.

She sat back up, breathing hard and wiping the tears from her cheeks. She popped the glove box door down and found some napkins—because that was where everyone kept them—and cleaned up a little. "Sorry."

"It's really normal, so don't worry about it." He squeezed her knee. "You should've seen me after my first firefight."

She brushed the hair back from her face, feeling the sting at the back of her head. And the stiffness in her hand. Other than a few bruises, she was all right. Definitely not in need of a doctor's assessment.

"It could have been so much worse." Her mind was having trouble catching up. "Now I'm all worried about Frankie and what might be happening there."

"Cops are on the way, and we'll be there in ten." He steered with one hand and reached over to hold hers with the other. "If there's something going down, we'll make sure it's resolved. All right?"

She shifted in the seat to face him. "That was really your brother?"

He nodded, glancing over. "Did he say anything?"

"Not to me," she said. "I didn't do anything to let Stuart know we knew each other either. I mean, not that we've met, but that I knew who he was."

"Didn't matter if you've never met him. He would've stepped in front of a bullet for you, no question."

"We should visit him." Then her mind flashed her right back to the prison, and her body washed cold. She instantly started sweating. "Maybe in a while."

He squeezed her hand. "It won't always feel like this. But for what it's worth, I'd love to go visit him with you after you've had some time to heal. When you're ready."

"I'm not hurt."

"That's not the kind of healing I meant."

She sighed. "I was a covert agent. Sort of. I shouldn't have been so scared. I should've known better how to handle myself and been all cool and calm under pressure."

"Instead, it turns out that you're a human being."

"You only say that because you're a superhero."

He chuckled. "I'm a *what*?"

"You heard me." She tugged her hand from his and folded her

arms. Being irritated—or just acting like she was—made her feel better, because she could push back. This wasn't about her inadequacies anymore.

He was still laughing. "I could train you, you know. If you want."

"We tried sticking together, and look how that worked out." She pushed out a big breath. "You probably should. Just in case. Not for superhero missions. I don't want to go on any of those."

"Noted." He glanced over, smiling at her. "It would be good for you to be able to protect yourself, and your family."

She wondered what family he was talking about.

"When you have one."

This handsome man beside her, this superhero, a warrior who would lay down his life for the people he cared about, was the person she wanted to do that with. She wanted to ask him if he was available.

Instead, she bit her lip.

Spending her life with a man who gave his time and energy to make this city safe for the people he cared about was everything she'd ever wanted or been looking for. The kind of man who would do that for his family.

"We're here." He cleared his throat.

She'd been about to ask him if he wanted a family when he pulled the truck over to the side of the road. Kira had given him the address, because if bad guys had found the shelter, then it would definitely need to be moved. But first, they needed to make sure everyone was safe.

The white farmhouse was set back from the street and barely visible through the trees that lined this side of the road. Down a short dirt lane, the house had a big front yard but not much except a patio at the back. The red metal roof could be seen through the trees.

Two gunshots sounded in quick succession.

Luca met her at the front of the truck, wearing a bulletproof vest. He held a second vest out toward her. "Put this on. But you're still going to stick behind me."

"Nowhere else I'd rather be." She spotted more than one cop car beside the house, in front of the separate garage, and lowered the vest over her head.

Luca didn't head toward danger. He turned to her, fixing the straps on her vest, then slid his arm around her back—his gun in his other hand—and leaned down with his face close to hers. "I love you. You face what comes at you with grace, and you have this ability to stand strong and still be vulnerable at the same time. It's amazing. You're sweet and beautiful and stronger than you know."

"I love you." She slid her hands from his chest to the sides of his neck. "Thank you for making me feel safe. For understanding who I am when sometimes I don't even understand it."

He tugged her close and touched his lips to hers, tipped his head to the side and asked her to accept everything he felt for her. Kira received it like the best kind of gift. Something she hadn't expected at this point in her life, and yet, how good was it to be blessed by God this way? All of it wrapped up in a surprise that blew her away.

She matched him every step of the way, showing him right back how she felt about him. What she wanted and what she hoped they could be.

Luca pulled back and kissed her one more time quickly. "Stay behind me."

They headed for the house, running toward the front door, which stood open. Up the porch steps. He slowed as they approached the door.

Kira ducked behind him, holding on to his belt. Grateful she usually lived a life where she didn't need to own a bulletproof vest in her size. Did they come in sizes? She wouldn't ever need to know, hopefully.

She was going to stick with this man and her job at the hospital.

Take the blessing God had given her and work on it, building something beautiful that she would never want to let go of.

Luca entered the house, and she kept pace with him, watching on the sides for people she could help. Another gunshot echoed through the house, followed by three answering shots.

Kira winced. *God, keep them safe.*

She heard running feet, then a thud. Luca tensed. "Stop!"

A bullet fired in their direction, and she felt Luca brace. The shot embedded in the wall to her right. He fired, and there was another thud.

"Clear!" Luca's yell echoed through the house.

"Clear!" The yell came from upstairs, followed by "We've got an officer down!"

Kira let go of Luca's belt. She spotted the man he had shot, a bullet in the center of his forehead. Lying in the hallway, jeans and a dirty white tank. Tattoos and a chain around his neck. Gang members like him came into the emergency department often, so she'd dealt with his type plenty of times.

Not men who looked the part but held down jobs and took care of their kids. This one was the kind who was angry at the world, dealt drugs, and didn't care who he hurt.

She raced up the stairs after Luca and saw the residents of the shelter huddled in a wide room with double doors, the main bedroom, which had bunk beds all around. Between the beds, a collection of women and a few kids stood in a group, huddled together. Fear stark on their faces. She spotted Frankie, but there wasn't time to talk to her now. That would have to wait until later.

"Is anyone else hurt?" She crouched beside the officer with blood on the left side of his chest. She did a quick assessment.

The other officer, kneeling on the other side of his friend, had sweat running down the sides of his face. "No, no one."

"You called it in?"

He reached for his radio, but his fingers slipped. Luca crouched by him. "I've got it." He squeezed the sides of the radio and called for an ambulance while she studied the patient.

"We need to put pressure on this." She looked at the residents. "Frankie, I need a towel!"

The young woman broke off and raced out of sight.

Kira leaned down and listened to the officer's breathing. One side, then the other. "His lung collapsed. The bullet let air in outside his lung that is crushing it."

"Here." Frankie shoved the towel at her.

"I need a straw."

"What?" Frankie didn't move.

"And a knife. Can you get me both of those?"

Luca pulled something out of his pocket and flipped it open. The blade of the knife glinted in the light.

"I need a straw. Something sturdy." She looked at Luca. "And some tape. Duct tape, electrical tape, anything like that."

"How about physical-therapy tape?" A young woman held out a roll of athletic tape. "Would this work?"

"Yes. Thank you." Kira leaned down and listened to his breathing again, then she used Luca's knife to cut the man's shirt open. "That needs to be cleaned now."

Luca stood in one fluid movement and headed into what looked like a bathroom. She heard him rummaging in the cupboard.

Kira pushed back the sides of the shirt to reveal his chest, the officer struggling to breathe. Air bubbles escaped the wound, red with blood from the gunshot.

He stared at her, blinking. In shock and unsure what was happening. She looked at his name badge.

"Officer Walters, I'm Dr. Kira Yassan, and I'll be treating you today." She smiled at him. "We're going to stabilize you so you make it to the hospital. They can fix you up and put you back together. All right?"

He nodded, a jerky movement.

"This isn't going to be the thing that kills you."

The residents huddled at the door. Beyond Luca and the cop on the other side of the injured man, she saw another gunman lying dead on the floor.

These two officers had walked into an unknown situation and put their lives on the line for strangers.

Kira wasn't going to let any of them down.

Frankie raced up the stairs. "Here." She handed Kira a wide metal straw.

"Perfect." Kira said, "If anyone is squeamish, don't watch this." She took Luca's knife when he held it out, and cut the wound just enough to comfortably get the straw in. As soon as the straw was seated in the wound, she wrapped tape around it, holding it in place.

He let out a wheeze, then took a full breath, both his lungs filling. The labored breaths began to equalize, and the officer started to breathe steadily.

"There we go."

"What happened?" Frankie asked, still beside her.

Kira said, "The air in his chest needed somewhere to go, so it escaped out the straw and his lung was able to reinflate. He can breathe now."

"You saved his life." Frankie's voice was full of awe.

"He needs to be at the hospital, ASAP. This is only a temporary fix."

Luca motioned over her shoulder. "The ambulance is here."

Two EMTs rushed up the stairs with their gear. Kira ran down all the particulars and handed the man off to them. She scooted across the floor to sit with her back to the wall. Luca moved over and sat beside her, gathering her into his arms.

"You're amazing."

She smiled to herself. "I've been thinking the same about you."

"Seems like God knew what He was doing, putting us together. We fit."

The EMTs rolled the officer to their backboard, and the other cop helped them carry him down the stairs.

Luca was right. They complemented each other in some of the best ways. She lifted her chin and looked at him. "Yes, we do."

NINETEEN

LUCA HEARD THE SHOWER SHUT OFF IN THE bathroom of his cabin, which he'd completely renovated. He'd gutted the whole place and rebuilt it over the winter while trying to wrestle with the particulars of this case. If it went on much longer, he was going to sand and restain the floors.

But having Kira here, in his place, just days after everything had happened, cleaning up and putting her comfy clothes on? Way more distracting than the investigation he still didn't have answers for.

After they'd left the prison, he had taken her to the hospital to have her injuries looked at. Once her wrist was bandaged, they'd gone to her place and he'd hung out awhile until she fell asleep. He'd headed over to the police station then so he could go over everything with Mike.

She hadn't wanted to be apart for too long, and neither had he, so as soon as she'd woken up and called him, he'd picked her up and brought her to his house. Since then, there'd been a whole lot of movies, tea, and comfort foods. Rowan, Sierra, and Huck had come by for dinner last night, and afterward, he'd camped out on the couch so she didn't have to go home so late.

She'd told him it felt like she was on a retreat, and he agreed.

Luca grabbed the seasoning and shook it over the two steaks destined for the grill out the back. He already had the chopped veggies cooking over the flame. After they'd gone for a short hike earlier, he'd changed his boots for tennis shoes and pulled on a sweater over his T-shirt, giving Kira the bathroom so she could wash up and they could spend this evening in the Adirondack chairs on his porch, watching the sun go down and enjoying each other's company.

Luca flipped the steaks with a set of tongs and seasoned the other sides. His phone rang behind him on the counter.

Jamie.

He answered, hitting the speaker button. "Hey, girl."

"You sound happy." Her alto voice sounded amused.

"Speak for yourself. How's Logan?"

"The doctor cleared him to fly out of state for a national con-ference where they talk about wildland firefighting and make a plan for the new season. He's pretty stoked to help represent the tracker-ring tech and get it on the market so more firefighters can be safe."

Luca smiled. "That's great."

"That's the good news."

"Okay, what's the bad?" He wiped his hands on a towel and stood with his belt buckle pressed against the counter, looking out at his leather sectional—the one that would give Kira's couch a run for its money. He wanted to hear the noise she made when she settled onto it.

He looked at the lamp he'd found at an estate sale and the print over the fireplace that depicted a long highway in Alaska with the peak of Denali in the background and the color of fire in the sky.

"The money I donated to this foundation of yours made its way through offshore accounts and into the hands of companies associated with the same cartel you mentioned."

Kira wandered down the hall in leggings and a long sweater, her feet bare and her hair down.

For a second, he forgot to breathe. He just stared at her, walking toward him in his house like she belonged here. Like she did this every day. Making him want to ask her if she might never leave.

Stay.

He was getting ahead of himself, considering this was technically their first date.

"Saxon?"

Kira smiled, easing next to him and sliding her arm around his waist. "He's here."

Jamie said, "Oh."

"I'm Kira."

Jamie cleared her throat. "Dr. Yassan. Of course. I mean, *Kira.* It's nice to . . . you know, meet you."

She smiled, and Luca quickly touched his lips together. Then to Jamie, he said, "So the money you donated to the foundation went to the cartel?"

Kira gasped.

Jamie said, "Most of it landed in legit accounts, ones connected to their organization or vendors they work with. Part of it was paid to the cartel. Or they needed to break up the amount and split it out so the government didn't see huge sums of money moving around."

Luca rubbed his thumb over Kira's shoulder, his arm around her back. "Whichever it is, the money connects the nonprofit to the cartel."

"But is it a payment, or are they just putting money in their 'other' account?" Jamie asked.

"There's no way Destiny is tangled up with a cartel!" Kira shook her head. "That's crazy. That would mean . . ."

"She paid to have her husband killed."

Kira pulled out of his arms and turned to face him. "Are you serious? That's not normal life, where the normal people live. That's part of your crazy superhero world where people are trying to destabilize countries and upset the balance of power in governments."

Luca lifted his brows. "My superhero world? The one where you copied information and handed it to MI6 or the CIA? That world?"

"Copying files is hardly the same as saving the world." She folded her arms across her front, giving him a look at the nasty blue bruise on her wrist.

"So what's the answer?" Luca shrugged. "Destiny was duped and she has no idea?"

Kira frowned. "Maybe someone who works in the foundation is the one connected to the cartel and she knows nothing at all. And *that* person had Ralph killed."

"Okay, that's a decent theory. Now we need proof."

Jamie cut in on their conversation. "I'm going to leave you two to . . . whatever is going on with this conversation."

Luca lifted the phone. "I appreciate all your help."

"There was more, if you're interested."

"I am." Luca would rather explore the pink tint to Kira's cheeks and the fiery look in her eyes that had him *very* interested in what kissing her when she was riled up like this would feel like.

Kira ducked her head and got two cans of soda water from the fridge.

Jamie said, "I can't dig more into the financials. I keep running into blocks, and I'm going to get noticed if I keep going. There's an active DEA investigation into the cartel, and I'll get in trouble if I'm interfering."

"Yeah, keep yourself secure, okay? Your husband and that family of his don't need you getting into trouble."

Jamie chuckled. "Exactly. I am going to find out what the investigation is about. I'll send you any info I find."

"Thanks."

"Have a good evening. Nice to meet you, Kira."

She lowered her soda can. "You as well."

The call ended.

Luca set his can on the counter and stalked to her, sliding his arms around her hips and lifting her so she could sit on the counter. Kira let out a little yelp. Luca stood close, pulling her to him. His lips against hers. "Have dinner with me."

Not what he wanted to ask, but *spend forever with me* might be a little too much for a first date.

She smiled. "I thought that's what we were doing."

"Right. I forgot."

She giggled, looking more comfortable here than he'd ever seen her before—even in her own home. Luca nudged her nose with his. "Do you like my place?"

"It's gorgeous. And I called the hospital just now. I have a whole week off to recuperate, and I plan to spend plenty of days here relaxing and reading a few books I've been meaning to get to."

"I like that idea a lot." He could drown in the dark pools of those eyes. "I'll take some time off as well. We can rest." Plan their wedding. Figure out their future together. Make a list of what they were going to name their kids.

He leaned his head down, near to hers.

"But I do want to talk to Destiny. I need to see the look on her face when I ask her if she's involved."

Luca nodded. "Okay. After dinner? The veggies are cooking, and I need to get the steaks on." He started to pull away.

She grabbed the sides of his sweater. "Not so fast there, superhero."

Kira pulled him back to her and held him there, close as he could get. She slid her hands up to the sides of his neck and he leaned down.

Swept her up, taking over, because that was the only thing he could do. Supporting her. Protecting her. Loving her. Making it so she felt like she could fly.

Kira sank against him, and he held on to her. Felt her fingers in his hair. All of it made him wonder if she wanted to pull the tie from his bun and spill the length over his shoulders.

He felt it come loose.

She leaned back. "I need to see what it looks like."

Luca stayed still. She touched the sides, shifting it over his shoulders, then ran a finger down the side of his face through the long strand at the front.

"I nearly cut it a month ago."

She gasped.

He smiled. "Now I'm glad I didn't."

"I mean, I'm not saying don't *ever* cut it. But I like it." Her gaze drifted over his face, down to his chest and the Midnight Sun Hotshots sweater he wore. "I like it a whole lot."

"The feeling is mutual."

She playfully pushed him back and hopped off the counter. "You said something about steaks?"

He bowed. "Yes, ma'am. Coming right up."

"I'll help."

"Good, because we might need a salad if the veggies are burned."

He took the tray of steaks and showed her to the back door, out onto the single concrete step. "This summer, I want to put a deck back here. Maybe get a hot tub."

Not something he would've done if it were just him, but right now he was thinking it was the best idea ever.

She stared up at the towering pines around them, inhaling the crisp mountain air and just taking in the scenery. "It's beautiful."

"Yes, it is."

Her brow furrowed. "Is someone . . ." She peered at the trees. "There's someone out there!"

Kira hurried over to stand with him, something he liked a whole lot since she could've run into the house instead.

"Stay here." Luca opened the door far enough that he could grab the gun from the shelf right inside the back door.

Kira ducked behind the grill.

"Check the veggies." He strode to the tree line, about twenty-five feet since he'd cleared enough space between his cabin and the trees that it made a natural firebreak. The person she'd seen walked toward him on the trail that was the closest route from the road at the bottom of the hill.

It was Dr. Torres, the sleeve of his suit jacket torn and sweat along his hairline. For a man who did cutting-edge research and had real-estate holdings all over the city, he didn't look boardroom ready right now.

"Can I help you?"

Torres came over, stopping a few feet away. "I was looking for you and Dr. Yassan. Hoping you'd help me."

"The police are looking for you. We actually thought you'd been kidnapped," Luca said. "What's going on?"

"I'm afraid I was backed into a corner and didn't make the right choice."

"Is the patient in danger?" Maybe he'd given Francisco Abalos a substance that would kill him.

Torres shook his head. "I would never endanger a patient." He seemed affronted by the idea. "I'm referring to some business dealings with unscrupulous people in town. This . . . shadow syndicate."

Luca said, "You know who they are?"

"I've had communication with them. But I can't talk to anyone except the Marshals, and not without some assurances." Torres lifted his chin. "If I don't have that, my life will be in danger."

Luca nodded. "I understand. I can call Deputy Marshal Butler and have him come here. The two of you can work something out. Does that sound good?"

Torres nodded. "I was hoping you'd be able to connect us. I seem to have misplaced my phone."

"What happened at your house?"

"I haven't been back there in days," Torres said. "I'm afraid I have no idea what you're referring to. It's my vices, you see. They get the best of me on occasion, when I need to solve a problem. Or when the ideas in my mind need to quiet down so I can rest."

Luca motioned to the cabin. "Let's go inside so you can sit and wait for Butler. I'll make the call, and you can talk to Kira."

"Thank you." Torres nodded. "For your help."

A week later, Kira finally felt rested enough to speak to Destiny Rousseau. Luca drove, acting like there was nowhere he'd rather be than chauffeuring her around the city so she could see her friends. Acquaintances.

They'd spent long days together, and apart from after that one late evening with their friends, each time, at night, she reluctantly went home. Even if he hadn't mentioned it, she wondered if they would be one of those couples who had a short engagement. A small wedding, maybe at Wiltmore House, with their closest friends. Jordan could come out and be her bridesmaid, proving that she was wrong about Luca and Kira—they fit. Her friend just needed to see it with her own eyes.

After the wedding, they would go somewhere fabulous for a week or two.

"Ready?"

She shifted in the front seat so she could look at him. All that strength and skill, and he was determined to use it to protect her. To make sure she always felt safe. "Thank you for driving me."

Luca leaned over and kissed her. "Let's go figure out if Destiny is in this shadow syndicate."

Kira rolled her eyes. "That's not why we're outside her house on a random afternoon. Anyway, have you heard from Butler about Dr. Torres? Has he said anything?"

"Unfortunately, the Marshals don't invite me to their briefings."

"Bummer." She pushed open the car door, listening to him chuckle, loving the sound of his amusement and knowing she was the one who brought lightness to his life. Enjoyment. A little bit of peace that was wrapped in the gift of God they were to each other.

Holding hands and walking into a church service together this past Sunday had been the best feeling. Kira felt like she was riding the biggest high of her life—and it was all because of Luca.

He walked with her to Destiny's front door and pressed the doorbell that echoed through the house like stately country church bells. "Not the tone I'd have chosen."

"I'm going to get one of those doorbell cameras. You never know who might come by with juice, trying to tempt you with a chocolate pastry."

A loud crash echoed through the house.

Luca tried the door, and it opened. He pulled out his gun and thumbed off the safety. "Stay behind me."

She knew the drill by now but was still surprised when he didn't order her to stay in the car or something like that. Kira stuck with him, matching his pace and sticking in the protected spot right behind him.

From deep in the house, Destiny screamed and a gun went off.

Luca started running. Kira fought to keep up, racing up the stairs and down the hall through the open doors of the main bedroom. Destiny stumbled back toward the door in the corner, a smoking gun in her hand.

"Mrs. Rousseau, put the gun down." Luca rounded a body leaking blood into the plush fabric of the carpet.

Kira knelt and pressed two fingers against the man's carotid. Nothing. "He's dead."

She retrieved her phone from her jacket pocket and called 911, asking for Detective Michael Martinelli and reporting a dead body.

Kira stood and gave the body a wide berth, moving to where the other woman would be able to see her. "Destiny? Put the gun down, please."

It tumbled to the carpet. The other woman gasped, her face pale. Hands shaking. Her blouse rumpled as if it had been tugged away from her body. One cheek red like she'd been slapped.

"Destiny, are you hurt?" Kira kept her voice soft, easing toward the other woman.

She sucked in a sharp breath, her eyes glassy.

"The police are on their way."

Luca squeezed Kira's hand, passing her and moving back to the body. "This is Antonio Abalos."

She glanced at him. "Francisco's nephew?" The one who'd forced him out of the cartel. What was he doing in Destiny's house?

"He was going to kill me." Destiny gasped again. "The cartel still wanted to deal, but if Ralph could stand up to them, then I wasn't going to back down. No way."

"Let's go into the hall, okay?"

Destiny moved with her, and Kira led her out of the room. Luca stayed with the body but came out when the cops showed up with Mike right behind them. The detective said, "I need to see the victim, then I'll be out to speak with Destiny."

"All right." Kira nodded.

Destiny had a bench beside the bookshelves at the top of the stairs, so Kira led her to it and had her sit.

"Can I get you anything?" She didn't know what else to do but get a glass of water. "I could call Roger for you."

Destiny shook her head. "He's on a trip."

Kira frowned. "It's okay to ask him to come home to be with you."

The other woman looked away. Mike came back from the hallway. "Mrs. Rousseau, is it okay if I ask you a few questions?"

Destiny sniffed, nodding slightly.

"How did that man come to be in your bedroom?"

"Well, you don't have to ask like that. As if it's something sordid." Her red-rimmed eyes flashed with anger. It seemed out of place since Destiny had just taken a life. "He was an associate of Ralph's. At least, he was trying to be."

"Can you explain that?"

"The cartel wants to get a foothold in Renegade, what with it being so close to Denver. And the airport and freight train network. They want to use it as a hub to transport drugs or something." She shook her head. "I don't know anything about it. All I know is that they were trying to force Ralph to turn over some of his businesses to them. They hacked the foundation accounts and his business accounts, all to make it look like we were in league with them. So we looked dirty."

"Trying to force you to cooperate?" Mike looked up from his notepad.

"They said if we agreed, they'd leave us alone." Destiny sniffed. "Ralph refused to back down. That's why they killed him. Antonio said it was a deadly plant from Roger's homeland so the police would think that the son poisoned his father."

Kira shook her head. "I'm so sorry. That's terrible."

Mike said, "Antonio killed your husband?"

Destiny nodded. "Because he wouldn't agree. And neither did I, even when he was taking my foundation from me." She lifted her chin, tears in her eyes. "If Ralph wasn't going to give in, then I never would. But he grabbed me. I had the pistol in my dresser, and I used it."

Kira started to speak. She didn't want to question this woman, but now that she was seeing through the facade, the whole story just seemed kind of convenient.

Destiny stood up, shaking her head. "I'm sorry. I have to go downstairs. I need some air."

"This officer will go with you." Martinelli motioned to one of the uniformed cops standing nearby.

The guy nodded and followed Destiny down the stairs.

Kira waited until she was out of earshot before she said, "This is unbelievable, right? The cartel trying to gain territory here in Renegade."

Mike shrugged, heading for the bedroom with his suit jacket flapping. She walked beside him. He said, "Maybe not as unbelievable as you might think, what with a shadow syndicate trying to maintain power. People caught in the crossfire. It feels like a turf war."

"Well, you heard Destiny. She and Ralph didn't want anything to do with it."

He glanced at her and nodded, then stepped into the main room.

"One shot, point blank." Luca shifted out of his crouch and stood, pulling off gloves that matched the officers.

"I'll get the crime scene techs in here." The uniformed officer moved to the window and got on his radio.

"Fits her story." Mike squeezed the back of his neck.

Kira looked at the scene. "She's distressed. Maybe she'll remember more details in the next few days."

"We usually conduct a follow-up interview." Mike glanced at her. "This isn't something you need to get into."

"Don't worry." Kira held up her hands. "I'm due back at the hospital tonight, and I'm more than ready to work."

Luca's expression softened. "All this ties it up neatly, huh, Martinelli?"

Mike shook his head. "I guess. But that doesn't mean I have to like it."

"Because you still don't know who the syndicate is?" Kira said.

"Looks like our case is . . ." Luca glanced at Mike. "What is it you guys say? Oh yeah. It's *ongoing*."

"Guess you'd better get used to being on retainer."

Luca clapped him on the shoulder. "Wouldn't miss it. Except today. Kira and I have plans."

"Sure, leave me to all the details and paperwork."

"What's that?" Luca put his arm around Kira's shoulder and walked her away from the murder scene. "Can't hear you."

"Get lost." After a second, Mike said, "I'm happy for you."

Kira smiled up at Luca as they walked together down the hall to the stairs. Destiny was on the phone in the entryway. As Kira approached, the other woman waved her away. The officer mouthed, *Her lawyer.*

Luca said, "We can come back tomorrow."

Kira nodded. "All right." But she wasn't sure she wanted to visit soon. Maybe after she had settled back at the hospital and was in the swing of her normal life, this time with Luca as a welcome addition.

The past three weeks—she couldn't believe it had been that long—were unlike anything she'd expected.

They stepped out into the afternoon light, and Kira raised her hand to shield her eyes. "We have plans?"

"Only in the general sense. Want to get an early dinner?"

"After seeing that?"

Luca shrugged. "Does it bother you?"

"Not really. I didn't know the guy, and there was no chance to save him."

Luca touched his lips to hers. "Let's go for a walk in the park." He beeped the locks on the car. "You sure you're good after that?"

She stopped by the car. "You were there. I wasn't afraid. I'm just sad that Destiny is going through so much, and I'd like to help her, but I don't know how."

"You'll figure it out. Or she'll call and ask."

He had so much faith in her. Kira said, "Thanks."

He came over and kissed her softly. "Anytime."

"A walk sounds nice." And normal.

Life didn't always have to be danger and investigations. Sometimes it could be a quiet movie night or coffee on the porch under the stars. Spending the day together just enjoying each other's company or one another's space. Meeting friends for dinner and playing cards with their family.

All things she hadn't had in so long . . . maybe ever.

But now they were hers. A gift of God she'd never expected.

Each day was a blessing, and she hoped that she and Luca had many of those to come.

EPILOGUE

Four weeks later

HAVE YOU SEEN THAT HANDSOME MAN OF YOURS?" Barbara stood behind the counter.

Kira shook her head. "Luca is here?"

She slid her phone into her lab-coat pocket. Jordan had been texting about a guy she'd just met on a blind date, and they'd been picking apart everything he'd said to her—of course. Jordan was hoping he would call soon for another date.

She looked around but didn't see Luca.

"Maybe he's in the break room." Barbara had an oddly blank expression on her face.

Kira got a weird feeling something was going on. She headed for the break room and saw Mack in the hall, wearing his EMT uniform of cargos and a polo shirt, texting on his phone. "Anything interesting happening?"

He whipped his phone down and looked at her. "Interesting? No. Nothing's happening."

"Give it up and I'll buy your sodas for a year."

Mack's brows rose. "There's Eric. Gotta go." He slipped around her.

"You can run . . ." Kira called after him.

She looked through the open door into the break room, the clock on the wall anxiously approaching eleven at night. Just about time for caffeine. But the room was wall-to-wall with people she recognized, all milling around holding red plastic cups of what looked like lemonade.

"Is this a party?" She stepped into the doorway.

Someone yelled, "Happy birthday!"

Everyone raised their cups, and the crowd parted, revealing Luca with a cake and way too many lit candles. She spotted her women's Bible study friends and an anesthesiologist she'd been having lunch with recently—the two of them liked the same kind of novels. Even Frankie was here, which was surprising since it had been busy getting the new shelter up and running.

"That's a fire hazard." She tried to look disapproving. "This is a hospital."

"Then blow them out." Luca grinned, and it took years off his features.

Kira scowled at him, and Barbara headed past her, making a beeline for the punch. She said, "You're supposed to make a wish first."

She closed her eyes and waited a second before she blew the candles out.

"Was the wish that Saxon would propose?"

She whirled around and spotted a face she hadn't seen in years. Beside Kane Foster, one of Luca's oldest friends, was a striking Hispanic woman who looked a little nervous.

"You're here!" She gave them both a hug. "It's so good to see you guys."

She'd been talking on video chat to Kane and Maria, who lived in Last Chance County. Planning a visit soon. And yes, she'd been hoping there would be a ring on her finger then.

Even Hammer—sorry, *Rowan*—and Sierra were here with Huck, the sweetest little ten-year-old cowboy ever.

She smiled at them all. "I can't remember the last time I had a birthday party."

Had she ever had one worth remembering? Kira didn't want to think about that when things were happy right now.

Luca shifted close to her side, having set the cake down on the table at the end. His fingers touched hers, and she felt something warm slide onto her ring finger. Then he laced his fingers in hers, holding her hand.

She looked up at him. Touched her free hand to his chest, waiting for it.

"Marry me."

Kira smiled. "Was that actually a question?" He seemed incredibly sure of himself. But then, he had reason to be, didn't he?

Huck called out, "Just say yes, then we can have cake!"

Kira dissolved into laughter, falling against Luca. Of course he held her up. She stayed there with her forehead to his chest, absorbing his strength. Her warrior. Her hero.

When she was ready, she lifted her head and said one word. "Yes."

The room erupted into celebration.

Luca swept her up into his arms and kissed her.

THANK YOU!

Thank you so much for reading *Warrior*. We hope you enjoyed the story. If you did, would you be willing to do us a favor and leave a review? It doesn't have to be long—just a few words to help other readers know what they're getting. (But no spoilers! We don't want to wreck the fun!) Thank you again for reading!

We'd love to hear from you—not only about this story, but about any characters or stories you'd like to read in the future. Contact us at www.sunrisepublishing.com/contact.

Don't miss what happens next with the Heroes of Renegade in *Protector*!

She's risked everything to save lives. Now someone wants to end hers.

Firefighter **Samantha Williams** knows how to run into flames but hiding in WITSEC takes a courage all its own. When her sister starts getting tangled in trouble, and a string of arsons threatens the community, the danger is only beginning.

He'll risk everything to protect her. Even if it means uncovering secrets she's kept buried.

Deputy US Marshal **Liam Roberts** has made it his mission to protect people whose lives are in danger. Newly named guardian to his niece, Liam battles the challenge of balancing his new role in Renegade with family responsibility.

Keeping witnesses like Sam and her sister safe quickly turns deadly after a fire breaks out at Sam's house and a dead body is discovered. What begins as professional duty quickly develops to more as the two navigate raising teens and facing a deadly threat.

When the final trap is set and escape seems impossible, Sam will discover that sometimes the greatest rescue comes from the One she thought had abandoned her long ago.

When enemies close in, nowhere is safe.

ONE

SAMANTHA WILLIAMS PULLED THE FIRE HOOD over her head, slid her arms into the self-contained breathing apparatus harness, adjusted the shoulder straps, and fastened the belt as Ciaran "Murph" Murphy cut the siren of Engine 4 and eased it to the curb. Once they were stationary, everyone deployed from the truck without a word about Sam's phone call just now.

The vibration from her elderly, busybody neighbor's call still tingled against her palm. If her crew saw the tension in her face, they might ask what was wrong. Normal people wouldn't be thrown by something as simple as running late; they'd wonder why it affected her so much.

Greer slammed the door shut. "Ready?"

"Am I ever not?" Sam tried to find a smile and go back to being their teammate rather than the guardian of a teenage girl. Right now they had a fire to fight. There was nothing she could do about the fact that Isabella had left for school later than usual. Harmless, really—what teenager didn't oversleep on occasion? But Sam's pulse spiked anyway. In their world, even small details could draw attention, and attention led to questions—questions she could never answer. Isabella relied on her to keep her safe, and Sam knew any slip could put them both at risk.

Sam donned her fire helmet, leaving the mask unsecured for now, and shook out her gloves before she jogged around to the hose compartment, grabbed a section, and let the roughly twenty pounds fall onto her shoulder.

This was always when she found her focus. When the weight of *this* job—and not motherhood—hit her. If she wasn't all-in, nothing-else-matters with the job of being a firefighter, someone could die.

Sam used her left hand to grab a loop of the hose behind her and maintain control. It would let her know if there was resistance because someone stepped on the line, if it got snagged, or if she'd reached the end. Then she could start dropping line from her shoulder.

She focused on running the line perpendicular to the engine and up to the front of the old commercial building. Was this another arson or just faulty wiring?

Mason Greer followed behind her, making sure the line wouldn't kink once the water flowed. Then he'd help advance the line into the building.

Captain Cole Bennett and Zachary Holt had already forced entry through the front door, giving her and Greer access to the fire.

She laid the nozzle on the ground long enough to put on her mask. Sweat had already started to form across her brow from the fire's heat. Once the mask was on, the flow of oxygen replaced the thick smell of smoke. All she needed now was the—

"Water!" Murph yelled over the radio.

Time to put out the flames.

Sam led the attack line through the building, dousing the flames while Greer supported the hose from behind. The fire grew in intensity as they neared the center of the building. As if someone had started the main fire as well as little ones on their way out. Another one for the Renegade arsonist.

If someone had asked her years ago where she would be right now, fighting fires in Renegade, Colorado, with a new identity would not have been her answer. No. She'd still be Madison Johanson the nurse. Probably working twelve-hour shifts in a hospital somewhere. Making sure her little sister had a better life than she'd had—three meals a day, weather-appropriate clothing, shoes that fit and weren't falling apart. Things the average person would consider necessities but which had been luxuries for Madison. No one else was going to do it for Anna—now Isabella.

Samantha shoved thoughts of her neglected childhood from her mind. No use bringing up the past when it was as dead as Madison. There was a job to be done—a job that meant saving lives and using her training to stay safe so she could get home, where her real job began. The one where she raised her sister better than their mother had raised Madison.

She'd done a bang-up job of that, considering they were in WITSEC now. One traumatic childhood traded for a slightly less traumatic childhood. At least Isabella had someone to fight for her.

Her teammates shouted out their progress as they pushed deep into the bowels of the abandoned building until the flames were extinguished.

"Keep the line charged while we do the overhaul. Williams, get ready to hit it if it lights back up," Captain Bennett ordered before inspecting the largest burn area. "This where it was the heaviest?" He pointed to a heap of debris in the middle of the open space.

"Yes," she responded.

He held the thermal imaging camera up to the area and then ran it around the room. "Thermal's clear."

Sam followed the crew as Captain Bennett thoroughly inspected the rest of the structure.

"Building's cold. Let's clean it up."

They filed out of the structure and started cleanup.

Sweat rolled down her back as she folded the hose. She couldn't wait to get back to the station and shed her turnout gear.

"Excuse me." A small voice sounded from behind Sam as she rolled the hose.

Sam turned and found a little girl with blonde pigtails and tear stains on her cheeks. She knelt down. "Are you okay?"

The little girl shook her head, sending her pigtails swinging. "My mommy said if I ever need help, to find a policeman or a fireman."

"Your mommy is very smart. Are you lost?" Sam looked up as a woman in khaki capris and a green T-shirt jogged up.

"Emily, there you are. Let the firefighters do their jobs."

"But Mommy, you said if I ever needed help, to find a policeman or fireman."

"I did, but I meant an emergency. This isn't an emergency."

Emily nodded furiously. "It is too."

"Not the type of emergency that I meant." The woman turned to Sam. "I'm sorry. Her kitten is stuck in the tree. I was looking for our ladder, and I guess Emily had other plans."

Sam smiled at Emily. "You came to the right place. Saving kittens from trees is our specialty."

Emily jumped up and down, clapping. "Yay!"

Emily's mother shook her head. "You don't have to. I'm sure the kitten will be okay until my husband gets home and can help dig the ladder out of the storage building."

"Nonsense. Let me put this hose up, tell my crew, and see what we can do."

Emily threw her arms around Sam's leg and squeezed. "Thank you!"

Sam patted the little girl on the back, then made her way toward the engine and ran into Greer. "Hey, there's a kitten stuck in a tree. I'm going to go see if I can help."

"That's so cliché. I'm in." Greer turned. "Cap, we're going to go do a citizen assist."

Captain Bennett looked around, most likely assessing the progress of cleanup, then gave a thumbs-up. He'd never let them go if cleanup wasn't mostly done, unless it was a medical emergency.

She started back to Emily and her mom and realized Greer was jogging right behind her. "I don't need your help."

"Oh, I'm not helping. I'm just coming for the entertainment. Cats are evil on a good day. Trap them in a tree and add in some fear and they become psychos. Once I'm done laughing, I'll tend to your wounds." He clapped her on the back.

She rolled her eyes. "Cats aren't that bad. In fact, some people love them."

"Talk to me after you've contracted cat-scratch fever." He fell into step next to her, then let out a low whistle as they got closer to Emily and her mother. "Wow."

Sam shoved him. "Oh no. We are professionals. We're saving a cat and making a little girl happy. There will be no flirting."

"I can't make any promises." He flicked his hair out of his eyes.

She gave him a side-eye. He may have sounded serious, but the twinkle in his green eyes suggested otherwise. "She's married."

"Disappointing." Greer was a good guy. Definitely a flirt, but it was mostly harmless. The fact that he looked like a young Elvis, minus the pompadour, didn't make it hard for him to charm the ladies. Rectangular face with full lips and black hair. He even had older ladies fawning over him.

He was the guy you went to shoot pool with after work. But not the guy you invited to help you move house, because it would take hours longer than necessary. And he was never serious about anything except fitness and nutrition.

"Okay, Emily. This is my friend Greer. Let's go see if we can get your kitten." Sam made it a point not to introduce him to the mother. And not just because she didn't know the lady's name.

They followed the duo.

"You really don't have to do this. The kitten will be okay until my husband gets home. It's not the first time he's done this." The woman brushed hair back from her face.

"It's not a problem at all."

Emily ran up to a tall cottonwood tree full of deep green leaves. "He's up there!" She pointed past the lower, thinner branches to the thicker, sturdier ones fifteen feet up.

Sam studied the tree. Definitely climbable, but not so much in her turnout pants, which were stiff and didn't allow the maneuverability she would need. She shrugged off her jacket, unfastened the waist of her pants, and loosened the suspenders while kicking off her boots so she could strip down to her duty uniform.

"Here we go. You climb that tree like a spider monkey!" Greer laughed.

"You really don't have to do this," Emily's mother said.

"Nonsense. Climbing trees is like riding a bike, right? You never forget how to do it."

Sam grabbed the lowest branch and tested its sturdiness before starting her ascent. The rough bark cut into her feet through her socks as she climbed. She maneuvered up the branches and made her way to the kitten. It mewed softly as she approached.

"Hey, little guy. Let's get you down from here. Emily misses you." She slowly reached forward, trying not to scare the animal any more than he already was.

The fluffy white kitten sniffed her fingers.

Sam had to wonder if this was a tactic she could use with Bella. Would the teen respond to gentleness? Sam didn't even know where to start with the girl, but she had to figure out something.

"That's a good boy." She inched her fingers closer, but the kitten stepped back. "It's okay. I'm here to help you."

She reached forward a little more, and the little guy didn't move. She gave him a small pet on his head, and he immediately purred.

"Come here." She scooped the kitten up and cradled him to her chest. He stayed still as she descended the tree.

Emily waited with arms wide open for his safe return. "Thank you!" She hugged her kitten.

Sam crouched. "You're welcome, Emily."

"That was awesome." Greer clapped her on the shoulder. "Were you in the circus before moving to Renegade?"

Sam's stomach tightened as she straightened. "I guess you'll never know."

She never talked to anyone about her past, and she never would. Her and Bella's safety depended on no one ever finding out who they really were or how Madison had testified in federal court and sent a dangerous man and all his cronies to prison for life.

If anyone discovered her past, she and Bella would be moved out of Renegade so fast their heads would be spinning.

For the sake of this life she had built, no one could ever find out her secrets.

———

Adrenaline coursed through Deputy US Marshal Liam Roberts's body as he shifted his weight from foot to foot, ready for the hunt. But this wasn't a fugitive apprehension task force. Nope. He'd given up that career, become the guardian of his niece, and taken a job at the Marshals office in the city of Renegade. He looked around the room, taking in his new coworkers, who were busy gearing up, all wearing some fashion of blue jeans, tees, and running shoes.

This was a far cry from his old life.

But if he didn't make this work, he'd be ruining more than one future.

Liam looked down at his black slacks and button-down shirt. Not his fugitive-hunting apparel. He'd been in his new office all of two minutes before his new boss, Supervisor Daniel Howard, had told him to grab his gear and meet in the conference room for a briefing about a fugitive apprehension.

He already had his vest and duty belt on by the time the others filed into the conference room. A whiteboard filled the entire right wall. Pictures of criminals were taped along the board, with notes written all around them. A table that seated eight was centered in the room. Instead of sitting, everyone stood behind a chair. Just as anxious to get the hunt started as he was.

Except he shouldn't be this excited. He'd kissed the late nights kicking in doors and arresting bad guys goodbye. The adrenaline-filled life of fugitive apprehension didn't mesh well with single parenthood. A role change in his personal life had required a role change in his career. Now he was supposed to spend his days guarding the courthouse, transporting criminals, and handling witnesses—all with the caveat that he could be called for fugitive apprehension if needed.

Not what I expected on the first day, Lord.

Maybe after Sophia turned eighteen and went off to college, he'd go back to that life. If it was still available. He'd been told Renegade was where good marshals went to die career-wise. Apparently, no one ever transferred out of Renegade.

Which was a small price to pay, seeing as his sister sat in prison because of him. He'd made a decision as a teen that had sent her running down the wrong path and straight to a life of crime. He'd made something of himself, becoming a marshal on the straight and narrow, trying to absolve himself of his guilt. His sister hadn't been so successful, no matter how he'd tried to help her.

In the end it had been a no-brainer to become Sophia's guardian. After all, it was another way he could make amends.

No way would he have let her disappear into the foster-care system. But he couldn't help feeling like God had thrown a wrench in where Liam had thought his life was going. He'd hoped to one day become a father; he'd just expected to start at the beginning—with all-nighters, diapers, and spit-up. The works. Not to be thrown immediately into the hormones and high school stage. And doing it as a single man, at that.

"Okay." A broad-shouldered man wearing stonewashed blue jeans, a simple black shirt, and a US Marshals ball cap yelled over the activity, pulling Liam from his thoughts. "We've got John Vickers. Number eight on the list."

The US Marshals' Most Wanted list: the fifteen criminals the Marshals considered the most dangerous. There were some real bad guys, and occasionally gals, on that list.

Supervisor Howard stepped up. "Before we get into the details, let me introduce you to our newest team member." He gestured to Liam, and all eyes turned to him. "This is Liam Roberts. He'll be our new WITSEC and court-security guy. He comes to us from the fugitive apprehension team in Virginia."

Supervisor Howard went around the room putting names to the new faces, starting with the broad-shouldered man. Ethan Butler.

Next, Howard gestured to a man in his mid-forties, close-cropped dark-brown hair graying at the temples. "Nick Stanton."

He then pointed to a woman with warm-toned skin and light-brown hair slicked back into a bun. "Emma Kennedy."

"Cody Albright." A man sporting a two-day beard was next.

"Finally, Jodi Glover." She was the shortest member of the team but not by much. Blonde hair tucked through the back of a US Marshals ball cap.

Each team member acknowledged him in some fashion, whether a wave or head nod.

"Okay, Butler, fill us in on Vickers." Supervisor Howard turned the room over to Butler.

"He's wanted on multiple counts of capital murder. Known to be armed and violent. The last encounter law enforcement had with him, he said he'd die before going back to prison. Word is he's here in Renegade. One of my informants just called and said he's at the Blue Moon Motel on Jefferson." Butler crossed his arms over his chest.

Great. Fantastic way to start his first day. Fugitive with a sui-cide-by-cop attitude.

"On a scale of Rendell to Lowe, what are we talking about?" Albright asked.

"Lowe."

Albright grimaced.

They threw around names like he should know who they were. "Someone want to fill in the new guy?"

"Rendell said he wouldn't be taken alive, but once we showed up, he gave up without issue," Glover supplied.

"Then cried for his momma." Albright chuckled.

"Silas Lowe was the complete opposite." This time Kennedy chimed in.

"*Was* being the operative word." Albright's jaw stiffened.

Lowe had obviously meant what he'd said and hadn't survived the encounter. Which one of Liam's new teammates had been the one to pull the trigger?

Butler tapped his upper thigh. "Roberts, you're with me. Stan-ton and Kennedy, set up on Lincoln. Albright and Glover, you'll set up on Pine. We go in slow and keep our distance until we know it's him. Once we've verified it is Vickers, we'll make the arrest. Let's go."

The other four agents filed out of the room while Butler hung behind. "Follow me." He didn't wait for a response. Just turned and walked away.

Liam followed him to the secure elevator to the first floor, where they exited into a secured parking lot. Butler climbed into a black pickup truck that was backed into a spot right by the exit. Liam climbed into the passenger seat.

Butler threw the truck in Drive and tore out of the parking lot.

"What's the plan?" Liam looked in the side mirror to see two black SUVs following behind.

"You heard it. Verify and arrest." Butler glanced over. "Figured you'd know by now what you're doing, Mr. Fugitive Task Force."

"Right, but what's the plan on the arrest? How's the hotel set up?"

Each department executed arrests differently. With Butler as the lead on this case, he'd be making the decisions.

Still, Liam pulled up a map of the area on his phone and took a look at the layout.

Butler gave him a side-eye and gripped the steering wheel tighter. "The hotel is in the shadier part of Renegade. It's on the corner of the lot. Stanton and Kennedy will be set up a block north to maintain visual on the back of the motel. Albright and Glover will be a block to the east, watching the front. You and I will be half a block west."

Sounded like Butler had a good perimeter set up.

"Once we verify it's Vickers, we'll make a decision on how to take him down."

"Okay." That's all he needed to know.

Because he was new in town, he had studied maps and knew general locations and roads, but he wanted to know what the maps wouldn't tell him. The things he'd learn working with this team and operating on the streets of Renegade.

His phone rang in his hand. The words *Marshal Samuel Dennison High School* filled the screen.

"I have to take this."

Butler nodded.

He slid the Answer icon across the screen. "Liam Roberts."

"Good morning, Mr. Roberts. This is Vice Principal Woodworth. I'm calling you regarding Sophia."

His stomach sank. "Is there a problem?"

"Well, yes. Sophia was caught with several young ladies vaping in the bathroom this afternoon when they were supposed to be in class."

Liam closed his eyes and took a deep breath. Skipping class and vaping in the bathroom? Next she'd be skipping school entirely. After that, how long would it be before she ended up like her mother?

"She was given lunch detention. We just wanted you to be aware of the situation. We know she's new to Renegade, and had hoped she would start off on the right foot, but this isn't it. Her records from Virginia indicate she's been in some trouble before the transfer. We'll be encouraging her to take this fresh start more seriously."

And so would he.

Liam cleared his throat. "She was having some difficulties in her home life that caused issues. We're working on making sure that trouble isn't repeated here."

"We're aware. Just know that we are a compassionate and understanding administration. If you need any assistance with locating services in Renegade, please let us know. We only want what's best for our students."

"Thank you. Sophia and I will talk tonight." He disconnected the call and shook his head. "That kid."

Renegade was a fresh start for him and Sophia. New lives in a new town. The past was behind them. More hope for a better future for Sophia. Starting over was going to be hard, and they'd both have to make adjustments. They were each nursing broken hearts. For different reasons though.

That hope didn't stop the little voice in his head questioning everything and worrying about the future. Liam knew he needed to take those thoughts captive and trust God's plan, even though it didn't make sense. It was hard, but he was trying. God would give them the strength to overcome the past and move forward.

"Did you get your business squared away?" Butler glanced over.

"For now."

"Good, because we're here." Butler eased the truck to the curb and killed the engine.

Silence filled the truck. Adrenaline coursed through Liam as he studied the motel, waiting for Vickers to make an appearance.

Tried to feel like himself, a marshal on a fugitive apprehension team.

Rather than a father with no idea what he was doing.

NOTE FROM AUTHOR

Thank you so much for joining with us on this new adventure!

Susie and I love to create series ideas that lend themselves to action-packed stories with plenty of heart. We love to infuse the things of the Lord in what we write, and pray that you'll be drawn to Him through these books.

Heroes of Renegade has been a labor of love since its inception, and with many more stories planned, I hope you'll join us as we revisit Renegade Colorado in the releases to come. We have partnered with some amazing authors who all bring their heart and their voice to these characters, their stories, and the town of Renegade.

Happy Reading!

Lisa Phillips

Lisa Phillips is a USA Today and top ten Publishers Weekly bestselling author of over 100 books that span Harlequin's Love Inspired Suspense line, independently published series romantic suspense, and thriller novels. She's discovered a penchant for high-stakes stories of mayhem and disaster where you can find made-for-each-other love that always ends in happily ever after.

Lisa is a British ex-pat who grew up an hour outside of London and attended Calvary Chapel Bible College, where she met her husband. He's from California, but nobody's perfect. It wasn't until her Bible College graduation that she figured out she was a writer (someone told her). As a worship leader for Calvary Chapel churches in her local area, Lisa has discovered a love for mentoring new ministry members and youth worship musicians.

Find out more at www.authorlisaphillips.com

Another epic series created by

SUSAN MAY WARREN
and LISA PHILLIPS

WE THINK YOU'LL ALSO LOVE...

Infiltrating a dangerous militia to save her troubled brother, Jamie Winters finds herself kidnapped. Only Logan Crawford, the man she once broke, can rescue her—but he demands a promise in return. As they navigate peril in the Alaskan wilderness, their unresolved feelings spark a chance for love and redemption.

Burning Hearts **by Lisa Phillips**

Stunt double Vienna Foxcroft's stunt team are the only ones she trusts. Then in walks Sergeant Crew Gatlin and his tough-as-nails military dog, Havoc. When an attack on a film set sends them fleeing into the streets of Turkey, Vienna must face the demons of her past or be devoured by them. And Crew and Havoc will be tested like never before.

Havoc **by Ronie Kendig**

When an attempt is made on Grey Parker's life and dead bodies begin piling up, suddenly bodyguard Christina Sherman is tasked with keeping both a soldier and his dog safe... and with them, the secrets that could stop a terrorist attack.

Driving Force **by Lynette Eason and Kate Angelo**

We solve the problem of what to read next.

**WHERE EVERY STORY IS A FRIEND,
AND EVERY CHAPTER IS A NEW JOURNEY...**

Subscribe to our newsletter for a free book, the latest news, weekly giveaways, exclusive author interviews, and more!

Shop paperbacks, ebooks, audiobooks, and more at
SUNRISEPUBLISHING.MYSHOPIFY.COM